BREEDING
EVIL

Liz
Wolfe

GOLD IMPRINT

Dedication,
To Keith Wolfe, for believing in me.

May 2004
Published by Medallion Press, Inc.
225 Seabreeze Ave.
Palm Beach, FL 33480

ISBN 1-932815-05-8

Printed in the United States of America

For more great books visit www.medallionpress.com.

Acknowledgments

I'd like to acknowledge the following people for their assistance and support:

My editor, Pamela Ficarella, who caught even tiny discrepancies and asked the questions that made this book better.

My husband, Keith, for complicating my plots and energizing my fight scenes.

My daughter, Alana, for her unwavering belief in me.

My mother and sisters for understanding that edits had to come before vacation fun.

My writing buddy, Karen, for endless hours on the phone and over coffee.

And The Bats, for their own unique brand of encouragement.

CHAPTER ONE

"Since when is the FSA hiring private investigators for black ops?" Shelby Parker closed the file and placed it back on Ethan Calder's desk.

"It isn't really a black op, Shelby."

"And I'm not really an FSA operative." She'd tendered her resignation to the Federal Security Agency six months earlier, after ten years of living on the edge. One op after another. Having no job skills that really applied in corporate America, other than being sneaky and nosy, she'd opened her own security and investigative firm. And here she was, back at FSA headquarters in Denver letting her former handler talk her into one more op.

Ethan hadn't changed a bit since she'd been gone, other than a little more gray at the temples of his dark hair, and a few more lines at the corners of his dark eyes. He leaned his elbows on the desk and tapped his long, slender fingers together. No, he hadn't changed.

He would wait for her to come around to his way of thinking, to agree to his proposal.

She had no doubt that he knew she needed this job. The check for her advance lay on his desk, and even though Shelby couldn't see the exact amount, the number of zeros she counted made her a little giddy.

For six months she'd been struggling to survive by keeping tabs on wayward spouses, investigating fraudulent insurance claims, and providing bouncer services to a local bar on wet tee shirt night. If she didn't get some decent cases soon, she'd be living on the edge of poverty. Still, it was an edge that *she* had chosen. She hadn't left the FSA because of Ethan, or even because she didn't like the work. At thirty-three years old, she'd decided that she wanted to run her own show. She wanted something that was hers, something that she controlled.

Shelby leaned back in her chair and looked at the majestic Rocky Mountains through the ceiling-to-floor windows behind Ethan's desk. If she decided to take the job, it would have to be on her own terms.

"I can give you whatever support you'll need," Ethan said.

"You just said that no one in the FSA knows about this. That you can't even use an FSA operative."

Ethan sighed and folded his hands on the desk. "I need you on this one, Shelby."

Shelby stood and moved to stare out the glass wall of his office, turning her back to him. Ethan Calder was the best handler in the Federal Security Agency. He had been hers the entire time she'd worked for the FSA. No one was more aware than Shelby that, while she was out saving the world, he was back at headquarters saving her butt with the latest intelligence and best support he could cajole, bribe, or beat out of anyone who might be helpful. But he was distant and cold, and he leaned a little too heavily on the need-to-know theory of information disbursement for her comfort.

Still, there was no doubt he would come up with some creative way to provide whatever she might require.

On the other side of the glass wall, people were hunched over computers, speaking urgently on phones or to co-workers. No one just strolled down the hallways created by the cubicles. Footsteps on the utilitarian, beige carpet were hurried and purposeful. The FSA offices were always intense. Because there was always something important on the line—like lives and national security.

Shelby reluctantly admitted that she missed being a part of it—but not enough to give up on her fledgling agency. And her fledgling agency could certainly use the chunk of money Ethan was offering for this job.

It wasn't like she was going back to the FSA. It would just be a case—a lucrative case—and wasn't that exactly what she needed and wanted?

"So, will you do it?" Ethan walked back to his desk and sank into the chair. It took her a second to bring her mind back to the conversation.

"Why me?"

"The op calls for a chameleon. And, you're the best."

"Is that your idea of a compliment?"

Ethan had often noted that her appearance was one of her greatest assets. Exceptionally plain was the only way she could describe it. Neither attractive nor unattractive. Five feet six inches tall, neither slender nor plump. Although she tended to have more muscle than most women, that wasn't noticeable in street clothes. Hair that was a combination of dark blond and light brown, eyes that were neither green nor brown, but somewhere in between. Her face might as well be a blank canvas. Eyes, nose, and lips in proportion to each other, and none of them outstanding in any way.

Shelby looked at her reflection in the glass wall. Totally unremarkable and utterly forgettable. Someone who was easily lost in a crowd. But given a few products readily available at the drugstore, she could transform herself into just about any kind of person she chose.

"Fifteen people missing so far?" Shelby turned away from her reflection and walked back to Ethan's desk. She slid a finger under the folder and flipped it open, scanning the first page.

"At last count. Including Shannon Masterson and her son, Sam. No death certificates. All of them had some connection to The Center."

"Dr. Jonah Thomas is the head of The Center?" She turned over another page in the file. "I've heard his name before. A scientist, right?"

"Years ago he headed up a government-funded research facility. He was supposed to verify the existence of psychic phenomena, which he did."

"Really?" That woo-woo stuff was a bit much for her to believe in. "I remember him losing the funding for some reason."

"Right. It turned out that not only was he verifying the existence of psychic phenomena, he was performing experiments on some of the research subjects. The government dismantled the research facility and sealed all the records."

"So, he's an evil scientist."

"And an egocentric megalomaniac." Ethan leaned forward. "We know that he's been doing research on psychics for years, along with Dr. Ruth Carlson. He has contacts outside the country that are less than reputable. The Center seems to have unlimited funds that we can't trace. What we don't know is what the hell they're up to."

"You're really hopped up about this." Shelby couldn't help grinning at him.

Ethan sighed and leaned back in his chair. "Shannon is a friend. She was my wife's roommate in college."

"Charlotte wants you to find her?"

"No, she doesn't know that Shannon is missing. Shannon's aunt is married to the Ambassador from the United Kingdom. The aunt called me about it because of Shannon's friendship with Charlotte."

"Has she ever disappeared before?"

Ethan swiveled his chair to look out the window.

"Shannon's what you'd call a free spirit. She's taken off before, but never without telling her aunt."

"So there was no indication she was taking off on some trip or whatever?"

"No. In fact when Shannon took trips in the past, she usually asked Charlotte to watch Sam for her."

"So, the niece of an Ambassador. Why, exactly, is this a black op again?"

"It isn't a black op."

"Okay, not a black op. Just a secret between you and me." She lifted her eyebrows in blatant disbelief.

Ethan turned his chair back, sighed, and shook his head. "All right. The deal is that Ambassador Watkins has already called in the FBI to investigate."

"So, it's a black op because the FBI is already investigating? Why not just let them handle it?" The boundaries between the FSA and the FBI were blurred at times, but if one agency already had control, the other agency usually didn't interfere unless they were asked. Professional and political courtesy.

"It's not a black op."

"Ethan, if the FBI is already investigating The Center, then sending me in could be the end of your career."

Ethan stared at her for a moment, frowned and pressed a hand to the back of his neck, kneading the tense muscles. Shelby bit back a smile. That was a sure sign that he was about to resign himself to actually giving her the information he'd been trying to withhold. She sat down in the chair across from his desk and leaned back, waiting for the story.

"FBI Director Fields and Ambassador Watkins have a history that is less than congenial. The Ambassador's wife is concerned that the FBI won't do everything they can to find Shannon and Sam."

"Must have been something pretty heavy in their history to make her feel that way."

Ethan nodded. "Ambassador Watkins. Evidently he's a hard dog to keep on the porch. He had an affair with Director Fields' niece."

"Oh. Isn't Ambassador Watkins around sixty or so?" Shelby bit back a smile, knowing that Ethan was sensitive about the fact that he was twelve years older than his wife, Charlotte.

"Fifty-eight. He's also tall, handsome, and debonair. Not to mention that he is an excellent gift giver."

"I see. And Mrs. Watkins is okay with all this?"

"I wouldn't presume to ask, but evidently she's learned to live with it. I believe she's willing to over-look certain behaviors that aren't entirely acceptable to her."

"So, she called you because of Shannon's friendship with Charlotte?"

"Precisely."

"Did you mention this to Chambers?"

"As director of the FSA, he can't do anything that would step on the FBI's toes." Ethan shrugged. "However, he made it clear that he doesn't want Ambassador Watkins accusing the U.S. of not doing everything in its power to find Shannon."

"I see. Chambers doesn't want to step on Fields'

toes so he's letting you bring in someone from the outside. If Fields finds out, he can't accuse the FSA of anything."

"I'm just investigating the disappearance of my wife's friend." Ethan spread his upturned palms and smiled.

Shelby shifted in the chair across from Ethan, picked up the file, and looked at the picture stapled to the inside. Shannon sat on a porch swing in a sundress, her strawberry blond hair curling softly around her face, and one arm around her towheaded son who stood next to her, blowing bubbles. It was obvious from the look on her face that her son was the most important thing in the world to her. What would it have been like to grow up with a parent like that?

Crap. She knew she was about to agree to the job.

"You know someone could recognize me in Tucson. I lived there for a while."

Ethan nodded. "It's about time you agreed."

"I would have agreed two hours ago if you'd just told me everything," she shot back. "You know, I totally trust you when I go on an op. Don't you think it's about time you returned that trust? Don't you think that maybe our collaboration would work even better—"

Ethan cut her off with a wave of his hand.

"We need to get you inside."

Shelby leaned back and sighed. "I can't believe I just agreed to a black op."

"It's not a black op." Ethan gave her a rare, one-sided grin. "Maybe a little gray, but it's not black."

"Good afternoon, Mr. Calder." Monique Peterson smiled and reached for the phone.

"Afternoon, Monique." Ethan returned her smile. Monique had been Chamber's secretary for well over a decade. She probably knew everything that went on in the FSA, since she had Don's total trust. She completely managed his life at the office, from getting him what or whom he needed to being his sounding board. She was the only person who had complete access to him. Away from Don, everyone referred to her as his office wife.

"Mr. Calder is here," she said in a cultured undertone. She replaced the phone and waved a graceful hand toward the double doors behind her. "Go on in, he's expecting you."

"Thanks, Monique." Ethan shifted the leather folder to his left hand and opened the door to a large, well-appointed office. The walls were paneled in dark, burled walnut. An expensive oriental carpet lay on the hardwood floor. Don Chambers walked around his desk, a phone held to his ear, and gestured for Ethan to come over to the table by the windows.

Ethan sat in one of the armless chairs covered in soft, green velvet and placed his folder on the table, watching Don pace back and forth as he completed the phone call. Don Chambers was a tall, light-skinned African-American. He had bulky shoulders and muscles that left the impression he'd played college or professional football at some time. His cropped hair was beginning to gray, but he still looked young. Too young to be the director of the FSA. He placed the phone back in the cradle and turned to Ethan.

"Is Shelby on board?"

"Yes. Although it took some time to convince her."

"I'll bet that she just let you think it took some time. That girl likes to play hard to get." Don walked to the windows and pulled the shades against the bright, Colorado sun. "It's a shame she decided to leave us."

"True. However, in this particular instance, it's lucky for us." Ethan opened his leather portfolio and took a pen from his pocket. "Do we have any other information?"

Don seemed lost in thought for a moment. "No. Nothing new." He sank into the leather chair behind his massive desk. "These people are pissing me off, Ethan."

"No doubt." Ethan was well acquainted with Don's moods.

"Whatever they're doing, it can't be good. Fifteen people missing! And the FBI has just been sitting on its hands. I still don't understand that." Don shook his head and sighed. "But all my inquiries have been brushed off. My only other option would be to go to the President, and I think he probably has more important things to deal with."

"Like you said, this is our chance."

"Our only chance." Don nodded. "I've made all the arrangements. All the department heads have been instructed to supply you with anything you need."

"And if anybody asks why later?"

"Obviously, your friends are doing this out of a sense of camaraderie." Don spoke with a perfectly straight face. "Your coworkers like and admire you. It's only natural that they'd want to help you locate your wife's friend and her child." A blindingly white smile split Don's mocha face, followed by a deep, resounding chuckle.

"God, I hope it never gets to that."

"Relax, Ethan. This is all for looks. If it comes right down to it, I'll take the heat for this."

CHAPTER TWO

Shelby stopped just inside the door of Streakers Dance Emporium and scanned the crowd through a haze of cigarette smoke. Everyone who was hip, cool, slick, or just a wannabe, came to Streakers on Saturday night. She'd been in Tucson for several days setting up the op. Everything was ready. Tonight was the point of no return.

Let the games begin.

The crowded club was warmer than the cool spring night in spite of the cold air that blasted through the vents. The loud music thrummed in her ears. Multi-colored lights flashed across the mass of writhing bodies on the dance floor, while the tables around it were cast in shadows. There didn't seem to be an empty table in the place. It was a typical Saturday night at Streakers and exactly the setup she wanted.

Shelby pushed and wiggled her way to the bar, smiling and murmuring apologies to the fashionably dressed bodies she bumped into along the way.

"Tall club soda with lime." She slid a few bills across the bar and took her drink. Turning back to the crowd, she looked for her target and found him just a few moments later, sitting at a table with two other men. All three of them wore tee shirts, baggy jeans, and sneakers. One had on an Arizona Diamondbacks baseball cap; another one wore old-fashioned, aviator-style glasses. Ted Ryan and his friends couldn't have been easier to spot in this crowd if they'd been naked.

Crap. She knew the man at the end of the bar.

Donnie Conroy. One of her dad's old cronies, a low life con man. He squinted his watery, blue eyes in her direction as if he was trying to remember her. Shelby had known Donnie since she was ten years old when her dad had first involved her in some of his milder scams. The last time she'd seen him had been at her father's funeral seven years ago. Shelby figured she probably hadn't changed much since then, but she also hadn't been wearing a spandex dress, blond wig, and a quarter inch of makeup.

She stood at the bar and sipped her drink for a few minutes, hoping he'd give up. No dice. He picked up his drink and cigarettes and moved to a stool next to her. A hard shot of adrenalin poured through her, and she felt her heart rate and breathing increase in response.

No way was she going to let a two-bit con man interrupt her op. Figuring the best defense was a strong offense, Shelby turned and looked at him.

"What're youse looking at, Gramps?" Her Jersey accent sounded pretty good, even to herself, and must have passed with him.

"I just thought I'd seen you somewhere before."

"You wish, old timer!"

"No, I didn't mean it like that. It's just that your face really looks familiar."

"Yeah, like I never heard that before."

"Can I buy you a drink?"

"Fuggedaboutit. Go find a nice old lady your own age at the bingo hall. Sheesh!"

"You got no class. You know that?" Donnie scowled and slurped his drink.

"Whatever." Shelby rolled her eyes, flipped a hand up toward his face, and turned away. She could feel him staring at her back for a few more minutes.

"Shelby?"

Crap. He'd made her. Shelby sipped her drink acting as if he hadn't said anything, until she felt his hand on her shoulder.

"Shelby."

She jerked reflexively when she felt his hand. "What is your problem, old man?" She batted his hand off her shoulder. "Do I have to get one of the bouncers or what?"

Donnie shook his head, then turned, and toddled back to his bar stool, mumbling under his breath. He seemed to be convinced that he didn't really know her, and she breathed a silent sigh of relief when he finished his drink and headed for the door.

Shelby sauntered off in the direction of her quarry and leaned against a faux-painted column within a few feet of Ted Ryan and his friends. The music continued to throb, and she let her hips and shoulders pick up the rhythm, moving slightly in time to the pulsating beat. She gave it a few minutes, letting them thoroughly check her out, then glanced over and flashed them a casual smile. Just a isn't-this-fun kind of smile. Nothing too personal, nothing too aggressive.

After a few more minutes, she caught Ted's eye, smiled again, and turned back to the dance floor, tugging at the hem of her extremely short dress. Shelby sipped the club soda and made sure to smile a little too brightly, a little too eagerly at everyone who passed by. The hip, cool crowd pointedly ignored her. Her dress was too short, her makeup too heavy, and her hair too big and way too blond. No one wanted to even catch her eye. Perfect. Shelby shifted uncomfortably from foot to foot for a moment, and then walked over to Ted's table with a stilted gait, mentally dropping the Jersey accent in favor of a soft, sexy purr.

"Do you guys mind if I take this chair?" She braced her hands on the back of the chair.

For a moment, the three men just looked at her, mouths gaping. Then they all scrambled up from their seats. Shelby smiled at each of them. "I just really have to get off my feet for a few minutes."

"You're welcome to join us." Ted pulled the extra chair out for her.

"Oh, that would be so nice." She sank into the seat

next to Ted and lifted a leg. "These heels are just killing me." She pointed to the four-inch, spike heeled sandal on her foot and wiggled her freshly painted toes.

"You mean those aren't your dancing shoes?" Ted grinned.

"I don't know what I was thinking, wearing these shoes." Shelby affected a giggle and slurped a little more club soda. "My name's Carla."

"I'm Ted, this is Matt, and Bob."

Shelby knew more about Ted than his friends probably knew. He was twenty-six, had a BA in computer science from the University of Arizona, and worked at The Center for Bio-Psychological Research. He smoked pot every day and drank a few beers on the weekends. Computers were his job, his hobby, and his life. He was heavily involved in several role-playing games over the Internet. Ted stood about five feet ten and, while not fat, had that softness of body that comes from too much desk time and not enough physical activity. His brown hair was already thinning a bit, but he had a nice face. Big, trusting brown eyes and a quick smile.

"You guys must be regulars here, huh?"

"Not exactly," Ted said. His friends snorted and laughed. "We just come here every few months. Just to check it out, you know? I haven't seen you around though."

"I just moved here a couple of weeks ago. Still living in a motel room."

"You get transferred here?"

"Yeah. It meant a promotion, so I figured why not?" Shelby lifted a shoulder in a delicate shrug and let her tongue slide around the straw in her drink. "You guys all work together?"

"We all belong to a users' group. Online."

"Oh, yeah? I do some chat rooms online. Well, I did until my computer bombed." She twisted a strand of her platinum wig and gazed at the dance floor.

"Took a dump, huh?" Ted grinned and shook his head.

Shelby leaned over, giving him a glimpse of miracle-bra enhanced cleavage, and placed her lips close to his ear so he could feel her breath. "What did you say?"

He swallowed hard. "Your computer. What happened to it?"

"Oh, I have no idea." She waved a negligent hand. "It just stopped working."

"Any error messages?" Ted grinned at her, and she could see his friends nudging each other.

"Oh, sure, lots. But I couldn't understand them."

"What operating system are you using?" Ted leaned forward, elbows on the table.

"Windows." She watched Ted glance over at her legs again, and then she crossed them, causing the blue spandex to ride up her thighs a bit more.

"What version?" His eyes were glued to her legs.

"Version? What does that mean?"

"XP, ME?" Ted's eyes returned to her face.

"Got me." Shelby shook her head, tossing the blond

17

hair around and pouting just a bit. "Pisses me off, though. I'd like to get it fixed, but that's so much money."

"I could probably fix it."

"Really?" Shelby put her hand on Ted's arm and widened her eyes. "You can do that kind of thing?"

"Sure. That's what I do for a living."

"Man, that is so cool!" She leaned toward him, letting the spandex brush against his arm. "But how much would it cost? I really don't have a lot of money to spend on it."

"Just parts, if it needs anything." Ted's gaze moved to her low neckline. "And it probably doesn't even need any. Besides, I have lots of extra parts. So, really, it won't cost you anything."

"I would be so incredibly grateful," she gushed. "I'm just in awe of anyone who can work with computers. Fix them and stuff, you know?"

"Well, I've been doing this for a long time." Ted puffed up his chest a bit. "When do you want me to look at it?"

"The sooner the better."

"How about tonight? Unless, you want to stay here. I mean, I can do it anytime, actually."

"Now is good. If you don't mind leaving." Laying it on a little thick, but Shelby thought it appropriate, given Ted's mentality.

"No problem." Ted turned and grinned at his friends.

"Oh, that'd be great. I really miss my email, you

know." She slurped the last of her club soda through the straw, threw the strap of her tiny purse over a shoulder, and stood on wobbly legs. "Man, that last drink kind of got to me. Do you mind driving?"

At that point, she had to turn away because she absolutely did *not* want to see the stupid grins the men would be exchanging. If they high-fived each other she was going to deck them. Ten more minutes— fifteen tops. She wobbled out of the club and followed Ted to his car, giving him directions to the studio motel unit, keeping up the inane chatter until they got to the door.

Crap. She really hated this part. Ted seemed like a really nice guy. Here he thought he was about to get lucky, and in a few minutes his whole life would change. She pushed a twinge of remorse down.

She had a job to do. Find Shannon Masterson and her son. This was part of it. It was necessary, and in the end it would be better for him. Better for a lot of people. She unlocked the door to her studio suite, stepped inside, and pulled him in after her.

"It's right over here." She pushed him a few steps into the room, threw the deadbolt on the door, and flipped on the light switch. Ben and Rick stood on either side of the small dinette table at the end of the room. They each held a Glock 9MM trained on Ted.

Crap!

Hadn't she told them to stay outside? Hadn't she made it clear that they were only here to do as she asked? Hadn't she explained to Ethan that she didn't want them here? Fat lot of good any of that did her.

"What the hell—?" Ted's head whipped from the men back to Shelby, his eyes wide with fear and confusion. She put her hand on Ted's arm and gave him a look that was meant to be calming and encouraging.

"Stay back!" Ted shouted. His hand fumbled in his jacket pocket and came out with a gun. A small gun, but Shelby didn't want even a twenty-two piercing her flesh. His hand shook and he backed up, waving the gun from Ben and Rick to Shelby.

"What the hell is this?" he demanded.

"It's not what it looks like, Ted. You aren't in any danger here. Just give me the gun." Shelby held her hand out.

"Sure, then what? You take everything I have on me?"

"No, Ted, it's not like that. Just put the gun down so we can talk."

"You get over there with them." Ted waved the gun at her, and she resisted the urge to cringe. He didn't appear to be really adept with the thing. His hand was still shaking, sweat had popped out on his forehead, and his voice was an octave higher.

Likely as not, he'd end up shooting one of them. Nothing against Ben or Rick, but she was really hoping it wouldn't be her.

Shelby turned slightly sideways to Ted and shifted her weight to her right leg. He waved the gun around in one hand. Shelby prayed that he still had the safety on. Her left leg snapped out, hitting Ted's hand before he realized she'd moved. The gun flew out of his hand and skittered across the hardwood floor, stopping under the dinette table. Ted blinked and looked like he might cry. Or scream.

"It's all right, Ted. We aren't here to hurt you." Shelby glared at the men dressed in black cargo pants and black tee shirts. "Out. Now." She jerked her head toward the door.

"Have a seat, Ted. We need to talk about a few things." She pulled a chair out and motioned Ted to sit. Ted slumped into the chair, staring at her.

Ted's expression was bordering on shock, and Shelby knew it would be a few minutes before she could get him to really understand anything she said. Ben and Rick were still standing by the door. She unbuckled the straps of her sandals, kicked them off, and padded over to Ben and Rick.

"What part of my orders did you not understand?"

"Sorry, Ms. Parker, but Mr. Calder told us—"

"I don't care what Ethan told you. I work alone. Always." Shelby jerked the door open and glared at them until they left, closing the door behind them. She looked at the clock. After midnight and this was likely to take several hours.

"You want some coffee or tea?"

Ted shook his head, glancing nervously about the room. He looked like he was about to wet himself. She measured coffee into the tiny coffeemaker the motel provided and flipped the brew switch.

"Relax, Ted. You're not in any danger here."

He looked really nervous.

"You Okay, Ted? Your breathing's a little funny. You need a paper bag?"

Ted shook his head.

"Just do this." Shelby put her hands over her nose and mouth and took a deep breath. Ted followed her example for a few breaths.

"Better?" Shelby asked.

Ted nodded, but his eyes were still huge.

"Okay, here's the deal. I'm from the FSA. Ever heard of us?" She kept smiling at Ted, trying to put him at ease. Ted shook his head.

"Not surprising. Not a lot of people have. It's the Federal Security Agency. Kind of like the CIA or the FBI, but different." She pushed a plastic coated card across the table to him. "Here's my ID, just so you can be sure."

Ted picked up the card and looked at it closely. He then carefully put it down on the table, sliding it back to her.

"You're you don't want some coffee?" Ted shook his head, still slack jawed and apparently speechless. "How about a beer?"

Ted nodded. Shelby got up and poured herself a cup of coffee, and then snagged a beer for Ted from the mini-fridge.

"Anyway, I'm investigating The Center for Bio-Psychological Research." She waited, but Ted only nodded.

"Ted, relax. You haven't done anything wrong, and you aren't in any trouble. Really." She pulled out a chair and sat in front of him, leaning forward to pat his knee. His head jerked up at the touch.

"I'm not?" His Adam's apple bobbed in his throat as he swallowed. "I've only been working at The Center for a year. I don't really know anything about them."

"I know and that's all right." She nodded and gave him a smile she hoped was both kind and encouraging. "It's just that they seem to be up to some things that aren't quite legal, you know?"

Ted nodded, and then immediately shook his head. "No, I don't know. I don't know anything about them." He took a pull on the beer and set it down. His thumbnail picked at the label, slowly peeling it away from the bottle.

"Don't worry about it. I just need some information from you, and then you're going to go away for a while."

Crap! She sounded like a gangster that was going to do away with him.

"Ben and Rick will take you somewhere really nice and see that you have everything you need." Ted still didn't look like he believed her. Who could blame him?

"I'll even get you some really good weed. Some of the good stuff from Oregon or Michigan. I know a guy in Michigan. Mike. He grows some really good stuff." Mike had been a gun dealer who sold a little too far south of the border. Shelby had convinced him to give up some information in exchange for a reduced sentence. With his gun business ruined, Mike had decided to go into small-scale agriculture.

"What do you need to know?" Ted asked. His fingers continued to pick at the label, adding to the pile of wet fuzzy paper on the table.

"You'll like Mike's stuff. It's really good. Not like this desert crap from Mexico."

Ted smiled tremulously and nodded. She'd figured him right. Just the mention of marijuana seemed to have relaxed him.

Shelby spent the next few hours asking him questions about The Center for Bio-Psychological Research. How he'd set up the computer systems and what the passwords were. Who he knew. Who knew what he actually did there. What his relationship was with Dr. Jonah Thomas and Dr. Ruth Carlson.

"Well, that's all I need." She drained her third cup of coffee. "I'll take it from here." She patted Ted's knee again. "You did really good, Ted." She opened the door and motioned Ben and Rick back in. "Now, these guys will take you somewhere you'll be safe until this is all over."

Ted nodded, still looking a little spooked. Hours of questioning hadn't really calmed his nerves all that much.

"But what will The Center think when I don't show up at work?" he asked.

"They'll be told you were in a auto accident tonight. They'll think you're dead."

"Dead? But what about—?"

"Oh, your parents? Your family?" Shelby couldn't remember anything about his parents from the intelligence

24

file on him. "Ben, has Ethan taken care of his parents?"

"No need, his parents are dead."

"Oh, good." She winced as the words left her lips. "I don't mean that it's good that your parents are—I mean it's good for us that—"

Shelby stopped and took a breath. She was really good at her job, but when it came to dealing with regular people, she was the first to admit that she sucked.

"I'm really sorry about your parents." Shelby reached out and squeezed his arm.

"That's okay, it's been a long time."

His voice sounded so sad, it made her chest hurt. The poor kid had to be terrified.

"Ted, it's really going to be all right. The FSA will take care of you until we have this resolved." She patted his hand. "Okay, I think we're done here."

"And the stuff from Michigan?" Ted whispered.

"Oh, yeah, no problem. Ben, we need to get some weed from Mike. Tell him I owe him one."

The men each took one of Ted's arms and walked him to the door. Just as they walked out, Ted turned back to her.

"So, after this is all over, you think we could get together sometime?" Ted looked so hopeful that she didn't have the heart to refuse him flat out.

"We'll see. I'm pretty busy, but maybe." Pretty gutsy of him to ask her out after what he'd just been through. "Ben, you're taking care of the car I left at the club?"

"Consider it done, Ms. Parker."

Shelby closed the door after them and threw the deadbolt. She picked up the discarded sandals and dropped them on the dresser on her way to the bathroom. The small clock next to the bed showed three in the morning. Her eyes were gritty with fatigue, and she wanted nothing more than to fall into a deep sleep until mid-morning. But first she had to wash Carla off.

She started the shower and stripped out of the glittery, blue, spandex dress and uncomfortable wonder bra with the gel inserts, tossing them on top of the sandals. The bright blue contact lenses went into a case, and the platinum blond wig landed on the dresser next to the dress. Makeup remover took care of the heavy eyeliner, mascara, and lipstick. As always, it was a relief to wash off the persona. After a hot shower, she gathered up the Carla disguise and stuffed it into a FedEx box.

The Carla persona was an easy one. It only had to fool a few people for a very short time. Carla was almost a caricature in her simplicity. She was exactly what one expected to see. But Cathy Silvers had to be much deeper, much more a real person. The people at The Center would be looking at her closely. If they saw anything that indicated Cathy was just a façade, Shelby would probably be dead before she knew she'd been found out.

CHAPTER THREE

Shelby pulled on a sport bra, tank top, and baggy shorts in deference to the desert heat and checked out of the motel shortly before noon on Sunday. Time to make sure everything was set up for next week.

At the FedEx office, she filled out the form, slipped it into the plastic envelope on the box, and dropped the box in the pick-up slot. Carla was on her way back to Parker Security and Investigation until she was needed again.

If everything went according to plan, The Center for Bio-Psychological Research would be doing a pre-employment background investigation on her soon, and she wanted it all to be squeaky-clean. No sign of the ditzy blonde who had picked up Ted Ryan at Streakers.

She stopped at the market to purchase some groceries and a newspaper, and then she drove to the furnished apartment that had been rented under the name of Cathy Silvers.

Stale, hot air poured out when she opened the door. She flipped on the air conditioning and started a pot of coffee. Taking a roll of paper towels and a spray bottle of all-purpose cleaner, she made her way through the place, wiping the desert dust from everything.

Along the way, she checked each room to make sure there were signs that Cathy Silvers wasn't a brand new person. The kitchen cabinets were stocked with an assortment of canned goods, partial bags of pasta, and half empty spice jars. Bedroom drawers held sensible cotton underwear, socks, and tee shirts, none of them appearing to be new. Bookshelves were filled with obviously used computer manuals, science fantasy and romance novels, and a few popular self-help books. The bathroom cabinet held half-empty bottles of over-the-counter medication, a partial packet of birth control pills with Cathy's name and old address on the prescription label, and a selection of used makeup.

When the coffee was ready, Shelby poured a cup, settled on the sofa, and punched the speed dial number for Ethan on her cell phone.

"Hey, everything's set here."

"Good. I had all the planted information double-checked. Cathy Silvers is a go," Ethan told her.

"I guess Ben told you what we got from Ted?"

"Yes. Too bad we can't have Josh hack in remotely."

"I know, but I'm not surprised they're using something like thumbprint security. Could be worse, could be retinal scanners. If I can't talk them into giving me access to their computers, I can still pick up their thumbprints and get in. Besides, being there will give me an opportunity to see things I wouldn't otherwise. How's Ted doing? I think we scared the crap out of him."

"He's fine. I've got him holed up at a resort hotel with unlimited pay-per-view and all the latest computer games. And we got the supply from Mike that you insisted on."

"I know you don't like that Ethan, but the poor kid was traumatized. I figured with the right incentives, he'd be less likely to try to bolt."

"I suppose you're right." Ethan sighed and then chuckled. "You know he's telling everyone that he has a date with you after this is all over?"

"Oh, please." Ted really was smoking too much pot. "Anything more from Mrs. Watkins?"

"No. She still hasn't heard from her niece, but she firmly believes Shannon is at The Center or that they know where she is." Ethan sounded frustrated.

"Let's hope I can get in there soon."

"You really think you'll get them to hire you?"

"I'm pretty sure that after I plant the virus, they'll at least want me to come in and fix it."

"I've got Josh Dalton on hold if you need him. I can have him there in two hours."

"I won't need anyone." Why did Ethan always think she needed help?

"Still, just in case."

"Like last night, Ethan?"

Ethan was so silent she almost wondered if they'd lost their connection.

"Is that why Ben and Rick were waiting in the motel room when I got there with Ted?" Shelby asked.

"Calm down, Shelby. I just thought you could use the backup."

"You know me better than that, Ethan. Let's get one thing clear. This is my case. I'm in charge here. You might have had some say in how I handled an op when I worked for the FSA, but you've hired me as a private investigator. I call all the shots."

"Fine. Just be aware that backup is here if you need it."

"You won't be sending any other surprises, will you?"

Ethan sighed. "We'll do this your way."

Shelby hung up and sipped her coffee as she thought about Ethan. Their relationship ran the gamut from antagonistic to symbiotic, with little in between. As much as he annoyed her at times, she honestly couldn't imagine being on an op without his support. However, this wasn't an op. This was a case. Shelby wasn't going to turn down backup as long as it was in the form of intelligence or equipment, and Ethan knew that she preferred to work alone. They'd argued about that a lot when she worked for the FSA, but now it was her case. And she'd do it her way or no way.

The Center for Bio-Psychological Research was located a few miles southwest of Tucson. A low-slung, modern building that sprawled over half an acre of desert.

The entire site was surrounded by an eight-foot stone wall that sported inlaid tiles in the shapes of lizards, coyotes, and cacti. Shelby supposed that was an effort to make it look less like a prison. Several men walked about the grounds dressed in khaki pants and white polo shirts. At first glance, they appeared to be employees. Attendants possibly, or lab personnel. Then she noticed how they watched everything.

Guards. Probably armed, although not obviously.

She stopped at the guard gate and showed her driver's license to the guard. After parking in a visitor space close to the door, she went inside. The lobby was small and well appointed with a contemporary sofa and matching chairs covered in a southwestern design. The coffee table and end tables held an assortment of current magazines. A small table in one corner held a coffeepot, and next to it stood a water cooler with disposable cups. The opposite corner was given over to child-sized furniture and an assortment of educational toys.

A young woman slid open a glass window and smiled at Shelby. "Can I help you?"

"Hi, I'd like to see someone in personnel." Shelby glanced at the receptionist's nametag that identified her as Mandy.

"We don't have a personnel department. If you're looking for a job, you can leave your résumé with me, and I'll see that the right person gets it."

"No, I'm not looking for a job. Well, I am, but not here." Shelby took a breath, letting it sound shaky. "I mean, I need to speak to someone about Ted Ryan."

"Ted? Regarding what?"

"He, uh, he was in an accident Saturday night."

"Oh, so that's why he isn't at work today. I hope he's all right." Mandy smiled sympathetically.

"Well, uh, no, actually, he, uh, he was killed." Shelby made her voice a hoarse whisper.

"Oh, my God!" Mandy stood up from her desk. "I had no idea. I'm sure Dr. Carlson and Dr. Thomas don't know either."

Shelby sobbed and added a sniffle, wiping her eyes. "I'm sorry, it's just still so weird to think . . ."

"Oh, honey, come on in here." Mandy opened the door next to the counter on which Shelby was leaning and motioned her in. "You just have a seat here, and I'll go get one of the doctors."

Shelby shuffled into the tiny cubicle, nodding and sniffling. Her thighs rubbed together from the padded underwear, and her head itched under the dark brown, curly wig.

Mandy left, and Shelby whipped a diskette out of her pocket, slipped it into the floppy drive, and entered the commands to run the virus program. She cocked her ear to the door, listening for returning footsteps. Nothing yet. She fished a tiny microphone out of her sport bra and affixed it to the underside of Mandy's desk.

"Hi, I'm here for my appointment."

Shelby jerked around at the deep male voice. "Oh, sorry. I don't work here."

"Is Mandy here? I'm scheduled for an electroen-cephalogram today."

"Mr. Harmon." Mandy smiled as she came into the receptionist's cubicle, followed by a stern looking woman in a lab coat. Dr. Carlson.

"Hi, Mandy, I think I'm a few minutes late."

"Chase." A slight smile cracked Carlson's face. "Just go on back to the lab. They'll get you set up." He nodded and moved away from the counter.

Although he probably wasn't important to the case, Shelby automatically committed his name and face to memory and watched him from the corner of her eye. He appeared nervous. His fingers twitched, and his eyes glanced around, taking in his surroundings.

"I'm Dr. Carlson. Come with me, please." Ruth Carlson was a tall woman with short blond hair. More striking than attractive. She wore a lab coat over khaki pants and beige heels and looked a bit younger than she had in the pictures Shelby had studied. Shelby obligingly followed her to a small room that contained a round table and several chairs.

"You say Ted was killed in an accident Saturday night?"

"Uh huh." Shelby nodded. "He'd been out to a club with some of his guy friends, and I guess it happened on the way home." She sniffled again, pleased that Dr. Carlson seemed a bit irritated by that. "I just wanted to let you know 'cause I know Ted was totally dedicated to his job."

"Really?"

"Oh, yeah. Completely. Ted and I met online about two years ago. He was so freaking excited when he got

33

the job here. We used to chat for hours about how he was setting up the network and the security protocols."

"Security protocols?" Oh, yeah, Dr. Carlson was paying attention now.

"Oh, sure. I'm a network admin, and Ted was kind of new to a lot of that stuff, so I helped him out."

"Helped him out?" Dr. Carlson's face was getting more pinched and pale by the minute. She pulled an inhaler from her pocket, placed it between her lips, and breathed in deeply.

"Oh, Ted did all the work. I don't want to give you the wrong impression. It's just that I helped him decide what kind of security protocol to set up and stuff."

"I see."

"Ted was so dedicated to this place. He kind of felt like you'd taken a chance on him. You know, since he didn't have a lot of credentials and stuff. But, he was so brilliant." Shelby nodded. "I told him that all the time."

"Yes, well, it was certainly considerate of you to—"

"Just the other day? He called, and he was so concerned about that new virus going around." Shelby let a little gasp escape as if she were trying to control impending tears. "That one that gets through firewalls. He was so worried about it."

"He was?"

"And you know what's really awful? I just emailed him the virus protection program for it the same night he was killed."

"As I said, Ms. . . ."

"Silvers, Cathy Silvers."

"It was very kind of you to come by and let us know what happened." Dr. Carlson stood and opened the door.

"Yeah, I thought you'd want to know. Thanks for seeing me." Shelby got up and shook Dr. Carlson's hand.

Crap. Dr. Carlson wasn't taking the bait.

"If you have any problems, just let me know. Like I said, I helped him work out how the network was set up, so I could probably troubleshoot any problems for you. And I've been a desktop support tech, too, so I know my way around computers."

"That's very kind of you, however—"

"Oh, it's the least I can do. It'd be like honoring Ted's memory, you know? And I'm in between jobs, so you can just call me, and I'll be right here. Until you get someone else." Shelby pulled a slightly crumpled card from her pocket and handed it to Dr. Carlson. "Really. I want to do this for Ted. And, no charge, of course." Cool it, she told herself. Don't press too hard.

"Well. Thank you for coming by Ms. Silvers. I'll be sure to call you if we need your help." Dr. Carlson gestured to the hallway. "You can get back to the lobby this way."

"Sure. It was nice meeting you. Someone else who cared about Ted, you know."

Crap.

Shelby hoisted her backpack over a shoulder and waddled down the hallway. Just as she touched the doorknob, Dr. Carlson called out.

"Ms. Silvers?"

Yes! Shelby turned back to her.

"I was just thinking, that if we were to need you for some computer work, we should go ahead and get some of the preliminaries out of the way."

Suddenly Dr. Carlson's voice sounded a lot friendlier. "Sure, do you want a copy of my résumé?" Shelby hastily opened her backpack and pulled out a résumé , walking back to Dr. Carlson. Suddenly, this didn't feel right. Dr. Carlson's face had suspicion written all over it.

"Oh." Dr. Carlson glanced at the résumé in Shelby's hand. "Well, yes, of course." She took the resume without looking at it. "But we also have a standard procedure that involves talking to our staff psychiatrist and taking a lie detector test. Is that a problem?"

The bitter taste of fear slid across Shelby's tongue. She swallowed hard and forced a smile.

"No, not at all."

CHAPTER FOUR

Shelby summoned a geeky grin. "Just want to make sure you're not hiring a psycho, huh?"

"Something like that." Dr. Carlson smiled tightly. "If you have time, I can have Dr. McRae interview you now. He'll also be administering the polygraph."

"Sure, now is good."

Like hell it was. She could evade a lie detector test, but usually liked to have a little time to prepare herself. Shelby followed her down the hall.

Dr. Carlson knocked on a door and turned back to Shelby when she heard an answer. "Just wait here a moment."

Shelby knew Dr. Carlson didn't have any intention of hiring her. Something had raised a question in the doctor's mind, and she wanted the psychiatrist to check her out. Okay. No problem. Just stay in character. Not like it was the first time this had ever happened. This was *not* a problem.

Shelby took a breath and closed her eyes, letting her thoughts evaporate. Cathy Silvers had nothing to hide.

Unfortunately, she couldn't hear their voices through the door to confirm that opinion. She took another breath and let her muscles relax. The door opened.

"Ms. Silvers, come in. This is Dr. Harrison McRae. His interview will only take a few minutes." Dr. Carlson left abruptly, and Shelby turned to the psychiatrist.

Good thing she'd taken a minute to concentrate on being in the character of Cathy Silvers. Otherwise, she just might have made a fool of herself. Dr. McRae was gorgeous. Delicious. Delectable. And totally, completely off-limits.

His short, dark brown hair stood on end as if he'd just run his hands through it. The rimless glasses perched on the bridge of his straight nose did nothing to hide startling green eyes. Firm lips, set in a square chin smiled politely at her. He appeared to be in his mid-thirties, tall and tanned, with an athletic build. Her idea of a total hunk.

"Ms. Silvers. Please come in."

Crap. An Australian accent. She loved an Australian accent.

Shelby wasn't arrogant enough to think that she was invincible. She had triggers, emotions, and preferences just like anyone else. She was aware of them and had trained herself to ignore them or circumvent them. Find a way to go beyond them. She reminded herself of that fact about three times in the next ten seconds or so.

"Do you mind if I use the restroom first? I had one of those extra large coffees on the way here."

"Certainly. You can use mine." Dr. McRae gestured to a door on the far side of the room.

"Thanks," she mumbled, dropping her backpack on a chair and walking across the polished tile floor to the restroom. She closed the door behind her and leaned against it for a moment, taking a couple of deep breaths and letting them out slowly, forcing herself to relax.

Shelby quickly constructed Cathy Silvers' entire life in her mind, making sure to add incidents that might be on a lie detector test. She concentrated for a moment on the story of how Cathy came to Tucson, her relationship with Ted, and why she had come to The Center today. She worked on the images and details until she could feel them and smell them and taste them. Shelby took another breath and let it out slowly, then tore off a length of tissue, dropped it into the bowl, and flushed the toilet. She turned the water on and washed her hands.

The tissue flushing and hand washing probably wasn't necessary, but her rule was to never leave anything to chance if she didn't have to. Looking in the mirror as she dried her hands on a paper towel, she saw Cathy Silvers. A slightly plump, plain-faced woman in her late twenties. No makeup and her dark brown, curly hair a bit unruly. Loose cotton shirt over baggy jeans and well-worn sneakers.

When Shelby came out of the restroom, Dr. McRae looked up and quirked an eyebrow. "Ready, then?" he asked.

"Sure." She sat in the chair he indicated, while he walked around his desk.

"The written test is fairly brief. Just go through it as quickly as possible and mark the first answer that comes to mind. There are no wrong answers." He pushed a sheet of paper across the desk. Shelby rummaged in her backpack for a pen and turned to the paper.

Did she prefer chocolate or vanilla? Had she ever committed a felony? Were cats or dogs better pets? Had she ever had violent thoughts? What was the longest time she'd spent at one job? Had she ever pretended to be someone else? Did she prefer television or books? Comedy, drama, or fantasy? Had she ever had periods of time that she couldn't remember what she'd done or where she'd been? Did she love her parents?

Shelby marked the appropriate answers and handed the paper back to Dr. McRae. He scanned the page and smiled.

"Very good. Now for the rest." He opened a set of bi-fold doors behind his desk and pulled out a chair and a small table. "If you'd be so kind as to have a seat?" He gestured to the chair and handed her a sheet of paper. "These are the questions I'll be asking."

Shelby settled into the chair and glanced at the questions, while he took a tangle of wires and bands from a drawer and plugged them into the small, sleek monitor on the table. There were no surprises on the list of questions.

Generally they wanted to know if she had a criminal record, if she'd ever been arrested for any act of violence, if she'd ever stolen from an employer, if she'd ever sold information for any reason. Luckily, Cathy Silvers hadn't done anything that interesting.

Shelby pushed up the sleeve of her shirt, making sure to catch the edge of the padded tee shirt underneath. "Is this like a blood pressure thing?" she asked.

"It's a little more complicated than that." He looked up for a moment and then went back to untangling the wires. He strapped a band around her arm just above the elbow and attached sensors to two of her fingers. He then wrapped a tubular strap around her chest and placed a microphone a few inches from her mouth.

"Just relax. First, I'll ask you a few control questions to determine a benchmark. Then a few more questions, and we'll be done."

"Sure." Shelby could see the scroll of paper that would print out the peaks and valleys of lines as she answered his questions. At least she'd know right away if she blew anything.

Dr. McRae looked at the résumé Dr. Carlson had left and made a note. "Have you recently moved to Tucson?"

"Yes." When he looked at the résumé , she took the opportunity to glance at the scroll of paper. So far, so good.

Have you ever climbed Mt. Everest?"

"No."

"Did you graduate from Yale University?"

"Uh . . ." Shelby looked at Dr. McRae and blushed. "I'm sorry, what was the question?"

"Did you graduate from Yale University?"

"Well, I, uh, I actually attended . . ." She grabbed the opportunity to convince him. "Listen, I didn't actually graduate, you know? I mean, I did one semester at Yale, and then I couldn't afford it. It's really expensive!" Shelby let the persona of Cathy Silvers take over and squirmed in the chair, casting a pleading glance at Dr. McRae.

"So, I had to drop out. I kept taking courses at the community college and stuff like that. But I had to get a job. And I just kind of taught myself computer stuff, and then I got a full time job with computers and—"

"Cathy, it's all right. I don't really need to know if you have a degree or if it's from Yale."

"You don't?"

"No, not really."

"Well, it's just kind of embarrassing, you know. I mean, I have all those certifications, but I just couldn't keep going to college. I put that on my résumé because I figured if you're gutsy enough to say you graduated from Yale, who's going to check?"

"Don't worry about it."

"Do you have to tell Dr. Carlson?" Shelby gave him her best worried look.

"I only have to tell Dr. Carlson if you lied and what my general impressions are." Dr. McRae flashed a conspiratorial grin that warmed her right to her toes. She smiled back. "Let's just forget about Yale, shall we?"

Shelby ripped off her clothes as she walked into the apartment. Padded underclothes and a wig! What had she been thinking? Unfortunately, everyone at The Center had already seen her in the chubby disguise, so she was stuck with the pads for a while. She pulled on a tank top and shorts with a sigh of relief and then retrieved an aluminum case from the closet, set it on the bed, and opened it.

The case held an assortment of electronic equipment snuggly packed in foam. Shelby punched in a phone number on the keypad and flipped the switch to the micro recorder and speaker. After a few minutes the sound-activated recorder clicked on. She heard the tail end of a phone ringing; then Mandy's voice answered loud and clear. Good, everything was working. She plugged in the adaptor to save on the batteries, turned off the speaker, and closed the case.

The hard stuff was over for the day, so Shelby stopped in the kitchen to grab a beer before settling on the sofa to call Ethan.

"Hey, they gave me a psych test and a lie detector test. Just in case they decide to hire me, or so she said."

"I assume you passed both without a problem?"

"Of course. Threw me for a loop for a minute though. The thing is, I don't think Dr. Carlson has any intention of hiring me. I think she just wanted to check something out."

"Not surprising. They're very secretive there.

Probably wanted to know if you're really a friend of Ted's or up to something."

"Well, hopefully, she'll be calling me when that virus worms its way through their system. In the meantime, the listening device is working. But I would have been much happier with a wire tap."

Ethan sighed. "Chambers flat out refused. No probable cause."

"There's something else."

"What?"

"They had a staff psychologist do the test. He wasn't in the intel packet you gave me, so he's probably new. Harrison McRae."

"I'll have him checked out. Watch your back, Shelby."

Excellent idea.

"Jackson." Chris answered her phone absently, still reading the weekly reports from her agents.

"Chris," the voice purred into her ear, sending shivers up her back and raising gooseflesh on her arms. "So nice to hear your voice again."

Chris dropped the report on her desk and removed her reading glasses. "Jonah. I'd really rather you not call here."

"Really, Chris, you're special agent in charge. I'm sure you have a private office."

"What do you want?" Chris hurried around her desk

to pull her office door closed and then twisted the lock.

"Just checking to see if there's anything new in the FBI's probe into The Center's activities." Jonah chuckled. "Your boy, Dr. McRae, isn't having much luck with his investigation."

"Wasn't that the whole idea?" God, she hated Jonah Thomas.

"Of course it was. And I really appreciate your help."

"I'm not helping you. You're blackmailing me." She couldn't believe she'd put herself in a position like this.

"I was just thinking about our arrangement, and it occurred to me that you might consider taking the risk of getting rid of me in order to eliminate the possibility of these photos being released."

"I wouldn't take that chance, Jonah." She would, in a heartbeat, if she thought she could pull it off. Nothing would please her more than to have Jonah dead. Even better if it were at her hands. Whatever he was doing at The Center had to be illegal and immoral.

"Possibly. Still, I have to be careful. My life's work is at risk here." Jonah sighed into the phone. "Anyway, I wanted to let you know that if anything happens to me, I've arranged for the photos to be sent to your family, your boss, and several national publications and newspapers."

Chris gasped audibly and then silently cursed herself. She hated showing any signs of weakness to Jonah. Not that it mattered. He had her right where he wanted her.

"I've taken the liberty of sending you some copies of the photos. Just in case you had any doubt as to exactly how incriminating they are."

"You did what? Where did you send them?"

"To your office, of course. They should arrive this morning."

Damn him. "I have to go, Jonah." Chris slammed the phone down and rushed to her door, hands fumbling with the lock. She reached the receptionist's desk just as Joann was opening the mail.

"Joann, I'll open my mail. No need for you to take the time to do that."

"It's okay." Joann handed her a stack of letters that she'd just opened. "I was just finishing." She picked up a large envelope and slid the letter opener under the flap, then turned it over. "Oops. Says confidential. Sorry."

Chris forced herself to take the envelope slowly, resisting the urge to snatch it out of Joann's hands. "No problem. I'll be in my office. No interruptions."

"Sure." Joann turned back to the mail that she'd sorted for the other agents.

Chris closed the door to her office and turned the lock on the knob. Maybe the photos weren't as bad as she feared. She dropped into her chair and stared at the open envelope for a moment. Her breathing was shallow, and her heart raced. Finally, she forced herself to reach in and jerk the contents out. Only her iron control kept her from crying out when she saw the first one.

She stood naked, wrists and ankles bound to a wooden rack. Her breasts, belly, and thighs showed angry red welts. A petite, busty blonde in full dominatrix getup held a whip in one hand and had the other shoved in between Chris' legs. The distinctive tattoo that banded Chris' upper arm was clearly visible, as well as the small strawberry birthmark on her left thigh. Even her face showed clearly. She'd never convince anyone that it wasn't she.

Chris felt herself detach as she looked at the other photographs. Pictures of her having sex with other women. Pictures of her and Jonah at the sex club—Jonah dressed as a woman, her as a man.

Damn him to hell! She'd had no idea the pictures had been taken. She'd have to find a way to get the negatives from him. She couldn't let Jonah make them public.

Of course, her sexual preferences, even her past involvements, shouldn't have any effect on her career. But they would. Chris returned the photos to the envelope, placed it in her briefcase, and spun the numbers to lock it. Everything she'd worked for would be taken from her. Her career with the FBI would be over even if they didn't fire her for moral turpitude. She'd be lucky to get a job as a meter maid. Twenty years in the FBI, working her ass off in order to get promotions, and finally making special agent in charge of the Phoenix division. Now this.

She cursed the night she met Jonah at the sex club in Virginia. It'd been almost ten years ago, and she'd just accepted the fact that she liked women a lot more than men. She was just experimenting, testing her limits, enjoying the freedom she felt with finally embracing her sexuality. Jonah had swooped down on her and pulled her into his kinky games. It had been fun for a while, but when she'd tired of it Jonah kept cajoling her back. The last time had been only a couple of years ago.

Chris pulled open her bottom desk drawer, rifled through the file folders and pulled one out. Opening the folder, she skimmed the information until she found the phone number she wanted, and then punched it in on the keypad on her phone.

"Bottoms Procurement Service."

"Hey, Jim, glad to see you're still in business," Chris said.

"Who's this?"

"Chris Jackson."

"Listen, I'm not doing anything illegal these days. Strictly on the up and up."

"That's too bad, Jim. I need to find someone."

"Who?"

"It's more what," Chris said. "I need something retrieved."

"I see. And what makes you think I'd be able to help? Or even be willing to?"

"I can make your life a living hell, Jim. And I can arrange for you to go back to prison."

"You don't have anything on me."

"I can manufacture it." Chris waited while Jim Bottoms considered her threat.

"What exactly do you need retrieved?"

"Some negatives. They are probably in a safe in a private residence."

"Security system?" Jim asked.

"Most likely."

"Yeah, I know someone who could do the job. You can meet her tonight at The Bashful Bandito on Seventh at midnight."

"What's her name?" Chris asked.

"Zoe. You can't miss her. She's a little thing but she gets the job done. Has long red hair. Usually hanging out with a bunch of bikers."

"I'll be there."

CHAPTER FIVE

Dr. Harrison McRae locked the door to his office, pulled the videotape out of the hidden camera, and fed it into the VCR. He watched intently as the interview and lie detector test with Cathy Silvers played before him. She hardly faltered during the lie detector test. Her eye blink rate increased slightly at some of the questions, but otherwise she'd seemed completely honest. Especially with that part about having not really graduated from Yale. But the interview portion was more telling. Several times her eye blink rate increased to the point that she had to be lying about something. And her gaze occasionally strayed to the wrong quadrant when answering a question.

Cathy Silvers most certainly had lied to him. The only question was just how she came to be so incredibly good at it. He turned the tape off and gathered his notes. Time to report to Dr. Carlson and tell a few lies of his own.

"Come." Ruth Carlson closed the laptop and turned toward the door.

"I have the results of Cathy Silvers' tests." Mac hesitated at the doorway.

"Let's have it, Mac." Ruth waved him in. Mac took a chair opposite her desk and shuffled the papers he carried.

"Her tests all came back normal." Mac shrugged. "She lied on the lie detector test about having a degree from Yale, but then explained that she didn't have the monetary resources to complete her education. Her personality profile test shows that she's as normal as most people."

"Really?" Ruth tapped a pencil against her lips. "Could she be faking it?"

"Fake being normal?' McRae shook his head. "Unlikely. Why do you ask?"

"I got the feeling she was hiding something. Something just didn't ring true about her offer to help with any computer problems that might arise."

"Someone with Cathy's lack of social skills would most likely display a certain nervousness. Especially with an authority figure, someone she considered above her station." That must have been the right button to push, because Ruth unconsciously straightened her shoulders, her lips lifting fractionally. "I think her offer to help might be due to the fact that she was in love with Ted Ryan."

"She was?" Ruth reached her hand out for the papers Mac held. "I suppose I hadn't thought of that."

"It's a way of maintaining contact with him. Rather, with something that was a part of him."

"Ted never mentioned her. Of course, he wasn't likely to talk to me about his love life." Ruth looked through the personality profile test that Cathy Silvers had taken.

"I'm not certain that her affections were returned. From the interview, I ascertained that she met him online and subsequently decided to move here. No doubt hoping to foster a deeper relationship with him."

"And that's normal?" Ruth asked.

"Well, it's not totally aberrant behavior." Mac chuckled. "She's a plump, rather plain woman who's a computer geek. It probably is quite normal for that type."

"Very well." Ruth stood to indicate that the meeting was over. "Thank you for taking time to do that on the spur of the moment."

"If you decide to call her in to work with the computers, I think you'd be safe. There's nothing to indicate she would have any inclination to do any damage. In fact, her affection for Ted might make her strive to do a better job."

"It's highly unlikely that she'll be called in for anything. If we have computer problems before we can hire another person, I'll call in a professional team."

"That's probably wise, Dr. Carlson."

"If you'll excuse me, I have a meeting with Dr. Thomas in a few minutes."

"Certainly. Glad to have been of help. These will be in a file in my office, if you've further need of them."

Mac stopped at the end of the hall and made random notes on a pad of paper, as he watched Dr. Carlson's office from the corner of his eye. She left her office just moments after him and turned down the hallway that led to the lab and surgical unit.

He moved to the alcove that held the coffee maker and water cooler. From there he could see the large window in the laboratory. He dropped a tea bag into a cup, still watching Dr. Carlson as she stopped to speak to one of the lab technicians. Mac lowered the cup and pressed the button to dispense hot water. Dr. Carlson left the lab and pushed open the door to the surgical unit.

"Damn!" Mac dropped the cup and jerked his fingers away from the scalding water. So, Dr. Carlson and Dr. Thomas were having a meeting in the surgical unit. Strange place for a meeting. Hell, it was strange that The Center even had a surgical unit.

When he'd questioned Dr. Carlson about it, she had said it was in case of an emergency and he'd appeared to accept that explanation. The surgical unit was small but state of the art. No clinic would install such a costly feature if they weren't planning on using it. And they certainly wouldn't use it for a meeting. What were they doing in there?

Mac glanced at the door to Dr. Carlson's office. He knew the door would be locked, and he almost twitched with frustration. For the past several weeks, he'd searched for information on Shannon and Sam Masterson and found nothing. But he hadn't been able to get into the offices of Dr. Carlson or Dr. Thomas.

Sam was one of his patients at The Center, although they'd presented him as Sam Matson, a four year old living with foster parents after the death of his mother three months earlier. He'd uncovered a record of death for a Sarah Matson, and he hoped that didn't mean that Shannon Masterson was dead.

Ruth changed into scrubs and lathered her hands and arms at the basin. When she entered the procedure room, she saw that Jonah had already arrived. Five years of working with Jonah had done nothing to mitigate her occasional irritation with him. It had, however, convinced her of his brilliance. Occasional irritation was a small price to pay to work with him. Especially on something so important.

"I assume you want to use electro-ejaculation in this instance." Jonah snapped on surgical gloves and pulled his mask up to cover his mouth and nose.

"Of course." Ruth made a note on the chart and then pulled on her gloves. "Unless you have another method you like."

Ruth pulled the hospital gown down to reveal the nearly hairless chest of Chase Harmon. That would make it easier to attach the electrodes that fed his vital signs to the monitor. Of course, it was a relatively simple procedure, and she could have done it without monitoring his vitals. But Ruth preferred safe to sorry. Especially on such a valuable specimen.

"Don't be ridiculous, Ruth. This is too important to leave to chance." Jonah opened several packets and pressed the adhesive backed snaps to the patient's chest.

Ruth attached wires to the snaps, then plugged the wires into a compact machine and flipped a switch. The machine whirred to life and emitted a series of soft beeps. A small screen displayed a graph of the patient's heartbeat and numbers flashed his blood pressure and oxygen level.

Jonah beckoned to Ruth with a long, slender hand. "Help me roll him onto his side."

Ruth placed her hands firmly on Chase's shoulder and back. Even though the room was cool, the warmth of his skin seeped through her latex gloves.

"He's a big one, isn't he?" She pushed Chase's shoulder as Jonah pulled from the other side. The surgical gown parted to reveal firm, muscular buttocks and massive thighs. His skin was dimpled with gooseflesh from the coldness of the room.

Perfection. The man was in exceptional physical condition. Something she could appreciate as a doctor and a woman. She glanced at the broad expanse of his muscular back and made a mental note to be sure all the adhesive from the electrodes was removed before he awakened. She didn't want him suspecting that they had harvested his sperm rather than performing the electroencephalogram. He'd been reluctant to agree to having an EEG done while he was sleeping, but she'd convinced him that it was a necessary part of testing his psychic abilities.

"Well, you know what they say," Jonah said. Ruth cocked an eyebrow at him in question. He chuckled. "The bigger the better."

"You are so juvenile."

"Oh, come on, Ruth. You have to take some pleasure in your work." Jonah glanced at the window that afforded a view of an identical procedure room, as the orderly wheeled in their other patient. "You're sure the time is right?"

"Absolutely. I've charted her cycle for two months. If we're going to get a baby, this is the best possible day for that to occur." Ruth opened the package of electrode probes, placed them on the tray, and picked up the speculum. More coldness for the patient, though he wouldn't be aware of it. "Although I'd feel better if there were an orgasm involved."

"Yes, wouldn't we all?" Jonah murmured.

"You know what I mean," she snapped, letting the speculum drop onto the metal tray with a clank. "There's better sperm motility if an orgasm occurs in the female. With insemination we need all the motility we can get."

"I understand. But we don't really have a choice, do we?" Jonah watched as she prepared the patient. "You did say the chances are better for a female child?"

"Yes. We've gone over this, Jonah. The acid/alkaline balance is correct; the timing is best for a female. Of course, there are no guarantees."

"I realize that, Ruth. I simply would prefer to have a female. The ability is usually so much stronger in females." He frowned, then shook his head. "I can only wonder why."

"I still think that's just a pet theory of yours. If we get a female with stronger abilities than the boy, I'll be amazed. I've never even heard of anyone with his kind of ability." Ruth glanced at Jonah and frowned. "Why don't you go prep our patient in there? This will be done in a few minutes, and we want to get the sperm into her while it's still fresh." She nodded toward the other room.

This was difficult enough without him watching her every move. Someday they would be able to do this with gene manipulation. But that was probably years off. They hadn't even identified the gene markers yet. For now, this was the best they could do. Combine sperm and ova from the same two people who created Sam. She still marveled at their luck in discovering that Chase was Sam's father. Shannon Masterson had insisted that she didn't know the name of the man who'd gotten her pregnant just before she graduated college. Then Chase had shown up asking about Shannon, although he'd seemed surprised to find that she'd had a child.

They'd told him they had no idea where she was, but he'd hung around and even volunteered for the psychic research program. By the time they tested him, they'd done enough investigation to know that Chase and Shannon had gone to college together and been involved for some time before Chase joined the Marines. A DNA test had confirmed that Chase was

Sam's father. She picked up the speculum again and waited for Jonah to leave.

"Certainly. We don't want to take a chance with stale sperm. Call if you need any assistance."

Jonah walked into the adjoining room and gazed at the young woman strapped to the table. Her red-gold hair spread across the small, paper-covered pillow, eyes closed in what appeared to be a deep, peaceful sleep. He pulled the surgical gloves off, discarded them in the biohazard bin, and then pulled on a clean pair.

"You don't know how lucky you are, young lady," he murmured. "You'll be the mother of a superior being. Several superior beings, eventually."

The beginning of a new breed. He'd spent most of his thirty-two year research career working on this. Years spent getting government funding for the research which took valuable time away from his experiments. Still, he had persevered. And he'd shown remarkable progress. His last research program had proved that there was a genetic link in psychic ability.

Of course, when the government idiots had taken offense at his unauthorized experiments and closed down the program, he'd not shared that information with them. They were too stupid to understand the implications anyway. But, that very information had made it possible to convince private individuals and other countries to fund him. Ten years of unlimited funding with the best equipment and methods had brought him to this point. And his benefactors didn't bother themselves with how he obtained his research subjects or what happened to them.

Jonah didn't deliberately harm the subjects, but accidents happened. Experiments went wrong. He firmly believed the means justified the end in this case. Because now, he could breed humans to produce a child with exceptional psychic abilities. Behavioral and drug therapy, along with brainwashing techniques, would then ensure the child would grow up to follow orders. To use his or her abilities in any way he or she was instructed.

Jonah gently lifted each of her legs onto the braces and placed her feet in the padded stirrups. Pulling her hospital gown up, he swabbed her abdomen, thighs, and genitalia with a disinfecting wash. "Can't take any chances with our new little one, now, can we?"

CHAPTER SIX

Shelby stood under the pounding shower at the gym and let the hot water massage her muscles. Forty-five minutes on the treadmill, running at the highest incline, an hour of free weights, and half an hour in the pool. Normally her workouts weren't so long or so intense, but she had no idea when she'd get back to the gym. She wrapped a towel around her hair and then dried off. The dressing room was empty, so she didn't have to hide in one of the large stalls to squirm into the padded garments she was beginning to hate.

As soon as she got back to the apartment, Shelby tore off the padded clothes and stepped into shorts and a tank top. She settled on the sofa with a thick manual on computer networking and munched on a chicken Caesar salad.

Two hours later she dug into a pint of gourmet, chocolate brownie ice cream, hoping the sugar and caffeine would restart her brain. Her cell phone chirped, saving her from returning to the dry technical manual.

"What?" Shelby asked.

"We've got the background check back on Harrison McRae," Ethan said.

"Shoot."

"Nothing very interesting until a few years back. Seems he was investigated for performing experiments on patients without their full knowledge."

"Yikes! What kind of experiments?" She closed the ice cream container and returned it to the freezer.

"Essentially, they consisted of brainwashing techniques. Dr. McRae defended his treatment saying that he was helping his patients overcome emotional blocks that were adversely affecting their lives." Ethan's voice sounded like he was reading from the report.

"Without their full knowledge." Scum. The handsome doctor was pond scum.

"There's more. He was also accused of having a personal relationship with a couple of his female patients."

"And he seemed like such a nice guy. What happened with the allegations?"

"The cases were resolved without going to court."

"He paid them off, then." Super scum. Pig slime. And he was such a hunk. That grin that quirked up one corner of his mouth. Those rimless glasses. Shelby inadvertently sighed.

"Looks that way." Ethan paused. "Is there a problem?"

"No, not at all." It's not like she'd ever *really* consider a relationship with anyone involved in a mission, regardless of which side they were on. "Just seems like the more I learn about men, the more disappointed I am."

"We're not all that bad," he chided.

"That's what you all say."

"And we all mean it. Hopefully, you'll be called in on an emergency network problem soon by The Center."

"I set the virus up so that it won't appear for a few days. Thought it'd be less suspicious that way."

"Good idea."

"In the meantime, can you find out where Dr. McRae hangs out?" Shelby asked. "Maybe I can get some kind of information from him."

"I'll check it out and let you know."

"Okay. Good night."

Zoe Drummond parked her Kawasaki Ninja a block away from her target destination. She pulled the custom cover from the saddlebags and draped it over the bike, hiding her helmet underneath. She didn't normally leave her helmet, but she couldn't take it with her, and there was little chance it would be stolen in this neighborhood of mini mansions. It might take a few extra seconds to remove the cover if she needed to get away in a hurry, but that was better than someone noticing the bike, and possibly remembering the license plate. A lot of the bikers at The Bashful Bandito liked to give her a hard time about her crotch-rocket. But in her line of work, fast was good. Getting away fast was sometimes imperative.

She crossed a backyard, careful to stay out of the range of the motion sensor lights mounted to the patio roof, and easily climbed the four-foot stone wall that stood between her and the next house. Zoe hugged the stone wall as she made her way around the yard to the back door of the garage. She peered in through the small window and breathed a sigh of relief when she saw the car was gone. He'd been gone last night when she'd cased the place, and it was almost too much to hope that he'd be gone again tonight. But her client had told her that he was a doctor and away from his home frequently.

Zoe inserted her lock picks into the lock and deftly opened the door. Inside, she pulled the cover off the master control box of the security system. In minutes she'd deactivated the system. Wouldn't it be nice if the safe turned out to be as easy as the security system?

Safes and security systems were her specialty. The combination brought her jobs that paid well, so she didn't have to do them very often. Just enough to pay her living expenses and her tuition. Six more months of school and she could leave her life of crime behind. That thought brought a feeling of anticipation mixed with fear, and she pushed it aside. This was no time to be distracted.

She slipped into the kitchen and felt a familiar rush of adrenaline. She tamped it down. Walking quickly through the kitchen, she ascended the backstairs and walked down the hall to a bedroom that had been turned into an office. The safe was in a corner behind the desk. She smiled when she saw it, familiar with the brand and the type of lock. She hadn't opened one of these in a long time. Placing an earphone in her ear, she kneeled in front of the safe and pressed a small disc against the door, next to the lock. When the lock clicked and the door swung open, she checked her watch. Four minutes and twenty-eight seconds. She was slipping. It usually took less than three minutes.

The safe held several envelopes, a couple of file folders, and two jewelry boxes. Zoe quickly opened the envelopes and went through the contents. The third one held photographs and a smaller envelope of negatives. She flicked on her flashlight and glanced through the photographs. The woman who had hired her was in most of them. And in several very compromising positions. Zoe shrugged and slipped the photos and negatives back into the envelope. She only had to be sure she had the right photos and negatives. She stuffed all the envelopes and folders inside her jacket and grabbed the jewelry boxes.

This job had an added advantage. Her client wanted this to appear to be a random burglary, so Zoe would take everything in the safe and a few items from the bedroom. Anything she got, she was free to keep. Zoe quickly flipped open the jewelry boxes. A Rolex watch, and a platinum and diamond ring. She stuffed the boxes into the pocket of her leather jacket and closed the door to the safe.

She then walked into the master bedroom. The top dresser drawer yielded a set of ruby studs with matching cuff links. She dropped them into a pocket and considered what else she could take.

Suddenly, pain exploded through her head, and she crumpled to the floor.

Friday morning Shelby still hadn't gotten a call from the people at The Center about their computer problems. She knew the virus had started worming its way through their system on Wednesday, just as she'd planned. Several times each day she checked the tapes from the listening device she'd planted at the receptionist's desk. The first problems had been talked about on Wednesday, and yesterday Dr. Carlson had complained to Mandy about it more. Were they going to wait until the damn virus had eaten everything on their computers?

Shelby also hadn't managed to run into Dr. McRae. Evidently, all he did was go to work and go home. He didn't hang out at bars and wasn't involved in any kind of sport. Hell, the man hardly even shopped for food.

Shelby opened the aluminum case, rewound the tape, and punched the fast button so she could listen to everything speeded up but still recognizable. After an hour of noise and meaningless conversations, she heard Dr. Carlson's voice and pressed the button to slow the tape down to regular speed. Dr. Carlson instructed

Mandy to call a company called InfoTech Professionals, and Shelby groaned. Now she'd have to change her plans.

She listened to Mandy's call to InfoTech Professionals. They assured her they would have someone out there that afternoon and that they'd work over the weekend if necessary to fix the problem. Shelby punched the speed dial number for Ethan into her cell phone.

"The Center is calling in a firm called InfoTech Professionals."

"How long do we have?"

"They said they'd be out there this afternoon."

"Okay. I'll have Josh there in two hours."

"No, I don't need Josh. I'll handle it myself."

"Shelby, it'll be easier with Josh there."

"I said I don't need him. Just have him email me the FTP program."

Ethan sighed. "I'd be happier if Josh assisted you on this."

"And I'll be happier if I'm doing it myself."

"I'll send him down, just in case." Ethan hurried on before she could interrupt. "You don't have to use him, but he'll be there if you need him."

"Fine." Shelby knew when to let Ethan think he'd gotten his way. Josh could just cool his heels while she got into The Center. Then he could go back to Denver. "Tell Josh I'll meet him at InfoTech's offices."

❖ ❖ ❖

"Shelby Parker, FSA." She flashed her badge and identification to the young woman. "I need to see the owner."

"Do you have an appointment, Ms. Parker?"

"I don't need one. This is official FSA business."

"I'm sorry, but Mr. Knowles is booked up today. Perhaps if you left your card, I could have him call you?"

"I don't think so. As I said, this is official FSA business."

"Is that Futuristic Software Associates?" the receptionist asked hesitantly.

"It's the Federal Security Agency. Like the Central Intelligence Agency or the Federal Bureau of Investigation."

Realization slowly dawned on the woman's face. "Oh, I see. Just a moment." She picked up the phone and punched an intercom button. "Mr. Knowles, there's a Ms. Parker from the FSA here to see you." She listened intently, then turned away and lowered her voice. "No, it's the Federal Security Agency." Her head bobbed up and down. "Yes, like that."

"Thank you." Shelby smiled at her and waited. Thirty seconds later she heard footsteps. Evidently, she could still count intimidation as one of her strong points.

"I'm Dan Knowles. Can I help you?"

Shelby turned back from her perusal of the aquarium. Early fifties, a little pudgy from sitting behind a desk for too many years, short hair, stylish clothes, and those tiny glasses that were the current fashion statement for the visually impaired.

"Can we talk in your office?"

"Certainly." Dan led her down a wide hallway to a large office. He opened the door and gestured for her to enter. "Susan said you're with the FSA?"

"Yes. Are you familiar with the FSA?"

"Oh, yes. I was quite the radical in college. I'm familiar with all the federal investigative agencies. May I see your ID?"

Liar-head. From his conversation with the receptionist, Shelby knew he'd thought she was with the Futuristic Software guys. She handed over the leather wallet that held her badge and identification.

"You know this could easily be duplicated."

"Actually, it can't. But someone could easily make a copy that *looks* like the real thing."

"I think I'll need more than this," Dan said.

"I'm not surprised. Here's a number you can call to confirm my identity. And you can call the local FBI office or your local police to confirm that the number is a valid one."

"And I suppose you have the number for the local FBI office too?"

Shelby grinned at him. "Of course, but I think it might be better if you look it up yourself. I wouldn't want you thinking that this is a ruse or anything."

Dan turned to the laptop on his desk. He clicked the mouse, typed in a few commands, and opened the home page for the FBI. He picked up his phone and punched in the number for the headquarters in Washington, DC.

Shelby looked around his office while he spoke to someone for a few minutes. InfoTech Professionals was obviously doing well. His walls boasted some original artwork, and his furniture was a tasteful rosewood. She heard his phone click and more buttons being punched. He spoke to someone again, mentioning her name. After a moment he replaced the phone.

"So, exactly how can I help you, Ms. Parker?"

"You were contacted early this morning by The Center for Bio-Psychological Research. They have computer problems, and you assured them you would have a team there this afternoon."

"Yes. I have one of my lead techs assembling a team now."

"Stop him. You won't be sending anyone out to The Center."

"I won't?" Dan raised his eyebrows, but didn't seem to be resistant to her instructions.

"No. I'm expecting an associate, Josh Dalton, here within an hour. He'll wait here while I go to The Center as one of your techs. If I need Josh, I'll call and you'll send him out. Your job will be to answer any phone calls from The Center and assure them that I am indeed from your office and highly qualified to take care of their problem."

"Can I ask what this is about?" Dan asked.

"Yes, but you won't get an answer." Shelby grinned again, pleased that he wasn't going to fight her on this.

"I'm not surprised." Dan sighed. "You'll need to

have an InfoTech identification badge and a shirt with our logo. All our techs wear them." Dan turned his palms up. "Anything else?"

An hour later, Shelby was enjoying some gourmet coffee in Dan's office when his intercom buzzed.

"Mr. Knowles, there's a Josh Dalton here to see you." Dan's receptionist sounded a little breathless.

"Send him back, Susan."

"Hey, Josh." Shelby gave him a finger wave from the sofa. "Sorry to drag you out here."

"Hey, no problem. Getting out of the office occasionally is good for me."

"Dan Knowles." Dan stood and held out his hand.

"Can I get you some coffee or anything?" Susan lingered at the door, obviously awed by Josh.

"Thanks, that would be great. Just black." Josh flashed her a smile.

Shelby shook her head. His smile was so guileless and charming, it should be classified as a weapon. Josh Dalton was an impressive piece of masculinity. Most men were intimidated by him at first, and most women were attracted. He stood about six four and had the kind of muscular build that came from good genes and some serious gym time. His blond hair was thick and wavy, and his blue eyes sparkled with humor and intelligence. A square jaw and quick smile completed the package. As if his looks weren't enough, Shelby knew Josh boasted an IQ in the genius range.

Josh set his thick laptop case on Dan's desk and shook his hand. "Nice to meet you."

"So, you're one of the FSA's computer guys?" Dan asked.

"That's me," Josh agreed.

"Man, would I love to see what you've got in that case." Dan made a forlorn sound that was halfway between a sigh and a chuckle.

"You boys get acquainted while I change in the ladies' room," Shelby suggested.

The men headed down the hallway, and Shelby made for the ladies' room with her backpack. Ten minutes later she was looking in the mirror at Cathy Silvers. Plump, plain faced, with dull, curly, brown hair, and now wearing an InfoTech Professionals shirt. She closed the backpack and joined Josh and Dan in Dan's office.

"And check this out," Josh said tapping on the keys of his laptop and then leaning back to allow Dan a better view of the screen.

"No way!" Dan's eyes were wide.

"Way! And this can—"

"You aren't showing Dan our agency secrets are you?" Shelby asked.

"Not the important ones." Josh grinned.

"Wow!" Dan looked at Shelby, his mouth gaping. "You don't even look like yourself!"

"Yeah, she's good at that," Josh grinned. "You should see this one get-up she has. Looks for all the world like a senior citizen. Frumpy clothes, gray hair, that shuffling walk that older people have." Josh shook his head. "You'd never know."

"I'm impressed." Dan nodded.

"Hey, don't I need an InfoTech shirt too?" Josh asked.

"Not this time, Josh. You're staying here. I'll call if I need you."

Josh sighed. "Ethan said I was going in with you."

"Ethan lied."

"I know." Josh held his hands up. "Your op, your way. Still, I could be useful."

"And if I need you, I'll call. In the meantime, you and Dan can tech-talk to each other."

"This is because of that first op, isn't it?"

Shelby smiled at him. "Leaving your equipment behind was a bad thing."

"It was only that one time. And it was my first op."

"I know. It isn't that, Josh. This is just how I work."

Josh sighed and sat down again. "I never get to have any fun."

"You know what to say if anyone from The Center calls?" she asked Dan.

"No problem. I didn't get to where I am today without being able to tell a little white lie occasionally." Dan winked and handed her the keys to one of the company vans.

"Hi, Mandy."

The Center's receptionist turned to greet Shelby. "Oh, Cathy, hi. What can I do for you?"

"I'm here from InfoTech Professionals to fix your virus problem."

"Hey, you got a job? That's great."

"Yep. Just temporary, but it pays good." Shelby shrugged.

Mandy lifted the phone and pressed the intercom button. "Dr. Carlson, the tech from InfoTech Professionals is here." She replaced the phone and looked back at Shelby. "She'll be right here."

"So, it seems like you guys got that mole virus," Shelby ventured.

"I don't know what you call it, but it's eaten up a lot of files. They're just gone!"

"Sounds like the mole virus, all right," she said. "Good thing is that we can fix that and get back all your files. It's tedious, but not difficult."

"Dr. Carlson will be happy to hear that."

"Happy to hear what, Mandy?"

Mandy jumped a little in her seat. "Oh, Dr. Carlson. Cathy's here from InfoTech Professionals." Mandy busied herself with stacking some papers as Dr. Carlson stared at Shelby.

"Hi, Dr. Carlson." Shelby held out her hand, hoping to end the awkward moment. "I just got hired by InfoTech Professionals. Is that weird or what?" She pumped Dr. Carlson's hand.

"Isn't it." Dr. Carlson pulled her hand away from Shelby's.

"Perhaps you could give me a little background on your problem," Shelby suggested.

"Certainly." Dr. Carlson turned and walked down the hallway. "The only problem we've noticed so far is that files just seem to be missing. I'm assuming that's one of the effects of this mole virus."

"That certainly sounds like the mole virus. Not to worry, though. I can not only get rid of the virus, but probably restore most of your files as well."

"That would be much appreciated. How long will it take?"

"No way to tell until we get started." Shelby shrugged. "It depends on how much damage the virus has done."

"Fine. Where do you want to start?"

"I'll start in the computer room. I'll need the administrative passwords for your servers, if you have them. Otherwise, I'll have to reset some of the controls. Might take a while."

"I thought as much." Dr. Carlson handed her a file folder. "Unless Ted changed the passwords recently, they should all be in there."

"Are there passwords on the desktops?"

"No." Dr. Carlson shook her head. "Except for mine and Dr. Thomas'. Our computers contain very sensitive information about our clients. I'm afraid it isn't possible for you to view anything on our computers."

"So, your computers aren't connected to the network?" Shelby asked.

"Well, of course they are. But we keep the sensitive files on our hard drives."

"Not for long. That mole virus will eat them up."

"What?" Dr. Carlson looked startled. "But there's been no indication that the virus has affected our computers."

"Not yet. But trust me, this mole virus is a nasty little bugger. If you've been connected to the network since the virus arrived, it's just a matter of time before your sensitive files disappear."

"Dear God." Dr. Carlson pulled the inhaler from her pocket and gave herself a shot in the mouth. Shelby took a perverse pleasure at seeing her composure crack a bit.

"It's not like I need to view any of the files in order to eradicate the virus, Dr. Carlson. Someone can be present while I work, if you're worried about anything."

"I see. I suppose that would be acceptable. Although Dr. Thomas and I are both very busy. I suppose I could have one of the guards stay with you while you work on our computers."

"Excellent. I'll start on the servers, and when the guard is ready, I'll clean up your computers."

The first time she'd been there, she had only seen the very front of the building that held the reception area and several offices. Dr. Carlson led her down a hallway, passing a set of double doors with windows that opened into what appeared to be a lab area. The computer room was at the end of the hallway.

Shelby worked on the servers for almost an hour before Dr. Carlson returned with a guard in tow. She followed them back to Dr. Carlson's office and sat down in front of the computer. Shelby pressed the space bar and waited as the screen glowed to life.

"Hey, Dr. Carlson, it's asking for a thumbprint. What's up with that?"

"I have to log on using my thumbprint for identification. It's a security measure." Dr. Carlson pressed her thumb against the glass front of a small box on her desk. A light flashed from behind the glass, and the laptop whirred and clicked.

"Wow, that's like real James Bond stuff."

Dr. Carlson ignored her. "When you're finished here, I'll log on to Dr. Thomas' computer for you." She gave the guard a meaningful look, which Shelby was pretty sure meant for him to watch her like a hawk.

Shelby fished the diskette from the pocket on her backpack and slid it into the slot. The guard stood so close, she could smell the garlic he'd had at lunch.

"What's that?" he asked.

"It's the software to detect and clean the virus. See?" She ejected the diskette and held it up so he could see the label. Like that had anything to do with what was on the diskette. He nodded, and she slid the diskette into the slot again. Shelby started a standard virus scan, just so something would be on the screen to distract the guard. Working quickly, she clicked on the buttons that would install the File Transfer Protocol Service Josh had programmed and clean up the virus she'd installed earlier that week. The guard seemed mesmerized by the virus scan program and didn't mention anything else she was doing. Josh's program took only a few seconds to upload, but she let the virus scan run through all the files.

"That's it. This machine is clean."

"Dr. Carlson will be happy to hear that."

Less than an hour later, Shelby assured Dr. Carlson that even though the mole virus had been present on both their laptops, she'd been able to eradicate it and they hadn't lost any files. Dr. Carlson rewarded her hard work with a tight smile.

"Have you finished with the servers?"

"I've installed a program that will search and clean all the files. It'll take a while to complete," Shelby said.

"I see." Dr. Carlson frowned, and Shelby could imagine how uncomfortable she was having someone poke around in her computer files.

"It'll probably take ten or twelve hours for the program to complete, but it beats having to do each one individually. That would take several days. How many other computers do you have?"

"About a dozen. Although some of them are in the laboratory and clinic area. We don't normally allow anyone back there."

Shelby shrugged. "If they haven't been on the network, it's not a problem. I can start on the ones out here."

"The receptionist is still working, so perhaps you can check Dr. McRae's computer. He's already left for the day."

After Dr. Carlson let her in to Dr. McRae's office, she settled behind his desk, pulled out the diskette, and started the program. That seemed to satisfy the doctor, and she departed without a word. Shelby smiled at her as she left. The woman could seriously use some social skills. At least she hadn't assigned one of the guards to watch her every move here.

Shelby looked around Dr. McRae's office. She'd need to be here for a while, just to make it appear that she was actually checking his computer for the virus. Might as well take a peek in his drawers. That thought brought up a visual that Shelby firmly pushed to the nether recesses of her mind.

She pulled open a drawer and scanned the file labels. Most of them were names, Cathy Silvers among them. Patient files, she supposed. Shelby pulled one out and glanced through it. Nothing of any interest, except some notations about levels of psychic ability. The next few were pretty much the same. A variety of both men and women, ages from teens to forties. The only thing common to all the files was the notation on their psychic abilities.

There were no files with either Shannon's or Sam's names. That in itself seemed strange. As the staff psychiatrist, Shelby figured he'd have some contact with every client at The Center. And according to the intel Ethan had given her, Shannon had brought Sam here at least a few times.

She replaced the files in the drawer, her hand lingering on the Cathy Silvers file, curious what the doctor had written about her. This seemed like a perfect opportunity to find out.

"Looking for something, Ms. Silvers?" Dr. McRae asked.

CHAPTER SEVEN

Shelby froze. Caught with her hand in the damn cookie jar. Dr. McRae closed the door softly behind him and leaned against it.

"Perhaps if you tell me what you're looking for, I could be of some assistance?" His voice was soft, but she definitely heard a menacing undertone.

"And maybe you'd like to tell me why you're keeping a file on me?" Shelby pulled the Cathy Silvers file out of the drawer and held it up to him.

"I have a file because if I just left interview notes and test results lying about, the place would be a mess," he answered with exaggerated patience.

"You know what I mean." She let her voice and hand shake a bit, hoping he'd interpret that as a combination of fear and anger. "You have no reason to keep a file on me. Dr. Carlson said that that interview and the tests were in case she wanted to hire me. So, why isn't that information in personnel instead of here?"

"We don't have a personnel department per se. So, there was nowhere to put your file but in my office."

Dr. McRae's eyes narrowed. "And aside from that, you still had no business going into my desk."

"I didn't go into it. Well, not exactly. I bumped into the drawer while I was checking your computer for the virus, and the drawer just kind of opened. I saw this file folder with my name on it."

"Really?"

Hard to tell if he was buying her story or not. Before he could say anything else, there was a knock on the door. Dr. McRae barely got out of the way before it opened.

"I thought you'd left for the day, Dr. McRae." Dr. Carlson stood in the doorway.

"I came back for something."

"Are you finished with Dr. McRae's computer?" Dr. Carlson asked Shelby.

"I just finished," Shelby said.

"So, you're done here."

"For today. I'll need to come back tomorrow and make sure the check completed successfully on the servers." Shelby shot Dr. Carlson a geeky grin. "Part of the service. Making sure that everything is handled completely to your satisfaction."

"I see. Then I'll see you tomorrow morning at nine." Dr. Carlson barely nodded, turned, and marched down the hallway. Shelby stared after her. She had the social skills of a wolverine.

"Dr. McRae, I'm really sorry for what happened. It was just weird seeing my name on a file, you know?"

"I can imagine. Next time, just ask."

At least she could come back tomorrow. Hopefully, there would be fewer people around on a Saturday, and she could nose around some. In the meantime, all their files would be uploading to an FSA server.

Shelby pulled the InfoTech Professionals van into the InfoTech parking lot and lumbered inside. The day had heated up, and Dan's office was refreshingly cool. She dropped her tech case on a chair, grabbed her backpack, and ducked into the restroom to change. Dan and Josh were waiting for her when she finished.

"How'd it go?" Josh asked.

"Not bad. I installed the FTP program on all the servers and individual computers except the ones in the lab area. Carlson said they weren't on the network and didn't need to be cleaned."

"So, by tomorrow morning, we should have most of their files uploaded." Josh grinned at her. "Have any problems?"

"Dr. McRae caught me looking at a file in his desk."

"Damn. How'd you get out of it?"

"I lied."

"Remind me never to date you or any other woman who lies for a living."

"I'm going back tomorrow. Told Carlson I had to check that the program cleaned the virus from all the files. That will give me a chance to look around the place a little more."

"Whatever you can get away with."

"Thanks for coming down, Josh. Sorry I didn't need you."

"Maybe next time." Josh shrugged.

Shelby smiled at him. Maybe, but unlikely.

"Jackson," Chris said as she punched the speaker button on her phone and continued reading the report.

"Chris, Mac here." Chris looked up from the report at the sound of his soft, Australian accent. "One minute." She quickly scanned the rest of the report, scrawled her initials at the bottom, and added it to the growing stack in her outbox.

"What's up, Mac?" Chris picked up the handset and leaned back in her chair.

"There's been an interesting development."

Chris straightened in her chair. "What?"

"A woman by the name of Cathy Silvers dropped by on Monday. Presumably, she's a friend of the computer tech who was killed over the weekend."

"Yes?"

"Dr. Carlson asked me to test and interview her under the guise of possible future employment."

"I remember. Your report said she appeared to be lying about something?"

"Exactly. She showed up again today, ostensibly working for a firm called InfoTech Professionals. Dr. Carlson hired them to eradicate a virus in our system."

"So, she ended up getting some contract work and went back to The Center. Could be a coincidence."

"I caught her going through my desk."

"Really? How'd she explain that?"

"Said it was an accident. The drawer slid open when she bumped into the desk."

"I'll have someone check it out and get back to you." Chris fiddled with a pencil, twirling it through her fingers. "Have you found anything since your last report?"

"Not really. They keep all the data locked up pretty tight here. I've had two counseling sessions with Sam, but they're taped, so I haven't had an opportunity to ask him anything."

"Can you get him away from the cameras?"

"I'm trying. I have another session scheduled soon."

"Keep up the good work, Mac, but listen, don't take any chances. You're only there to gather information. Don't try to be Super Spy."

"No worries." Mac sighed. "It's just frustrating."

"I understand. This kind of assignment usually is. If you even suspect they've made you, we're pulling you out."

"There's been no indication of that. I think they bought the cover background and think I'm a real sleazeball."

"Keep me posted." Chris replaced the handset, rose from her chair, and moved to close the door to her office. She poured a glass of water from the carafe on the credenza and lifted it to her lips with a shaking hand.

Mac wasn't going to find any information at The Center, because she'd alerted Jonah Thomas the minute

Mac had been assigned to the case. She'd been surprised that they were letting Mac have sessions with Sam, but then what could the boy tell Mac? All he knew was that his mother was dead, and he was living with foster parents.

She still didn't know exactly what they were doing at The Center. All she knew was that they were investigating the disappearance of Shannon and Sam Masterson. And as long as Sam appeared to be in no danger, they weren't going to extract him until they found out if Shannon was still alive.

But this Cathy Silvers could be a problem. Chris turned to her computer and did a search on InfoTech Professionals. She opened up the company's web site, scanned the information, and then punched the number into her phone.

"Dan Knowles, please. This is Chris Jackson, Special Agent in Charge with the FBI."

"Dan Knowles here."

Chris introduced herself and explained that her office was investigating The Center, and then asked about Cathy Silvers.

"Oh, you mean Shelby Parker."

"Shelby Parker?"

"With the FSA." Dan paused. "Maybe I wasn't supposed to say anything."

"No, that's okay. We're working this case parallel to the FSA." Chris forced herself to chuckle. "You know how it is with government bureaucracy. I think I'm missing a couple of reports from them. I just wasn't aware they were sending someone in."

"Oh, I see. What do you need to know?" Dan sounded hesitant, and Chris didn't want him dwelling on this.

"Nothing, really. I was just investigating the appearance of an unknown person at The Center." Chris used her most professional voice. "We really appreciate your help in this matter. I'm sure Ms. Parker emphasized the necessity for discretion.

"Of course."

"The information you gave me isn't a problem, but you might want to watch how much you say to someone. I really could have been anyone."

"Of course. I'll be more careful in the future."

"Good. Again, we appreciate your help." Chris figured she'd intimidated him enough that he wasn't likely to give out any information over the phone to anyone. At least that was in her favor. Getting more intel on Parker and what the hell she was doing there would be easy.

But first, she had to take care of another problem. The thief she'd hired to retrieve the photos and negatives hadn't been in touch. Chris had expected to hear from her by now. Although Zoe had told her that she didn't know how long it would take, it'd already been several days.

And Jim Bottoms hadn't heard from her either. What the hell was taking her so long?

Saturday morning Shelby was back at The Center shortly before nine. Dr. Carlson arrived a few minutes later and let her into the building. The Center wasn't open for regular business on Saturday, so there were very few people around. Shelby saw only two guards on duty. One sat at the receptionist's desk watching the front door; the other walked the halls.

"Morning, Dr. Carlson." The guard actually stood up when she walked in. He could've just been a gentleman, but Shelby's first thought was that it was part of his job description.

"Earl." Dr. Carlson nodded to him and continued on to the door that led to the rear area of The Center.

"Uh, Dr. Carlson."

"Yes, Earl?" She paused with her hand on the doorknob.

"Just wanted to let you know that they're changing out the security cameras today. They took the old ones, but they had to go back to get some missing piece in order to install the new ones."

"So, we're without the security cameras for a while?"

"Correct. Until about five. They promised they'd have them working today."

Dr. Carlson sighed. "Very well. I doubt it's a problem."

Earl nodded, and for a moment Shelby thought he was going to salute or something.

Dr. Carlson let Shelby into the computer room and told her to call when she was finished. She then disappeared. Shelby logged on using the administrative password she'd gotten yesterday and opened the FTP program.

Shelby squinted at the short list of files. Only a few files had been copied, and the program had stopped.

What the hell? It looked like the program had been disabled. There was no record of files being copied after six last night. Which meant the program had only copied and transferred files for about two hours. Not nearly long enough to be complete. She dinked around in the files trying to figure out what had happened until her cell phone vibrated in her pocket.

Shelby looked at the number on the display screen. Ethan. Well, this couldn't be good.

"What?"

"Shelby, can you talk?"

"I guess so. I'm in the computer room, and it seems that I'm alone. So, unless they have the place bugged . . ."

"Josh is here in my office. He says that the FTP program stopped uploading files at six last night."

"That's what it looks like from here too."

"Damn."

"Took the word right out of my mouth. What does Josh think the problem is?" She heard Ethan talking to Josh and Josh's muffled response.

"He doesn't know. Possibly, they have some kind of detection program running that shut it down."

"Hold on a sec." She clamped the phone between her ear and shoulder and typed in commands. A bright red window popped up with a big exclamation mark in the center. "He's right." Shelby felt like throwing her phone through the monitor. A mature, controlled response to being thwarted.

On the other hand, it was a piece of luck that the warning seemed to be limited to the administrative ID. Unless Carlson or Thomas had received the same message and were stomping their way down the hall this very minute.

"Ethan, it looks like there's a detection program that found the FTP program and disabled it. Right now, I need to find out if anyone else has seen the message. Have Josh talk to Ted and see if he knows anything about it." She turned the cell phone off and slipped it into her pocket.

If that bright red message had appeared on anyone else's computer, they were tipped off to what she had done, and that meant that she was up to her neck in hot water. Unfortunately, the only way to find out was to check Dr. Carlson's and Dr. Thomas' computers. Unless there was some other computer offsite that might get the message.

Cold sweat trickled down her neck. She turned back to the computer and searched the network architecture. If they had an offsite computer linked to the network, it was well hidden. Ted hadn't had any knowledge of it, and she had to believe that he would have known. Now, to find out if the doctors' computers were being alerted.

First, she needed the perfect prop. Failing that, she needed anything that would do. Ah, ha! A dirty glass was perched on a high shelf. A further search turned up some duct tape. Shelby grabbed both and headed to the ladies' room.

God only knew what had been in the glass earlier. A strange orange, slightly crystalline substance was caked in the bottom. A lot of hot water and several paper towels later, she had a perfectly clean glass and an instrument for getting thumbprints. Shelby reached inside her padded clothing and pulled out a small aerosol can of spray fixative. Holding the glass carefully, she sprayed the outside, gave it a few moments to set, and then filled the glass with water. She washed her hands using the abrasive soap in the dispenser and dried them thoroughly, first with paper towels and then with the hot air dryer.

Crap. This was going to hurt, and she chastised herself for not having thought about it earlier. She could have taken care of the problem with a razor at home. Oh, well. She tore off strips of the duct tape and pressed one firmly to the back of her hand. Clenching her teeth, she ripped the tape off, taking all the tiny hairs with it. She repeated the process twice again, just to make sure. Then, more washing with the abrasive soap. Finally, she sprayed a coating of the fixative on the back of her hand, let it dry and repeated it several times.

Now, she needed the doctors and a little serendipity. Shelby knew where the doctors were, and she'd probably have to supply the serendipity herself.

CHAPTER EIGHT

Zoe fought her way through a thick grogginess to semi-consciousness. Her eyelids were heavy and opening them proved to be too much, so she stopped trying. A wave of nausea washed over her, and she had a flash of memory. She'd had this sick feeling a few times in the past few days. Days? Her thoughts drifted in and out. As soon as she tried to grasp one, it would drift away. She gritted her teeth against the nausea and forced her eyelids open. She was lying in a hospital bed. What the hell was she doing in a hospital bed? The room was small and sterile. Light poured in through a window with bars on the outside. She blinked against the bright light. Her vision blurred and then came into focus again.

Zoe swallowed, wishing she could reach the water glass on the table next to her bed. Memories drifted in and out. Someone holding her up in bed, placing a straw into her mouth. The sting of a needle in the back of her hand. More injections in her upper arm. She raised her left hand as far as the restraints would allow and saw an IV taped to the back of her hand.

Then she remembered the man. The one she had been stealing from. What had she been stealing? She closed her eyes and concentrated on remembering. Photographs and negatives. It was all coming back, but none of it explained where she was or what was happening. She drifted to sleep again, only to be awakened by the door to her room opening.

"And how is our patient today?"

Zoe opened her mouth, but her throat was too dry to speak. Just as well, since her first inclination was to swear at the man. He cranked the bed up and held a glass of water so she could drink from the straw. The movement made her dizzy and her stomach lurched, but she sucked down as much water as she could before he took the glass away.

"It's good to see you awake. I think we can take the restraints off now." He snapped open the leather that encircled her wrists, and Zoe flexed her fingers. "What do you remember?"

Zoe shook her head. "The last thing I remember is riding my bike. Did I have an accident?" She wasn't about to admit that she'd been stealing from this man.

"Exactly." Jonah Thomas nodded. "I'm afraid you had some serious internal injuries, and you'll need to stay quiet for some time."

"How long have I been here? What day is it?"

"We brought you here early Wednesday morning after your accident. It's Saturday now." He smiled at her in a way that made her want to hit him. "You'll probably have a little nausea from the nasty bump on your head. But that will clear up soon. Just rest and get better."

Zoe lay back against the pillows and let her eyes close. The sooner he left, the sooner she could check out her surroundings. At least he seemed to buy her story of not remembering what had happened. Not that he'd probably tell her if he didn't.

She forced herself to wait a few minutes after she heard him leave, and then sat up carefully, waiting until the dizziness passed. When her feet touched the floor, her knees buckled and she had to hold onto the side of the bed for support. Damn, she was as weak as a kitten. After a few minutes, she felt stronger and shuffled over to the door, pulling the IV stand with her. She couldn't see much from the small window. Just an empty hallway with a rolling file cart full of what looked to be colored folders. She turned the doorknob, not surprised to find the door locked.

Tears of frustration stung her eyes. She'd always thought the worst that could happen on a job was that she'd be caught and arrested. She'd been wrong.

Dr. Carlson had been headed down the hall that led to the lab after she left the computer room, so Shelby headed there as well. The double doors to the lab and clinic area had large windows, and she could see several people walking around. They all wore scrubs or lab coats. The lab and clinic area were larger than she'd originally thought and looked like they took up most of the building. The doors were locked and had a security keypad and a doorbell to one side. Shelby pressed the doorbell and waited. A few minutes later Dr. Carlson appeared and opened the door. Shelby thought she might try to squeeze in, but Dr. Carlson was firmly planted between her and the interior of the lab.

"What is it, Cathy?"

"I have a problem. The program that I installed to fix all the files infected by the virus isn't working the way it should. It seems to be stalled somewhere."

"Dear God. Has it destroyed more files?"

"No. Not yet. The thing is, I need to go through the files individually to clean them, and I can do that—no problem. But I really need to be able to isolate those files so there's no danger of further infestation." Shelby nodded at the doctor expectantly.

"Then do it." Dr. Carlson turned away, but Shelby pushed the door open behind her.

"Oh, I will. It's just that I wanted to let you know that I have to leave for a while, but that I'll be back." She pulled a floppy diskette from her pocket. "I thought I had everything I needed here on this floppy. But it's just the file that actually cleans the virus." Shelby jostled her right arm, letting some of the water spill onto the floppy.

"Oh, my God!" Shelby shoved the glass of water

into Carlson's hand and wiped the droplets off the floppy. "Can't let this get damaged. Then I wouldn't be able to clean up the virus." Dr. Carlson looked agitated. But she was holding the glass, and that's all Shelby was concerned about.

"Is there a problem, Ruth?" A tall, slender man walked around the corner. This had to be Dr. Jonah Thomas. She had really hit pay dirt. Before Dr. Carlson could reply, Shelby lurched forward holding out her right hand.

"You must be Dr. Thomas. Nice to meet you." Shelby shoved her hand toward his and, as she expected, he automatically grasped her hand and shook it. He had a wimpy handshake and that was exactly what she'd been hoping for. Shelby turned her hand just a little so it was almost lying in his palm. He unknowingly cooperated by gripping her hand, allowing a perfect thumbprint to imbed itself in the fixative on the back of her hand.

"I'm Cathy Silvers with InfoTech Professionals."

"Cathy is working on our computer virus problem," Dr. Carlson said to him. "Cathy, do whatever you think is necessary. I'll be here until two this afternoon."

"Perfect. I just need to get that diskette, and I'll be back in under an hour." Shelby grabbed the glass from Carlson's hand, being careful not to smudge the prints the good doctor had left on it.

Fortunately, she had the equipment she needed in the trunk of her car, so she didn't even need to drive back to Tucson. She dumped the water from the glass, set it in the cup holder of the console, and drove to the closest gas station. The bathroom provided everything necessary to cast the thumbprints she'd gotten from the doctors. Shelby locked the door and opened a small case, taking out the items she needed. When the polymer was mixed into a smooth paste, she applied it to the glass and to the back of her hand. The hand dryer supplied the heat she needed to cure it quickly. Both prints lifted neatly, and it only took a few more minutes to transfer them to the special molds she'd prepared earlier.

Shelby now had portable thumbprints from both doctors. Of course, she had to get into their offices and manage to use the thumbprints without them knowing about it.

Less than half an hour later, she walked into The Center, latex sleeves with the doctors' thumbprints tucked safely in her padded tee shirt. She hated the hot, padded clothes, but there were some advantages, like being able to store a lot of equipment.

The guard let her in and called Dr. Carlson. The doctor stomped into the reception area and motioned Shelby to follow her. Evidently, she disliked being interrupted. Shelby thanked her and pretended to log onto the network. As soon as she left, Shelby turned her cell phone on again. There was one missed call from Ethan. Great, maybe he had an answer that meant she wouldn't have to skulk around trying to get into the doctors' computers. She punched in the number, and Ethan answered.

"Sorry, Shelby."

Crap. That didn't bode well for her fantasy of being able to fix this easily.

"What?"

"According to Ted, it's a software program the doctors asked him to install. It's hidden and sends an alert to the doctors if it's disabled."

"Crap." She thought that summed up the situation succinctly.

"I know. It looks like the only option is for you to try to download as much as you can."

"Crap."

"You already said that."

"Yeah, but I really mean it this time. Did Ted mention how the doctors are alerted? I need to know if they're going to get the big red warning sign on their computers."

"Hold on, Josh is talking to him." Shelby said a little prayer while Ethan posed the question.

"Ted says it will appear on Dr. Carlson's computer when she logs into the network, but not on Dr. Thomas'."

Shelby mumbled a few expletives, which didn't make her feel any better, but let Ethan know that they had a big problem. "Okay. I have to get into Dr. Carlson's office and log her computer onto the network, before she has a chance to."

"Is that a possibility?"

"I've got the thumbprint already. I just have to get past the security lock on her office door."

"What about her network password?"

"I memorized it when she logged on for me yester-day. If it doesn't work, I'll reset it as the administrator and tell her there was a glitch in the network, and she'll have to change it." Sure, no problem. As long as Dr. Carlson didn't come into her office for anything while Shelby was in there.

"Can you manage to hang around there long enough to get the files?"

"Downloading from the network isn't a problem. I just need to bring in my equipment." She patted her puffy abdomen. Plenty of room there. "I'll have to get into the doctors' offices again to get their files. But first things first."

"Let me know when you get that message off Dr. Carlson's screen."

Shelby ended the phone call and headed back to the lab. She almost forgot to breathe when she saw Dr. Carlson and Dr. Thomas leaving the lab.

"Is it two already?" Shelby asked.

"Not quite, but Dr. Thomas and I are leaving for a while."

"Oh, I got the diskette, but it's going to take a while to clean up all the files."

"Then you'll just have to finish up tomorrow. I can't stay around all afternoon waiting for you."

"There's no reason you have to be here, Ruth. One of the guards can let her out when she's finished," Dr. Thomas suggested.

Dr. Carlson seemed to consider the idea. She didn't look too happy about it, but she finally nodded. "Very well. I'll have the guard check in on you. How long will you be staying?"

"It's going to take several days to get the whole job done."

"I see. Well, be out of here by four today. I'll let the guard know that you'll be leaving then." Dr. Carlson pulled out the ever-present inhaler and took a good whiff, motioned to Dr. Thomas, and walked toward the reception area. Talk about your lousy bedside manner.

Shelby could barely keep the smile off her face. She'd have plenty of time to get into the offices. Too bad she didn't have the equipment to download the files today. On the other hand, Carlson was probably going to have the guard watch her like a hawk, so she still needed to be careful.

Shelby headed back toward the computer room to give the doctors time to get out of the building and drive away. She checked her padded tummy pouch to make sure she had the equipment to decode the door lock and walked back down the hallway.

"Where are you going?"

Crap. The guard.

"Ladies' room. Is that a problem?"

The guard grunted, glanced into the computer room, and then turned back to the reception area. So much for having all the time in the world. He hadn't taken long to check on her, and Shelby had no idea how often he planned to repeat it.

She hurried down the hall, pulling the equipment out as she ran. It only took a few seconds to attach it to the security lock and less than a minute for the code to be displayed. She committed it to memory and punched in the numbers. While the laptop booted up, she slipped the latex sleeve over her thumb. As soon as the login screen appeared, she pressed the print against the reader and held her breath. It worked. Shelby punched in Carlson's password and jumped up to see if anyone was coming down the hallway.

Dr. McRae was standing at the far end of the hall, looking at a chart attached to a clipboard. As soon as the laptop beeped, she hustled over to the desk. Sure enough, the bright red warning sign was on Carlson's screen. Shelby typed in the commands to delete it, logged out, and turned off the laptop. Now to get back to the computer room.

Dr. McRae was still in the hall. He'd put the chart away and was talking to the guard. The restroom was just around the corner from Dr. Carlson's office. But Shelby had to get there without either of them seeing her. Dr. McRae looked up, straight at the pane of glass in Dr. Carlson's door. Shelby jerked back. Crap. When she looked again, Dr. McRae was pointing to something and talking to the guard. Both men had their backs to her. Seizing the opportunity, she scuttled out and around the corner into the restroom. She gave herself a moment to calm down and then walked out into the now empty hallway, edging over to the door that led to the reception area and poked her head in.

"Hey. Just wanted to let you know I'm going back to the computer room now." The guard grunted, and she closed the door. Shelby hurried over to Dr. Thomas' door and attached the decoder module. Might as well get his code, too, while the security cameras were out of commission. As soon as the code flashed, she memorized it and disconnected the equipment.

"Ms. Silvers." Dr. McRae turned as she walked into the computer room, sounding surprised to see her there. "I'd forgotten that you were coming in today. Any luck with the virus?"

"Some. The program I used wasn't working completely, so I have to go through all the files individually."

"I see. Well, I won't keep you." He nodded and turned back to the door.

"Did you need something?"

"No. I just saw the light on and wondered who was here on a Saturday."

"Just me." She dug into her backpack and fished out a slightly squished tuna sandwich. "If you need to work in here, I was about to go eat my lunch."

"No, I don't need anything in here. But I'll join you for lunch, if you don't mind."

"Sure." Shelby smiled. The scum doctor was being so very nice.

"There's a little courtyard outside. I'll meet you there in a few minutes. Can I bring you anything?"

"Uh, yeah. A soda would be good."

Shelby thought it was highly unlikely that he was looking for a lunch companion, which meant he wanted something.

She chose a seat in the sparse shade, ever mindful of

her sweltering disguise. Dr. McRae joined her a few minutes later with an ice-cold soda and a bag of chips. For his own lunch, he'd purchased a pre-packaged sandwich that claimed to be turkey and cheese according to the wrapper.

"So, are you adjusting to the weather here?"

"Yeah. It's kind of hot, but I guess that's just going to get worse, huh?" Shelby opened the squished sandwich and took a big bite. With her mouth full the conversational ball was in his court.

"That's what I hear. I've only been here for a month myself." Dr. McRae nibbled on his sandwich.

"What made you come here?"

"The Center made me a good offer. And it's a chance to work with children. They do quite a bit of research with gifted children."

"Really? You like kids, huh?"

"I find them easier to deal with than most adults." McRae shrugged. "Children are so much more open and up front about what they're feeling and what they think."

"I guess they don't have as much to hide yet." That comment earned her a sharp glance.

"Back in DC, I coached a soccer team. The kids were great. Biggest problem I had was dealing with the parents."

"You coached a soccer team?" That bit of intel didn't exactly fit with his background check.

"Sure. Great way to keep in shape."

"I've got to get back to work. It's going to take

some time to go through all the files individually to clean up the virus."

"So, you'll be around for a while?"

"Oh, yeah. For a few days at least."

"Then we'll have to have lunch again."

"Sure." Shelby wadded her sandwich wrapper up and tossed it into a trashcan. She then headed back to the computer room wondering why Dr. McRae wanted to be so damn friendly. Not that she had a problem with that. There were worse things than listening to that accent and looking into those bright green eyes. But she couldn't help wondering what he was getting out of it.

There really wasn't much she could do back in the computer room. She didn't have the equipment with her to download files, so she just nosed around the network. She tried some searches to see if there was anything with Shannon Masterson's name on it, but came up with nothing.

Dr. Carlson had sounded like they were coming back at some point so Shelby didn't want to risk breaking into one of their offices again. But with the security cameras out of service, she might as well take the opportunity to check the place out. She pulled a diskette out of her backpack and quickly installed a couple of harmless viruses that Josh had made for her, then started the virus scan. Anyone who looked at the screen would assume that she was cleaning the mole virus from the files on the network.

She opened a few doors along the hallway, but found

only janitor and storage closets. The double doors to the lab were at the end of the hall, and she approached cautiously since they had big windows. As Shelby inched up to the doors, she could hear voices. One was definitely Dr. Carlson.

"There's no way he could be aware of what we did," Dr. Carlson said.

"I know. It's just that he's asked some rather probing questions." The voice sounded like Jonah Thomas, but Shelby couldn't be sure.

"About what?"

"He said he remembered some strange dreams that he'd had during the EEG and wondered about them."

"What were they about?"

"They were sexual in nature. And unusual. That's all he would tell me." The man's voice sounded disappointed.

"I was sure we'd given him enough anesthesia that he wouldn't remember anything," Dr. Carlson said.

Whoa! What had they done to this guy? And who was he?

"The electro-ejaculation procedure had to feel unusual to him. His mind would register that even if he had no real memory of what happened."

"I suppose. I just didn't think this would be a problem." Dr. Carlson sounded agitated.

"It isn't a problem. At least not yet." It was definitely Dr. Thomas' voice. "I told him that it was probably just that he'd been uncomfortable about having an EEG done while he was sleeping, and that it was nothing to worry about."

"And he believed you?" Dr. Carlson asked.

"He seemed to. Don't worry so, Ruth. If it becomes a problem, we'll deal with it."

"I don't want to get rid of him. I'd hoped to use his sperm in further experiments."

Eeeuuwww! Sperm? What were these people doing?

"I know, Ruth. No need to panic. At the very worst, we'll have to sedate him and harvest his sperm over a period of time. It isn't the best case scenario, but it will work."

"Well, we knew that it would come to that eventually. There's no other way to produce the babies we need for the program."

"I keep searching for other donors who are suitable. That's very important for the long term."

"And we still need more mothers. That's actually more important than the men."

"I have a lead on several right now," Dr. Thomas said. "We should be able to bring them in within the next few months."

The door handle turned, and the door opened a crack. Shelby scanned the wide, empty hallway for a place to hide. There wasn't so much as a water fountain in the hall.

Crap.

CHAPTER NINE

Shelby awakened at four on Sunday morning still thinking about the conversation she'd overheard right before she'd made a mad sprint down the hall. If Carlson hadn't turned back for a minute, she'd have been caught for sure. Not that she wouldn't have talked her way out of it. Still, it was a close call.

When she'd reported in to Ethan, he had the same reaction. The Center was doing something really wrong. But they still didn't know exactly what or why. And she still had no clue as to where Shannon and her son were.

Shelby slugged down a couple cups of coffee, wondering what to do at the crack of dawn, and then she remembered—she knew where Dr. McRae lived. She hadn't had any luck finding him out and about before, but if she got there before he got up, she could certainly follow him around for a bit. Might be handy knowing what he did with his free time.

McRae confused her. The intel from his background check didn't mesh with what he'd told her about himself at all. Ethan had probably just done a basic background check, and that wouldn't necessarily turn up something like coaching a soccer team. And, of course, McRae could be lying. But why? He certainly had no need to impress Cathy Silvers.

At least Shelby wouldn't have to wear the padded underwear today. She threw on a tank top and shorts, pulled her hair into a ponytail, and then shoved on a baseball cap and added large sunglasses. A quick check in the mirror assured her that she'd blend in with the general Tucson population. Certainly McRae wouldn't suspect that she was Cathy Silvers. She drove to the airport, parked her Firebird, and rented a new white compact that looked like more than half the cars in Tucson.

McRae turned out to be a morning person too. She'd only been parked across from his apartment for half an hour when he came out. Following him was a little tricky since there weren't many cars on the road at seven on a Sunday morning. He stopped at a small bakery and café for breakfast, and she was able to jog across the street to a fast food place and get an egg sandwich for herself.

He'd bought a newspaper, and she expected him to linger over breakfast. But as soon as he finished eating, he returned to his car carrying several large boxes of pastries. Shelby followed him north on Oracle to a small nursing home in a residential area. She knew he'd moved to Tucson recently, so it was unlikely that he had a relative in a nursing home here. Besides, there were enough pastries in those boxes to feed a lot of people.

Shelby hadn't planned on getting too close to McRae, but curiosity got the better of her. She gave him about ten minutes and then followed him into the nursing home. The lobby was decorated with a couple of vinyl sofas left over from the seventies, not quite matching chairs, and a small reception area desk. Next to the dining room door was a sign that read: *You are in Tucson. The month is May. Today is Sunday. Your next meal is Lunch*. When she needed a sign like that, Shelby decided she was going to eat a bullet.

"Hi," she said to the middle-aged receptionist. "I'm checking out nursing homes for my grandmother. Do you have a brochure or anything like that?"

"Oh, certainly, dear. Let me just find it for you." The woman opened a drawer and rummaged around.

"Looks like a party in there." Shelby nodded toward the small cafeteria area where she could see people gathered around tables

"Every Sunday Dr. McRae brings in some dough-nuts and pastries for the residents. They just love it."

"He must really care about his patients," Shelby said. She could see McRae through the open doors talking to one of the nurses.

"Oh, he does. They aren't his patients, though. Not really. He doesn't work here. But he's a psychiatrist, and he comes in and talks to the residents. Such a sweetheart." She pulled some brochures out of the drawer. "Now, is your grandmother already in a nursing facility, dear?"

"Huh? Oh, no, not yet. But we know it's just a matter of time, so I told my mom that I'd check around."

"That's a good idea. You really don't want to leave these things until the last minute. I could have the director give you a little tour, if you have time."

"Oh, maybe later. I'm kind of in a rush today." McRae was walking toward the doors, and the last thing Shelby wanted was to run into him. He probably wouldn't recognize her without the Cathy Silvers disguise, but there was no point in taking chances. "Thanks for these, though." She turned and headed for the front door just as McRae came out of the cafeteria.

Back in the car, Shelby waited for McRae to leave. Coaching kids' soccer teams? Taking pastries to nursing homes? This definitely didn't fit with what she knew about Harrison McRae. Shelby drove back to the airport, returned the rental car, and drove the Firebird back to her apartment. A quick call to Ethan assured her that she'd have a more detailed background check on McRae in a few days. Maybe that would answer some of her questions.

Monday morning Shelby pulled on her padded underclothes and frumpy wig and headed out to The Center again. She had a couple of flash drives tucked into her padded tee shirt along with the latex thumbprints. The Center's computers were pretty state of the art, and all of them featured USB ports right in the front, so she could plug in a small flash drive and download files quickly. The only problem would be getting into the doctors' offices undetected.

Getting Shannon and her son out of there was a priority, but she had to locate them first. Shelby suspected they were being kept in the lab section. Only the doctors and a few others had access to that area. She'd just have to find a way in.

After Dr. Carlson left her in the computer room, Shelby plugged one of her flash drives into the network server and copied files while she considered the possibilities of getting into the lab area and the doctors' offices. By noon, Shelby had to admit that both would have to be done after hours. There were just too many people around to make it feasible during the day.

Shelby chatted with the receptionist and a couple of the guards during the afternoon. Amazing how much people like to talk about themselves. Where they work, where they live, who their friends are. Maybe her job had made her too paranoid to do that. The receptionist told her that they lock the place up at six, although the doctors usually work a couple hours later than that. The two guards revealed some information about their shift changes and security procedures. Just amazing. Shelby smiled and chatted and took it all in.

She saw McRae late that afternoon, taking a break in the courtyard. He was studying some papers in a folder, probably a patient chart. She stayed at her own table, slugging down a bottle of water and eating cookies, which tasted faintly of peanut butter and were as hard as concrete, that she'd gotten from the vending machine.

McRae still confused her. Especially after yesterday. What Ethan had turned up in the background check just didn't mesh with what she was learning about him. Shelby still wasn't totally certain that he hadn't seen her in Dr. Carlson's office. But if he had, surely he'd have mentioned it. At least asked her what the hell she'd been doing in there.

Shelby turned her mind back to the idea of breaking into The Center later that night. She didn't see any other way she'd be able to get into the lab or the doctors' offices and have enough time to do what she needed to do without being observed. She scanned the grounds surrounding The Center. The walls were about eight feet high topped with iron spikes that were supposed to look decorative, while keeping the riff-raff out.

She'd learned from the guards that they changed shifts at midnight, did a complete sweep of the building every hour, and checked the grounds every two hours. After the midnight shift change, there were only three guards on duty. One manned the front gate, another made the rounds, and a third was positioned at the reception desk where he watched displays from three security cameras. One camera scanned the entrance, another the main hallway, and the third the interior of the lab.

Not insurmountable. She finished her cookies and went inside, stopping at the receptionist's cubicle for a little chat. Mandy peppered her with questions about computers, while Shelby checked out the display on the security monitors. It only took a couple of minutes to see exactly how she could avoid the cameras. Shelby gave Mandy some vague answers to her questions and left. Breaking in tonight would be a piece of cake.

"What do you want to talk about today, Sam?" Mac took a seat across from the small table where Sam was positioning figurines in a shallow box of sand.

"I don't know." Sam frowned. "I don't wanna talk. I wanna do something."

"Good. What shall we do then?"

"Read." Sam jumped out of his chair and ran to the sofa where he'd left his small backpack. He pulled the zipper open and drew out some folded sheets of paper. "Read this to me."

"What? Something you can't read yourself?" Mac opened the crumpled papers and scanned them. They were pages from a medical chart. Sam's medical chart. His eyes locked on several words and phrases. Halcyon. Sleep deprivation. Emotional dependency. Experiment P-15. Total Control. He quickly folded the papers and slipped them into his pocket.

"I can read it, but I don't know what some of the words mean."

"I see. Well, before we do that, I'd like to play a drawing game with you. You up for that?"

Sam shrugged. "Okay."

Mac pulled a box of markers and a few sheets of paper off a shelf and laid them on the table next to the figurines. He moved his chair around so that his back was to the hidden camera that recorded all his sessions.

Sam scooted into the chair next to him and opened the markers, spilling them onto the table. A marker rolled onto the floor, and Sam held his hand out toward it, frowning. The marker rolled and then lifted into the air, landing in Sam's chubby hand. Mac watched in amazement. No matter how many times he'd seen Sam using his abilities, he was still stunned by them.

"Why don't you draw me a picture of you and your foster parents?"

"Okay," Sam sighed and pulled a sheet of paper over. Mac tapped on the table to get Sam's attention, and then moved his fingers to send him a message in sign language.

This is a secret. May I keep the papers for a while?

Sam watched Mac's fingers, put down his marker, and signed back to him.

Okay. But why is it a secret?

Mac shifted again, making sure that their signing was hidden from the camera.

I'll tell you later. Don't forget it's a secret, Okay?

Okay. Sam signed back to him.

"Here's my drawing."

Mac smiled and patted Sam's arm. "Well, let's see. This is you?" Mac pointed to the smaller character Sam had drawn. "And these are Jill and Victor?" Mac smiled as Sam nodded. He'd drawn Jill and Victor extremely large on one half of the paper. They were holding hands, and Jill had a particularly vicious expression. Victor had been drawn with no mouth. On the other half of the paper, Sam had drawn himself rather small, and there was a woman's face drawn over his head.

"Who's this?"

"Mommy," Sam said.

"I see. You miss your mother, don't you?"

Sam nodded. "I can hear her, but I can't see her."

Mac quickly signed to Sam. *Agree with me.* "You mean you can remember her voice, but you can't remember what she looks like?"

Sam looked at Mac for a moment, and then nodded. "Uh huh."

"Do you have a photograph of your mother?"

Sam nodded. "I keep it in my room."

"Then you'll always know what she looks like, won't you?"

"I guess."

"How about another picture?" Mac asked. "Draw something that makes you feel safe and happy." Mac pushed another sheet of paper in front of Sam and signed to him.

Does your mother talk to you in your head?

Sam nodded and turned back to his drawing. Dear God. Shannon must be communicating with him telepathically. Mac knew that Shannon had psychic abilities too, but he'd never thought about them communicating with each other. At least, this meant that she was still alive.

"That's very good." Mac tapped the drawing with a finger. "It's your teddy bear, Rocky, isn't it?"

Sam nodded and picked up a black marker. Holding his lower lip between his teeth, he carefully marked out one of the ears. "I forgot, he has only one ear now."

"What happened to it?" Mac asked.

"Jill—it came off one day." Sam's lip trembled. "Next time it could be worse. It could be a leg or something. But it won't, because I won't forget next time."

"Yes, you must take care of your toys." Mac briefly touched Sam's arm and signed to him again.

I'm sorry about Rocky. I'll see what I can do.

Sam smiled at him, and Mac's heart hurt so much he had to bite his lip. "Well, our time's up. I'm sure Jill is here to pick you up. But I understand you're coming in tomorrow. Maybe we can have an ice cream together." He needed to be able to talk to Sam away from the hidden camera and microphone.

"Strawberry!" Sam crowed.

"Strawberry it is, then." Mac opened the door to his office and watched Sam walk over to Jill Stone.

"Hey, Doc, ready for me?"

Mac automatically smiled at Chase Harmon. "Of course, please, come in." Mac closed the door behind them.

"I really appreciate you seeing me on such short notice." Chase sat in one of the oversized chairs in the corner and waited for Mac to join him.

"You sounded like it was urgent. Having problems?"

"I don't know if I'd call it a problem." Chase

shrugged his beefy shoulders. "It's just weird."

"Please tell me about it."

"Well, it's kind of embarrassing."

"That's all right. I've heard a lot of embarrassing things, and nothing will leave this room."

"Yeah, well, it's about a dream I've been having."

"You've been having the same dream repeatedly?"

"Pretty much. It started the night after I had the EEG here, and I've had it every night. Sometimes more than once a night."

"Is the dream about the EEG?"

"Not really, it's just that it started right after I had it." Chase hunched forward, elbows on knees, fingers laced together. "The dream, well, it's very sexual."

"Dreams about sex aren't uncommon, Chase. Even dreaming about a sexual practice that you'd never do isn't unusual."

"Yeah, well, this one is." Chase took a breath and blew it out slowly. "It involves some weird stuff."

"Like what?"

"Anal probes," Chase said softly.

"I see. Chase, men have glands that are easily aroused in their anal cavity. Perhaps that's what—"

"No, it isn't like that. There's nothing pleasant about it at all. It's cold and uncomfortable. There are some beeping noises and some conversation that I can't really hear; then I ejaculate and the dream is over."

"Do you actually ejaculate or is that just in the dream?"

Chase blushed. "It's just in the dream. But there's

no pleasure with it. In fact, I wake up feeling, I don't know, violated or something." Chase rose and shoved his hands in his pockets. "I spoke to Dr. Thomas about the dreams. He said that it was probably just a reaction to having the EEG while I was sleeping."

"A reaction?"

"Yeah, I wasn't real comfortable with that, and he figures it's just a control issue."

"I see. That's possible. I could prescribe a mild sedative for you. It would help you sleep and probably suppress the dream somewhat."

"No, thanks. I don't like taking drugs."

"Fine. We can try some hypnotherapy. That might reveal something." Chase still looked reluctant. Mac would have had more questions for him, but he knew that this session, too, was being taped. "Actually, in all likelihood, the dream will diminish and disappear soon."

"That'd be good."

"Why don't we give it a few days and see?" Mac stood. "If it doesn't diminish, then I'd suggest the hypnotherapy."

"Sure. That sounds like a plan." Chase held his hand out to Mac. "Thanks again for seeing me."

"That's what I'm here for. I just wish I could be of more help." Mac shook his hand and opened the door for him. He couldn't imagine what had happened that caused Chase to have such disturbing dreams. There were just too many things going on at The Center that had no explanation.

CHAPTER TEN

Shelby parked her car behind a couple of Palo Verde trees and secured a grappling hook to the tow bar. Using the nylon rope attached to it, she quickly lowered herself down the side of the steep ravine that separated the desert from the stone wall at the rear of The Center. At the bottom of the ravine, she took another length of nylon rope off her shoulder and opened the grappling hook at the end. She swung it in a circle a few times, building up enough momentum to carry it up to the stone wall. A satisfying clank followed by a scraping sound told her she'd connected.

Shelby pulled herself up the rocky, sandy ravine and scrambled over the top of the stone wall. Pulling the grappling hook free, she dropped to the ground and reeled in the nylon rope, leaving it in a dark shadow. Eleven fifty-eight. The guards should be changing shifts now.

She unzipped her fanny pack and pulled out the equipment she would need. The door at the rear side didn't appear to have any electronic devices attached, but she double-checked it with her sensor anyway and attached the electro-magnet to the door. Then she flipped the switch. The light glowed green, and she turned the small knob to move the steel deadbolt. The noise almost made her heart stop. She waited a minute, but didn't hear any alarms or heavy footsteps pounding down the hallway. Moving the magnet down lower, she repeated the process and pushed on the door as the magnet turned the knob on the other side. She slipped inside, stowed her equipment back in the fanny pack, and threw the deadbolt. So far, so good.

Shelby moved down the hallway and stopped at the corner that led to the main hallway with the camera. Using a small mirror on a rod, she watched the movement of the surveillance camera, waiting until it swung away. She had three seconds to sprint to the other side of the cold drink machine. She let the camera swing around again, using the time to psych herself up.

When the camera swung away, she propelled herself forward at full speed, barely making the safety of the vending machine in time. She checked the position of the camera again with her mirror. As soon as it swung away, she dashed for Dr. Carlson's door, punched in the code, and leapt through the door, hoping she got it closed before the camera swung back. Leaning against the door, she took a few deep breaths and listened for the sound of boots pounding down the hallway.

Shelby quickly logged onto Carlson's laptop, thanking the powers that be that the doctor hadn't taken it home. In a few minutes she'd plugged in her portable hard drive and downloaded the files. Checking the security cameras again, Shelby timed her run into Dr. Thomas' office. Slipping the latex sleeve over her thumb, she pressed it against the glass panel. Nothing. Crap. She could feel her heart thumping as she inspected the purloined print. Maybe his thumb was bigger than hers. Shelby slipped the sleeve off, wrapped a strip of tissue over her thumb and tried it again. It worked, and she started breathing again.

Now for getting into the lab. This would be trickier because she didn't have the code for the security lock. The thirty or forty seconds it would take to get the code would put her in danger of being seen on the security cameras. From the narrow window in Dr. Thomas' office door she could see the camera as it swung around. She dashed over to the lab doors, looked in the window, and ran for the corner that the camera couldn't view.

Crap.

There were two people in lab coats in the lab. Taking them out wouldn't be a problem—except that she needed to come back here tomorrow.

Mac spread the papers out on the coffee table and looked at them again. The implications of what he was seeing were enormous. How the hell did Sam get his hands on these anyway? Mac ran his hands through his hair and picked up the phone, punching in Chris' cell phone number.

"Mac. What's up?"

"I've discovered some disturbing information."

"What's that?"

"Evidently The Center is planning some experiment on Sam. I have some papers here from his chart. They indicate the use of some extremely dangerous drugs, sleep deprivation, and mind control techniques."

"You're sure?"

"Of course, I'm sure." Sometimes Chris Jackson just really annoyed him.

"Well, now, don't get all defensive. I just want to make sure what we're dealing with here. Any sign of the mother?"

"Some." Mac took a breath to calm himself. "Sam told me that she speaks to him in his head. I think that means that she's communicating with him telepathically." Mac heard Chris sigh and knew he had a hard argument ahead of him.

"Well, Mac, I don't know how much I trust this psychic stuff, you know?"

"I understand your reluctance. But, believe me, I've seen solid evidence of psychic ability in both Sam and Shannon. I have no doubt that Shannon is able to communicate with her son telepathically."

"If you say so."

"So, what are we going to do about getting Sam out of The Center?"

"I can have a team set up to recover the boy in a few days."

"That's not good enough. They're starting the experiment on him day after tomorrow."

"Now, listen, Mac. I know you're concerned about the kid. I am too. That's why I agreed to letting you go undercover down there. But these things take time."

"Sam doesn't have any time."

"I know it seems dire, but really, we'll have everything in place before they can do much to the kid. Besides, we need to get his mother out too. If we only take Sam, it's just going to be harder to get Shannon out later. I wouldn't want to rush in and have the whole thing blow up in our faces, you know."

"I can understand that." Mac felt like his head was about to blow up from the frustration. "However, knowing Shannon, I'm certain her wishes would be to protect her son."

"I understand that, as his mother, she would certainly feel that way. However, as the SAC, I have to consider her safety as well. I doubt Ambassador Watkins or Director Fields would be pleased if our actions saved Sam at Shannon's expense."

"I understand."

"So, you just sit tight for a few more days. Maybe you can do something to delay the experiments on the boy."

"Yes, I will certainly try to delay them."

"Good. I'll let you know when we're ready to move."

"Fine." Mac hung up the phone and looked at the papers again. He couldn't wait for Chris to send a team in. Not if it was going to take several days. Even one dose of the drugs they were planning to give Sam could have a terrible effect on him.

Sam was the center of Shannon's life. He'd seen the total devotion she had for Sam when they'd worked together at The Center for Deaf Children. Shannon would expect him to keep Sam safe no matter what the cost to herself. He had to find a way to get Sam out of The Center immediately and hope they could still rescue Shannon. He had another session with Sam tomorrow. All he had to do was get him out of the building and to his car without anyone noticing. He could drive straight to the FBI offices in Phoenix. And then he'd have to deal with Chris Jackson.

Shelby spent the following morning pretending to clean more files of the mole virus, while checking the network to make sure she hadn't missed anything. By two she knew she'd gotten everything she could this way. From now on, she'd have to use more covert methods. Assuring Dr. Carlson that all their files were clean, Shelby turned in her temporary access badge and headed to her car. Might as well get a nap this afternoon so she'd be alert for breaking into the lab tonight.

Shelby pulled out of the parking lot and drove down the drive that turned and ran alongside the building to the exit gate. Something didn't feel quite right. Shelby slowed the car and looked around.

The security guards seemed to be out in full force. All of them wore lightweight jackets in spite of the warm day, their hands obviously clasped around guns in their pockets. They all appeared to be looking for something—or someone—and a number of them were headed across the parking lot to the side of the building.

Shelby turned her car at the corner of the building and saw McRae trotting along the side of the building, carrying a young boy. Shannon's son. She recognized him from the picture Ethan had included in the file. She turned the corner, sped up, and braked in front of them.

"Get in. Now!"

McRae paused, seeming uncertain until a bullet whizzed over his head. He jerked the rear door open and piled in with Sam.

As soon as she heard the door close, she gunned the car and sped toward the exit gate. The gate normally stood open during the day, but now it was slowly swinging closed. The guard who usually sat in the little enclosure was standing in the middle of the drive holding up his hand.

"Stay down!" she yelled at McRae when she saw his head pop up in the rearview mirror. She could hear gunshots and was surprised that none of them had hit the car yet.

Shelby gunned the car and aimed for the still-moving gate. The guard realized her intention at the last minute and leapt to the side, landing in some decorative cacti. She saw two white SUVs pull out of the parking lot and kept the gas pedal pressed to the floor, while the car smashed through the metal gates as they were closing.

"They aren't shooting at us," McRae said. "They wouldn't take the chance of hitting Sam." Shelby glanced at him in the rearview mirror. That explained why none of the shots had hit the car.

The road from The Center to Tucson was straight through the desert, and her only hope was to outrun them. Although the sixty-nine Firebird she'd chosen for Cathy Silvers to drive had faded paint and rusty dings, the engine was restored to factory condition. The speedometer markings went up to one-eighty, and she was about to test that. She knew the Firebird could out-run the SUVs, and the worst that would happen was that she'd get a ticket.

"We need to go to the FBI," McRae said from the backseat.

"No FBI," Shelby said as the car fishtailed out onto the road.

"Then the local police."

"No police either." Shelby glanced in the rearview mirror at McRae.

Mac turned to fasten a seatbelt around Sam, and then leaned forward. "I'm an undercover FBI agent."

"You must be pretty new, because you sure weren't prepared for this scenario."

"Well, for a computer geek, you certainly seem rather adept at this sort of thing," Mac shot back.

"Just keep the kid safe back there." She had to think, and the conversation wasn't helping. The speedometer had reached one-twenty, but Shelby was sure she could coax a little more out of the car. She was about five miles from The Center when the cop pulled out with his lights flashing. Crap.

Shelby pulled over to the side of the road and stopped. The two SUVs didn't pass them. She assumed they'd stopped around the curve, out of sight. Pulling her FSA ID and driver's license out of her padded tee shirt, she waited for the cop to walk up.

"Ma'am, I'd like to see your license and registration, please." The cop was young and squeaky-clean looking. Blond crew cut, starched and pressed uniform, leather and metal accessories highly polished.

"FSA Agent Shelby Parker." She handed him her FSA ID. "I'm on official FSA business. You might want to call your chief before we go any further. Mind if I get out of the car?"

"I'd prefer that you stay inside. And keep your hands on the wheel." The cop examined her ID and then walked back to his cruiser. While he talked on the radio, Shelby turned and scanned the roadside for signs of the men from The Center. She thought she saw some movement and squinted until she could make out a man trying to conceal himself behind a scrawny Saguaro cactus.

"FSA?" McRae asked from the backseat. Sam sat scrunched up beside him. His eyes were wide, but he didn't seem particularly frightened. Then again, what did she know about kids?

"We'll talk about it later," she said as the cop returned.

"Chief says I'm to forget this ever happened, escort you to your destination if you'd like, and assist you in any way you deem appropriate." He grinned and handed her ID back.

"Thanks. Just behind that curve back there, there's one, possibly two white SUVs following me. If you could arrange for them to be delayed, I'd sure appreciate it."

"No problem. Are we talking a few minutes or should I find a reason to take them in?"

"I just need to get into town without them following me. If you can delay them for ten or fifteen minutes? Just don't let on that you know anything about me other than I was speeding through the desert."

"No problem, Ms. Parker." He touched his hand to his forehead in a salute and trotted back to his cruiser. He then backed up on the road with his lights flashing.

Twenty minutes later, Shelby pulled up at the storage facility where she'd parked her yellow and white Mini Cooper. While the attendant brought the car around, she pulled out her cell phone and dialed into the phone connected to the recorder of the listening device she'd put in the receptionist's cubicle. The phone automatically picked up. Shelby punched in a twelve-digit code and heard a series of answering beeps.

"Who are you calling?" McRae asked.

"No one. I just activated the destruct sequence on some equipment that I don't want the people at The Center getting their hands on."

"What kind of equipment?"

"A recorder for a listening device I planted at the receptionist's desk."

"You don't want them listening in on their own conversations?" McRae looked puzzled, and she laughed.

"I don't care what they hear. I just don't want them to have the equipment." The attendant arrived with her Mini, and she handed him the keys to the Firebird with instructions to store it until someone contacted them. McRae put Sam in the backseat and fastened his seatbelt. He then slid into the front with Shelby.

"What now?"

"We go to a safe house." She glanced over at him and smiled. "I'll make a pot of coffee, and we'll sit down and figure this out."

"Coffee sounds good," McRae said.

"Well, first we have to buy some." Shelby turned onto Palo Verde and headed for the huge Wal-Mart. "I'll get some food while you get some clothes for you and the kid."

"What about clothes for you?" McRae asked.

"I've got clothes with me. You have cash?"

"No, I'll charge it."

"You really are new at this aren't you?" She parked the car, opened the trunk, and punched in the security code on an aluminum briefcase. The case contained a packet of IDs and a considerable amount of cash. Shelby pulled out a few hundred in twenties, handed them to McRae, and then took another bundle for herself.

"Don't use your credit cards for anything. At all. They can trace where you've been using them."

"Right." McRae frowned and nodded. "I knew that."

"Meet me at the food check-out when you're done." They went their separate ways—McRae to the kids department and Shelby to the grocery department.

She knew the safe house would have some canned foods, but little else. She wheeled the cart to the frozen food section and grabbed a bunch of frozen dinners, some ice cream, and a few frozen veggies. Now for the kid. Shelby thought for a moment about what kind of food kids eat, and then decided to go with what she'd seen on television. She picked up some cereal, milk, juice, cookies, bread, peanut butter, and jelly. On the way to the checkout stand, she grabbed a six-pack of beer and a bottle of wine.

Wait! Did kids use special soap or something? She headed over to the toiletries aisle and checked out the offerings. She threw in some baby shampoo, guaranteed not to make the kid cry, and some bubble bath in a bottle that looked like a cartoon character. There didn't appear to be a special soap for kids, so she assumed the bubble bath took care of the dirt. Or maybe kids just used the same soap as adults.

McRae met her at the exit, and they piled their purchases into the trunk. The safe house was only a half hour north of Tucson, and they pulled into the driveway before five. As soon as they got in, Shelby made a pot of coffee and checked out the back of the house, while McRae fixed a peanut butter and jelly sandwich for Sam.

The house had two bedrooms; one contained a full-size bed, the other a twin. The front room was furnished with an old sofa, two chairs, and a bargain-basement coffee table. There was a small fireplace, full of ashes. Usually FSA safe houses were better kept than this, but it didn't matter, as Shelby didn't expect to be here for very long.

She grabbed a change of clothes from her suitcase, along with shampoo and soap, and headed to the bathroom. She stuffed the dark wig and padded clothes into a plastic bag and then stepped into the shower. As good as the hot water felt, she didn't linger, taking just enough time to shower, shampoo, and rinse. The towels smelled a little musty, and she figured the house hadn't been used for a long time. She pulled on shorts and a tee shirt, ran a comb through her hair, and went back to the front room.

"My, that's quite a difference," McRae said as he handed her a cup of steaming coffee.

"So, you're an FBI agent." Shelby sipped the coffee, set the cup on the scarred pine coffee table, and then plopped into a chair.

"And you're with the FSA." McRae grinned at her.

"Want to tell me why you're here?"

"I could ask you the same question."

"We could do this all night."

"You don't think we'd need to stop to sleep at some point?"

"Let's cut to the chase." Shelby leaned forward. "I'm with the FSA. I'm here to recover Shannon

Masterson and her son, Sam. Both believed to be held against their will at The Center."

"Fair enough. My story is pretty much the same."

"The FBI sent you in to extract them?" she asked.

McRae shook his head. "I was supposed to determine if Sam and Shannon were actually there. I'm not actually an FBI *agent*. I'm a psychiatrist with the FBI."

"Ah, that explains this afternoon. And it explains how you got into The Center. I assume most of the background check we got on you was manufactured?"

"God, I hope so." McRae chuckled. "The FBI went to a lot of trouble to make me look as sleazy as possible."

"They did a good job."

"I actually had to beg for this assignment."

"Interesting. Why?"

"I met Shannon and Sam last year. She was visiting her aunt in DC, and we were both volunteering at The Center for Deaf Children."

"And you and Shannon fell in love, and then?"

"No, nothing like that." Mac shook his head and smiled. "Sam is an exceptional child. As we worked together I became aware of his special abilities. Shannon didn't want to admit it at first, but she finally came around."

"Special abilities? Is he a genius or something?"

"Sam definitely has a genius level IQ, among other things."

"And the other things are?"

"Sam is psychic."

CHAPTER ELEVEN

"Did you say that Sam is psychic?" Shelby asked.

"Actually, he's rather exceptional. His abilities far surpass those of most persons with psychic abilities."

"Exactly how is Sam psychic?"

"He can read emotions in people. I suspect he can even pick up thoughts and affect emotions in others. He can move things with his mind."

"All that at the age of four?" Shelby sounded skeptical even to herself. Move things? Affect emotions?

"Actually, children usually show a much stronger psychic ability than adults. Unfortunately, our society manages to convince most of them that what they are experiencing is impossible. By the time they're adults, they've dulled their senses to the point of being practically useless."

"And the FBI sent you here to rescue this miniature psychic and his mother?"

"At my insistence." McRae nodded.

"Yeah, you want to elaborate on that part?" That should be interesting.

"Dr. Mac, I'm done!" Sam called from the kitchen.

"Just a moment," Mac said, holding up a hand. He disappeared into the kitchen and came back a few minutes later holding Sam in his arms.

"Sam, I'd like to introduce you to—" Mac stopped and raised his eyebrows in a question.

"Shelby," she said. "How're you doing Sam?"

"I'm okay. But mommy needs me."

"Where's your mom?" Shelby asked, trying to ignore the sorrowful look on the kid's face.

"Back there. They wouldn't let me see her."

"I see."

"You look like you could use a bath, Sam. Let's go." McRae swung Sam around, making him giggle. "Can you bring me those bags?" He nodded toward the Wal-Mart bags on the floor next to the sofa.

Shelby picked up the bags and followed him into the bathroom. McRae plugged the tub and turned the water on, checking the temperature.

"Here we go." McRae pulled Sam's shirt off, and then his shorts and underpants.

"Oh, just a minute." She ran back to the kitchen and rummaged through the bags of food until she found the bubble bath.

"How about some bubbles?" She waved the bottle at Sam.

"Yay! Bubbles!" Sam sat in a couple inches of water as McRae opened some plastic toys he'd bought.

"Spiderman!" Sam squealed and held his hand out. The plastic Spiderman figure lifted out of McRae's hand and floated through the air, landing securely in Sam's chubby fist.

"Holy crap!" Shelby couldn't believe what she'd just seen. McRae shot her a smug I-told-you-so look.

"Sam, will you be okay in here for a few minutes?" Sam nodded, still intent on his Spiderman toy. "Just yell if you need anything." McRae grabbed her hand and pulled her back out to the front room.

"Did you see that?" Shelby was still shocked. "Of course you saw that. That's what you were talking about, isn't it?"

"Well, yes, actually."

"He really can move things with his mind!"

"As I told you, Sam is an exceptionally gifted child."

"This is incredible."

"Exactly. When I asked for this assignment, I believed that The Center wanted to test Sam's abilities and possibly Shannon's as well." Mac sipped his coffee. "But once I got hired at The Center, I started to think that maybe that was just a part of it."

"Sam's mother is psychic too?" she asked.

"Yes. Certainly not as strong or as varied as Sam, but she has psychic abilities. I'm very worried about her."

"Sam said that his mom was still at The Center. Do you think that's true?"

"Yes, I do. I believe that Sam and Shannon can communicate psychically. I'm not sure to what degree though."

"Like you and I would have a phone conversation?"

"It could be that, or it could be very different. But I'm convinced from what Sam has said that he is definitely in communication with her."

"And she's still at The Center?" Shelby asked.

"Yes, I'm sure of it."

"Crap."

"I beg your pardon?"

"I just wanted to take a hot shower, have a glass of wine, and relax for the rest of the night. Now, I have to break into The Center again."

"Again?" Mac asked.

"Oh, yeah, I broke in last night to download some files."

"I see. Why do you have to do it again tonight?"

"To get Shannon."

"You think you can actually break into The Center, take Shannon, and get out?" Mac shook his head.

"Of course."

"You're mad."

"Not really. A little irritated about not having a relaxing evening, but . . ." McRae was looking at her as if she'd lost her mind. "Really, it'll be fine." Mac wasn't buying her assurances.

"But since I took Sam today, they'll increase security. They'll be expecting something else to happen."

"Probably not." She almost wanted to laugh at his concern, but she didn't think he'd appreciate it. "Actually, they probably won't do anything to increase security—tonight." McRae lifted an eyebrow at her.

"They're still dealing with Sam's disappearance," she explained. "Most likely they won't expect me to try to take Shannon tonight. In fact, why would they even think that I know Shannon is there?" It was a line of bullshit, but she was hoping Mac would buy it. There was no way he was going to talk her out of this.

"You can't be serious?" Mac stood and walked to the middle of the room. "These people are evil but they certainly are not stupid! They have Shannon for a reason. Otherwise, they'd have just disposed of her. We took Sam, and they'll expect us to try to take Shannon too."

"My job is to get her out of there."

"I understand that. I just don't see how getting yourself caught is going to accomplish that."

"I won't get caught."

"Is that confidence or arrogance?" Mac demanded.

"I'm not arrogant. I'm just good at what I do."

As soon as the hallway lights were dimmed, Zoe got out of bed and started exercising. First deep knee bends, then pushups, and finally, jumping jacks. Her strength was almost back to normal. She didn't know if it was the four days she'd been strapped to the bed or the drugs they'd given her that had made her so weak. They'd taken the IV out, but they still gave her some kind of sleeping pills at night. So far, she'd been able to fake the nurse out and not swallow the pills. She was still having nausea occasionally, and she felt extremely bitchy. But that could just be the circumstances. Who wouldn't be bitchy about being locked up? Eventually an opportunity to escape would present itself, and she was going to be ready. And if the opportunity didn't present itself in the next twenty-four hours, she'd have to create it herself.

Jonah Thomas visited her twice a day. He'd explained that the room was locked for her own safety. She continued to appear meek and complacent. She agreed with everything he said and thanked him profusely for saving her life. Maybe that was causing the nausea. Zoe chuckled at the thought. No one had ever accused her of being meek, much less complacent.

Today Dr. Thomas had told her that they would need to run some tests in a couple of days. Something to do with her head injury. They'd be putting her to sleep for the test.

Not without a fight. Zoe didn't know why they wanted to put her to sleep or what they planned to do, but she was certain it had nothing to do with her supposed head injury. The only injury she'd suffered was when someone, probably Dr. Thomas, had conked her on the noggin while she'd been tossing his dresser drawers.

She finished her exercises and filled a glass with water from the bathroom faucet. At least they'd finally brought her some cotton pajamas, and they'd given her a pair of slippers to wear. It wasn't exactly her jeans, boots and leather jacket, but it was better than bare feet and the hospital gown she was in when she had awakened.

Dr. Thomas had told her that her clothes had been destroyed in the accident, but he'd given her an envelope with her wallet and a silver chain inside. She pulled open the drawer in the bedside table and picked up the tri-fold wallet. They'd left her cash—all seventeen dollars of it. More importantly, they'd left her driver's license and credit cards. She'd need all that when she got out of here. Of course, they weren't planning on her leaving. Probably, they only gave her the wallet to make her feel like she would get out someday.

Zoe crawled into bed and pulled the sheet over her shoulders. The night nurse would be in soon to make sure she was asleep.

"Hi, sweetheart. How have you been?" Chris forced her tone to be casual, flirty, but she wanted to scream out the questions, get answers immediately. That wouldn't work.

"Chris. I, uh . . . I'm surprised to hear from you."

Surprise. That was good. "I know, hon. I meant to call a while back, but I thought maybe you didn't want to hear from me."

"It isn't that. Not really. I just needed some time."

"I understand. It was hard on me, too, you know. I never wanted to break up."

"We've been over all this Chris. I just couldn't

maintain such a long distance relationship. With you in Virginia and me in Denver, it was just too hard."

"I know, I know. But I'm not in Virginia any more. Denver isn't that far from Phoenix."

"It's far enough, Chris. I'm with someone else now."

"Oh, yes, Charlie, isn't it?"

"How did you know?" Surprise again. Good, keep her off balance.

"I checked. I have my sources, you know." Chris chuckled, but not unkindly. "I hope you're happy."

"I am. It's not the same as it was with you, but Charlie and I are happy."

"That's good to hear." Chris paused a moment. "I'm actually calling to ask you for a favor."

"Of course, anything."

"I have a problem, and I need some information. My career is on the line."

"Your career? Chris, what's happened?"

"I can't go into all of it now, but I'll tell you everything after it's all said and done."

"Chris, you've got me worried."

"Well, I'm worried too. But if you can give me the information I need, I can get it all cleared up."

"What do you need?"

"I need to know why the FSA is investigating The Center for Bio-Psychological Research in Tucson."

"Chris! I can't give you information on our investigations. You know you can get what you need through the usual channels."

"Not this time. I know the FSA is investigating The Center. I figure it's a black op because it's supposed to be the FBI's case."

"Don't ask me to do something I can't."

"You can. In fact, you're the only one who can. You know everything that goes on there."

"Yes, I know, but I can't tell you."

"Would you rather explain me to Charlie?"

"What?"

"I have pictures that Charlie would like to see too."

"Chris, you wouldn't!" Chris waited through the pause. "Charlie is very important to me." Another pause. "What we have is very special. I don't want anything to screw up this relationship."

"Then tell me what I need to know. No one will ever find out. It won't compromise the op, I swear." She'd swear to anything at this point. She had to know why an ex-agent was doing a black op for the FSA. If Parker was successful, if she brought Jonah down, then the photos would get released. That was not an option.

"Why do you need to know?"

"I told you, my career is at stake—maybe even my life." That was laying it on a little thick, but she had no regrets about the lie.

"Ethan hired Shelby Parker to get Shannon Masterson and her son out of The Center."

"How is she going to do that?" Chris asked.

"I don't know. Shelby has never done anything by the book, and now she doesn't have to since she doesn't work for us."

"Does Chambers know what Ethan is doing?"

"Of course, he knows everything. It's just set up like Ethan is doing this on his own in case someone finds out."

"So, Chambers planned the whole thing?" Chris didn't wait for an answer. "What's Parker doing now? I know she got into The Center disguised as a computer tech."

"I just overheard that she got Shannon's son out of The Center this afternoon. They went to a safe house in the area. I don't know anything else. Really, Chris."

"I see. Listen, sweetheart, I really appreciate this. You're saving me. Just like you always have."

"No more, Chris. I can't do it anymore."

"Just a little more. I'll call again. I'll need to know where Parker is and what she's going to do."

"I don't know that I can get that information."

"Of course you can. You have access to Chambers' email, his voice mail. Find a way." Chris almost hated herself for doing this. "Don't make me call Charlie."

CHAPTER TWELVE

Shelby climbed over the stone wall in back of The Center at midnight when the guards were all busy with the shift change. She peeled off her coveralls and left them with the grappling hook and rope. Access to the building was just as easy as the previous night, so maybe she'd been right that they didn't expect anything to happen.

Before she'd left The Center, she'd been able to get the code to the lab area by watching someone punch it in while she was supposedly getting a soft drink. Dressed in scrubs and a lab coat, with paper booties covering her boots, Shelby looked just like everyone else she'd seen go into the lab.

Shelby walked slowly by the lab doors and looked in the windows. One woman sat behind a desk reading a newspaper and glancing occasionally at a monitor. Last night there'd been two people in the lab. She walked back, punched in the code, opened the door, and walked up to the woman sitting at the desk. Fortunately she had a clear view of the woman's nametag.

"Hi, you must be Rose." Shelby held her hand out, and Rose took it, looking a little surprised. "Dr. Carlson told me you'd already be on duty when I got here."

"She did?"

"I'm Karen. She said you'd show me the ropes."

"Are you working the night shift now?"

"Didn't she tell you?" Shelby asked. "The doc said they were expecting some new patients in a couple weeks. I guess she figured it'd be too much without extra help at night."

"I'm amazed that she even thought of it. Did you work days before?"

"Just occasionally. When someone was on vacation or something. It's nice to have a regular schedule for a while."

"Well, nights are pretty quiet here, and by this time the patients are all usually asleep. Of course we only have the two women right now." Rose scribbled a number on a piece of paper and handed it to her. "This is the code to the patients' rooms for this shift."

"Thanks." Shelby slipped the code into her pocket. That was a piece of luck. She hadn't known what the security code was for the patients, and this would make it much easier.

"You just missed all the excitement," Rose said as she folded her newspaper.

"What was that?"

"Some guy came in here like a demented commando and tried to take one of our patients."

"Tonight?" Shelby tried not to sound as anxious as she felt about that.

"Just a couple of hours ago. I guess it was some boyfriend who thought we were keeping her prisoner." Rose shook her head. "Sometimes family and friends just don't understand when a woman admits herself to a facility like this."

"So he thought she was here against her will, huh?"

"That's what it sounded like. The guards caught him and called the doctors."

"Did they call the police?"

"You really are new here, aren't you?" Rose chuckled. "The doctors don't hold with involving the police in these situations." She shrugged. "It just complicates everything, according to Dr. Carlson. Usually they just take the person away and talk to him. You know, explain why the patient is here and how we're helping her."

"Does that work?"

"It must. I've only seen it a couple of times, but they've never come back." Rose shrugged again. Shelby figured she was the kind of woman who shrugged a lot. "Hey you want to check on the Masterson woman? I already gave the other one her meds."

"Sure. I haven't been here in a while, where's her room?"

"Number three, down that hallway." Rose seemed

to enjoy having someone there to do her job for her, and Shelby was happy to let her take advantage of it.

Shelby stopped at the door of Room Three and peered in the small window. The bed was empty. Covers rumpled and thrown back. She could see a sliver of light from under a door that probably led to a bathroom. Shelby punched in the security code Rose had given her and went in. There was only one security camera that she could see, and it had a view of most of the room. She shuddered at the thought of having her every move monitored twenty-four hours a day.

Wait. If they had a security camera in the room, why were they checking on the patient every two hours? Crap. Rose was probably calling Dr. Carlson right now to verify that Shelby was supposed to be there.

Shelby positioned herself with her back to the camera just as Shannon came out of the bathroom. Pressing her finger to her lips to indicate Shannon should be silent, Shelby motioned her over and handed her one of the notes she'd prepared in advance. Shannon was wearing cotton pajamas and terrycloth slippers. Not the best escape outfit, but it could have been worse. She read the note and nodded.

Shelby opened the door and looked down the hallway. Rose was standing at the desk with her back to them, phone held to her ear. After a few seconds, she punched in a number and hung up. She was probably paging Dr. Carlson, which meant Shelby needed to disable her before the call got returned. She motioned for

Shannon to keep the door from closing and to wait for her. Then she hurried down the hallway.

Rose was watching the monitor and had picked up the phone again. She turned just as Shelby reached her. A sharp uppercut to her chin, and she crumpled like a rag doll. Then Shelby saw the number on the phone display. Rose had called the guard. She took the receiver from Rose's limp hand.

"Hello?" the guard answered.

"Oh, sorry, I hit the wrong number on the speed dial." Shelby lowered her voice and made it sound raspy.

"Who is this?" the guard asked.

"It's Rose. I have a cold."

"Everything all right back there?"

"Sure. I'm just out of it with this cold."

"Okay." He hung up. Shelby ran back down the hall and flung open the door to Shannon's room.

"Hey! What's going on out there?"

Shelby saw light coming from under the door next to Shannon's room. Whoever was in the room was pounding on the door. Must be the other patient Rose had mentioned.

"Quiet!" Shelby ran to the door and punched in the code. The pounding stopped as the door was jerked open. A petite woman stood at the door in pajamas and slippers, curls of red hair escaping from the braid that hung over her shoulder. Her green eyes narrowed at Shelby

"Who are you?" the woman demanded.

Shelby ignored her question. "You want to get out of here?"

"Damn straight."

"We have to hurry. But be as quiet as you can." Shelby grabbed Shannon's hand, and they ran to the lab doors. She spared a moment to make sure the guard wasn't around, and then they ran down the hallway to the rear exit. Shelby didn't bother relocking the door this time. In a few seconds she had the grappling hook attached. She ripped the paper booties off her boots, stuffed them in a pocket, and tied the coveralls around her waist.

"I'm going to give you a leg up to get over the wall. Just drop down to the other side and wait for me."

Shannon nodded. Her eyes were wide with fear, but she seemed determined.

"Wait. Let me go over first, then I can help her down." The redhead placed her foot in Shelby's cupped hands. Shelby lifted her up, and she scrambled to the top of the wall, stepped over the iron spikes, and dropped to the ground with a soft thud. Shelby cupped her hands again and boosted Shannon over, and then secured the grappling hook and started pulling herself up the stone wall.

"Hey!"

Crap. The guard had seen her.

Shelby dropped back to the ground and turned toward him slowly, hands raised over her head. When he was in just the right position, her right leg snapped out and landed a heavily booted foot in his midsection.

The air whuffed out of him but he kept coming, just a little more slowly. She threw a punch with her right arm, causing him to swing around to avoid it, which put his right hand in easy reach of her left. She grabbed his wrist and pulled him toward her, delivering a quick chop to a nerve cluster on his neck. He slumped to the ground, looked at her for a second, and then his eyes rolled back in his head and he fell over.

Shelby grabbed the rope again and hoisted herself over the wall. Shannon looked terrified. The other woman already had the rope and was lowering herself down the ravine. Shelby bent slightly at the knees and braced herself.

"Climb onto my back and hold on."

Shannon didn't move, just stood there shaking her head.

"Do it! Now!"

Shannon climbed on and wrapped her arms around Shelby's neck. Shelby had to take a few seconds to reposition Shannon's arms so she wasn't choking her, and then she lowered the two of them down the steep incline. The other woman had found the rope Shelby had left and was more than half way up the other side by the time they reached the bottom. Shannon was able to pull herself up the other side of the ravine with a little help, and they made it to the car before anyone came to check on the missing guard.

"You all right?" Shelby asked as she drove toward Tucson. Shannon was shivering although the night was only mildly cool. Shelby turned up the heater.

"I guess. Who are you? How did you know I was there?" Shannon burst into tears.

"It's okay. You're going to be fine. We have your son."

"Sam? Is he all right?"

"Sam's fine. He's been living with some foster parents The Center put him with. I don't have all the answers yet, but we will. Soon."

"I knew he was with Jill and Victor." Shannon clamped her lips into a thin line.

"I understand you can communicate with Sam?"

"You know?"

"Dr. McRae told me. That's how I knew you were still at The Center. Sam told us."

"Dear God, this has been such a nightmare."

"It's over now. We're going to a safe house, and tomorrow we'll make plans to get you to the FSA. They'll take care of you and Sam until we can close down The Center."

"They took you *and* your son?" the other woman asked from the backseat.

"Who are you?" Shelby asked, catching her eye in the rearview mirror.

"Zoe."

"Shelby Parker." Shelby introduced herself to the two women.

Shannon leaned her head back and closed her eyes. Tears streamed down her face.

"It really is going to be okay," Shelby tried to assure her.

"They have Chase."

"Chase Harmon?" Shelby asked. She remembered him from the first day she'd gone to The Center.

"He tried to rescue me tonight, and they caught him." Shannon gave Shelby a quizzical look. "How did you know his name?"

"I ran into him at The Center. Is he family or a friend?"

"Both, I guess. Chase is Sam's father, although he doesn't know that."

"Sam doesn't know who his father is?" Shelby asked, slightly confused.

"No—yes." Shannon shook her head. "I mean, Sam doesn't know, but also, Chase doesn't know that he has a son."

Oh, boy. Shelby had read about this kind of thing in confession magazines that some of her dad's girlfriends had lying around. But, even back then she'd known that those stories weren't true. Did women really not tell men that they were carrying their children? Well, evidently, it happened.

This man obviously still cared enough about Shannon to try to rescue her. There was surely an interesting story behind all this, but right now Shelby had other things to concentrate on.

"We'll get Chase out too."

"How can you do that?" Shannon's eyes were clouded with fear and hope. "I doubt they even have him at The Center."

"I got you, didn't I?"

Shannon seemed to relax at that reassurance.

"What were you doing at The Center, Zoe?" Shelby asked.

"It's kind of a long story. I don't know why they had me there. All I know is that I couldn't get out, and I was nauseous all the time. God knows what they're up to there."

Shelby decided she could get Zoe's story later. "Can you tell me why they were holding you, Shannon? Were they doing anything to you?"

"I don't really know. The entire time I was there, I was kept in that small room. They'd come in and take blood samples and ask for urine specimens." Shannon started to shake again. "Sometimes, they'd give me something, and I'd go to sleep and not wake up for hours. I don't know what they were doing. Sometimes, afterwards, I'd find something. Like some adhesive stuck to me, or once I had a bandage on my hip. I didn't know why, and they wouldn't tell me anything."

"I know it's been really hard on you. We can go over this later. The good news is that you'll see your son in less than half an hour."

Shannon collapsed into tears again. Happy ones, Shelby assumed—or hoped.

"Anything yet?" Dr. Carlson asked.

"Nope." Frank typed in another command and punched the enter key.

"I thought this tracking system was supposed to work."

"It works, it just has limits," Frank explained.

"We don't have time for limits."

"Well, you got 'em anyway. Here's the thing. The GPS tracking device is accurate within twenty miles. Up to thirty miles, we might or might not get something on it."

"So, you're telling me the tracking device is at least twenty miles away?" Dr. Carlson asked.

"Exactly. If you want to find it, you need to get one of the portable receivers within twenty miles of the thing."

"Damn!"

"It's a good system, Dr. Carlson. But it ain't Star Trek," Frank said.

"How many portable receivers do we have?"

"Half a dozen."

"Give them to me," she said.

"I have to get them all activated first."

"I'll have someone pick them up within an hour." Dr. Carlson ran her hand through her hair. "You can do that in an hour, right?"

"No problem. So, I take it this isn't just a test?" Frank asked.

"Hardly." Her cell phone beeped, and she pulled it off her belt clip.

"Ruth, what's going on?" Jonah's soft voice irritated her even more.

"We have a problem." Ruth walked away from

Frank so she wouldn't be overheard.

"I assumed that. You rarely call me at one in the morning."

"Someone took the Masterson woman tonight and your new surrogate."

"What?"

"Frank's getting the mobile tracking devices ready, and I'm about to check the security tapes to see who was in here. The night nurse was found knocked out with a bruise on her chin. One of the guards was found in a similar condition at the rear wall. There was a grappling hook with a rope left attached to the wall. I assume that's how they left."

"Dear God. We can't lose her now, Ruth!"

"I know that, Jonah." Did the man think she was stupid? The pregnancy test had just come back—positive.

"I assume there's been no word on Sam?"

"No. I'll call you as soon as I hear something."

"No need. I'm coming down now."

"Fine." Ruth punched the end button on her cell phone and returned it to her belt clip. Losing Sam had been bad enough. Why the hell had McRae taken Sam anyway? Chris told them that he was just there to gather information. What had caused him to run off with Sam? Jonah had been trying to call Chris all day, but she hadn't answered. And it appeared that Cathy Silvers had helped McRae. She didn't know what to make of that.

Ruth rubbed her eyes and ran a hand through her hair. Now Shannon was gone as well. And the new surrogate.

That the thief Jonah had caught carried the recessive gene had been a stroke of luck. The people funding the program were not going to be pleased about this.

"What the hell is going on, Ruth?" Jonah rushed into the control room.

"Why don't you ask your friend Chris?" Ruth shot back. Jonah's cell phone beeped, and he pulled it out, glancing at the number.

"I will." He flipped the phone open. "Chris. I certainly hope you have something to tell me."

"I got your voice mail that McRae had run off with Sam. I haven't heard from him."

"That's only part of what's happened. Now Shannon is missing too. Someone broke into The Center and tried to take her. We have that bastard. But a few hours later, someone else managed to get her out."

Chris wanted to ask Jonah why Shannon and Sam were so important to him, but she didn't dare. "Shelby Parker," Chris said. "Ex-FSA agent. You know her as Cathy Silvers."

"And you just found this out?" he demanded. "Where did the information come from?"

"I won't implicate my source, Jonah."

"The hell you won't!"

Chris ignored his outburst. "I have more information for you. Parker and McRae took Shannon and Sam to a safe house."

"Where?"

"I don't know. But since they took Sam several

hours before they took Shannon, I'd assume it's not far away."

"I need more than that, Chris."

"I checked the records. There's an old FSA safe house a little outside of Tucson, on the northwest side. I don't have an address."

CHAPTER THIRTEEN

"You want a beer?" Shelby asked Mac.

"Sure. Sounds good."

She poured a water glass half full of wine for her-self, and one for Shannon, and popped the cap off a bottle of beer for Mac. She didn't normally drink during an op unless it was part of her cover, but it had been a really rough day, and there was no way The Center knew where they were tonight. She handed the beer to Mac and set the glass of wine for Shannon on the coffee table.

Zoe was already asleep on the twin bed in the second bedroom. Shelby figured she could question her in the morning. They'd probably both feel more like talking then.

"He's asleep, finally." Shannon pulled the door to the bedroom closed and joined them, sinking down on the sofa. "He's exhausted."

"You look pretty tired yourself," Shelby said, handing her the glass of wine.

"Wine." Shannon looked pleasantly surprised. "Thanks."

Shelby didn't think Shannon even looked old enough to drink wine, dressed as she was in cotton pajamas with her hair pulled back in a ponytail.

"I thought you could use it. And I figured you for more of a wine drinker than a beer guzzler."

"True." Shannon smiled, looked down the hallway, and shook her head. "God, I want to run back to the bedroom and look at him again. It's been so long."

"Just over two months, right?"

"Seems like years, but yes, just over two months." Shannon gulped, then gasped. Shelby thought she was going to start crying again until she put the glass down, clamped a hand over her mouth, and ran for the bathroom.

They could hear the retching from the front room. Mac and Shelby exchanged glances. She scowled at him.

He shrugged at her. Evidently, his expertise didn't extend to sick women. Shelby took a healthy slug of her wine and went to the bathroom. Shannon was running water on a washcloth.

"Sorry about that." Her voice sounded shaky.

"You okay?" Shelby asked.

"I'm fine."

"Maybe it was the wine on top of all the excitement today."

"God, I hope so."

"Huh?" Shelby asked.

"Just a joke." Shannon shook her head and pressed the washcloth to her neck. She then ran it under cold water and wiped her face. "When I got pregnant with Sam, I was puking three times a day within a week."

"You know exactly when you got pregnant?"

"Down to the day and hour. Chase and I had decided not to see each other. I knew that he was leaving for the Marines. Anyway, I ran into him at a bookstore. He was leaving the next day." Shannon shrugged. "Well, one thing led to another, and a week later I was pregnant and puking. I figured if he didn't have room in his life for a relationship, he certainly didn't have room for a child."

"Men really have the easy part of procreation."

"Tell me about it." Shannon rinsed out the washcloth. "I'm probably just a little too tired and too stressed to drink wine right now. I think I'll just go to bed."

"Good idea. See you in the morning." Shelby stepped out of the bathroom. "Oh, sorry you have to share a bed with your son. I didn't expect the house to be so small."

"No problem. I'd sleep with him anyway tonight. But where are you and Mac going to sleep?"

"We'll manage. Just get some rest. Tomorrow will be a busy day."

"Is she all right?" Mac asked when Shelby came back to the front room.

"Yeah, just tired, I think. She's going to bed now. I think mostly she just wants to be close to Sam right now." Shelby sipped her wine and considered Mac. He looked tired and worried. His hair was sticking up in places, and the lines on his forehead seemed deeper.

"You were saying earlier that you had to beg for this assignment?"

Mac grinned. "Yes. The director wasn't keen on the idea of a psychiatrist going undercover at The Center. But I convinced him that it was the only way we'd get in there."

"Why did you think they were at The Center?"

"Shannon and I emailed each other after she left DC. The last couple of emails I'd gotten from her mentioned The Center. She said she was taking Sam there for IQ testing, and she was going to be counseled on how to deal with a genius child. She was very positive about it."

"And then you stopped hearing from her?"

"Exactly. Shortly after that, her uncle contacted us."

"Her aunt contacted the FSA. That's basically why I'm here."

"Don't we have a conflict of interest or something here?" Mac asked.

"Not technically." Shelby considered Mac for a moment. "I'm not with the FSA."

"You said you were an FSA agent."

Shelby shrugged. "I lied."

"I have a feeling that you lie easily."

"Depends on what I'm lying about. Actually, I was

an FSA agent until a little over a year ago. I left and started my own investigation and security firm."

"So, how do you happen to be here?"

"My former handler called me in on this. It's complicated."

"So you really are working for the FSA."

"I guess." Shelby suppressed a sigh. Her first big case. But it felt like a step back. "Now that we have Shannon and Sam, I have to do something about Chase."

"Chase Harmon?"

"You know him?" Shelby asked.

Mac nodded. "He was being tested at The Center for psychic ability. But why was he rescuing Shannon?"

"Chase is Sam's father, although he doesn't know it."

"Really?" Mac lifted his eyebrows. "Shannon pretty much refused to speak about Sam's father. I assumed they'd had a falling out at some point."

"Well, he cared enough about her to break into The Center and try to get her out."

"He always seemed out of place at The Center. I just assumed that he wanted to find out if he had any psychic ability. He'd volunteered for the research program." Mac shook his head. "And now he's there?"

"They caught him, and the night nurse said the doctors took him somewhere to talk to him."

"I'll bet."

"Earlier you said that you originally thought they wanted to test Shannon and Sam."

"That was before Sam gave me some papers from his chart."

"How did he get papers from his chart?"

Mac shrugged. "The papers indicated that The Center was about to perform some strange experiment on him."

"Experiment? Like a lab animal?"

"Exactly. I'm not sure what the entire experiment was, but it included the use of some very powerful and dangerous drugs."

"On a child?"

"Horrifying, I know." Mac shook his head. "There were also indications of some brainwashing techniques."

"What the hell are these people up to?"

"I can't imagine. But it's bad. It's really bad."

"And how did Chase Harmon know that Shannon was there? *I* couldn't even be sure she was there," Shelby asked.

"No idea." Mac shrugged. "Perhaps she was able to get word to him."

"Mac, why did you take Sam out by yourself? It sounds like you were just there to gather information."

"That was the original plan." Mac took a swig of beer and leaned his head back, closing his eyes. "I'm probably going to be in big trouble."

"You mean you didn't tell the FBI what you were doing?"

"Worse. I told my SAC, and she instructed me to do nothing."

"Oh."

"She said they'd come in and take Sam in a few days." Mac lifted his head and grinned. "I didn't find that acceptable."

"I see."

"They were going to start the experiment immediately. I couldn't leave him there knowing that.

"I'd have done the same thing." Shelby nodded.

"Thanks. That helps. Can I use you as a reference on my résumé?"

"I doubt you'll need to start looking for another job. Probably your SAC will just yell at you for a while. Threaten to demote you to the mailroom, or possibly the janitorial staff. That's what usually happened when I ignored direct orders. They don't threaten to fire you until at least the fifth or sixth time."

"You sound like it happened regularly." Mac grinned at her.

"Often enough." Shelby grinned back at him.

"I'm exhausted."

"It's been a long day. We need to get some sleep. Tomorrow I'll call Ethan and tell him where we stand."

"We seem to be a little short on sleeping space."

"The sofa pulls out to a bed. If you don't mind sharing, we can both sleep on it."

"I've never turned down an invitation to sleep with a beautiful woman."

"Sleep is the operative word here," Shelby warned him.

Shelby woke up at five, all senses alert. Someone was coming into the safe house.

Crap.

Mac was snoring softly beside her, and she realized that their legs were intertwined. She gently disengaged hers and sat up. The noise was coming from the kitchen. Shelby put her hand over Mac's mouth and shook his shoulder. Mac's eyes flew open, wide with fear, tinged with panic. She put her finger to her lips and then whispered to him.

"Someone's breaking into the house. Keep quiet and stay here."

Mac nodded. Shelby swung her legs off the bed and slipped her feet into the boots she'd left on the floor. She quickly zipped them up, grabbed her gun from the end table, and stepped silently to the doorway leading to the kitchen. They must have chosen the kitchen window because it was the only one without bars on it.

How the hell had anyone found them? No one had followed her when she left The Center. That left only two options. Either Mac told someone where they were, or there was a leak at FSA headquarters. She'd left Ethan a voice mail telling him where they were, but little else.

Two men had entered the kitchen. That was good. She could certainly handle two. Of course, there could be more outside. The moon was shining through the kitchen window casting their shadows on the wall as they moved about. She glanced back at the sofa bed. Mac wasn't there, and Shelby figured he'd gone to alert Zoe, Shannon, and Sam. Although she'd told him to stay put and stay quiet.

She moved back against the wall and looked around the room. They'd moved the small coffee table over when they pulled the sofa bed out, and it was within easy reach. She tucked her gun into the back of her shorts, bent over, and grasped the end of the small table.

The shadows indicated that the two men were almost at the doorway and walking side by side. She waited until she could see them turning the corner into the front room. She blew out her breath, lifted the table, and slammed it into them.

The table was too light to stop them, but at least she heard the satisfying whoosh as she knocked the breath out of them. Her body performed the offensive moves without conscious thought—left fist slamming into a neck, right foot connecting with a jaw. She took a blow to the midsection and stumbled. She regained her balance and spun into a roundhouse kick, catching one of the men in the head. The man dropped to the floor, but his buddy was coming at her. Suddenly his head snapped forward, his eyes rolled up into the sockets, and he crumpled. Zoe was standing behind him holding a fireplace poker. Shelby ran to the back door and wrenched it open only to see a third man scampering over the fence.

Crap.

Shelby rummaged in the kitchen drawers and found

a roll of thick twine. "Here, tie them up," she instructed Zoe.

"Who are they?" Zoe asked.

Shelby quickly frisked the men and found no identification, but one had a piece of notepaper with The Center's logo on it. Not surprising. How they'd found the safe house was still disturbing, but she'd have to deal with that later.

"Thanks for the help," Shelby said to Zoe. "But I could have handled them myself. I'd rather you stay back if this happens again."

Zoe shrugged. "Staying back isn't in my nature."

Shelby could understand that. It wasn't in her nature either. She stepped to the back of the house and found Mac, Shannon, and Sam in the bathroom.

"Next time I tell you to stay put, do it," Shelby said to Mac.

"I just thought—"

"We need to leave here, now!" Shelby interrupted him.

Mac pulled Shannon out from behind him. She was holding a sleeping Sam in her arms. "I'll get the stuff."

Shelby led Shannon and Sam outside to the car. Mac and Zoe arrived moments later with all the bags of stuff he'd bought at Wal-Mart. Five minutes later they were on I-10 headed north.

"What the hell happened back there?" Mac asked.

Shelby glanced in the rearview mirror and saw that Sam was sound asleep in Shannon's arms. Two women and a child in the backseat of the Mini was a bit cramped, but Sam didn't seem to mind sitting in his mother's lap. "I knocked them out." She saw Zoe frown. "With Zoe's help. Evidently they were from The Center."

"How could The Center know where we were? I thought that was a safe house."

"It was until they found us. Did you call anyone?"

"Of course not!" Mac looked genuinely offended.

"Me neither," Zoe added.

"Then they found us some other way. I'll have to deal with that later. Right now, we need to get to someplace that is really safe," Shelby said.

"Is there such a place?"

"Oh, yes. There's a place that's as safe as your mama's arms," Shelby assured him.

"Tell me you aren't taking us to some FSA maximum security site."

"No, we're going to a retreat in Sedona."

"A retreat?"

"Hot tubs, mud baths, meditation, herbal wraps—stuff like that." Shelby smiled brightly, but Mac didn't look convinced.

Four hours, six cups of coffee, and two rest stops later, Shelby turned into the driveway of *Serenity Haven* on the outskirts of Sedona. The long drive led up to an eight-foot high stone wall. She rolled to a stop at the gate, lowered the car window, and pressed the intercom button.

"How may I help you?" a smooth, deep, male voice asked.

"I'm here to see Mel."

"And your name?"

"Falcon," Shelby answered.

"Falcon, I apologize for the delay. Please enter."
The iron gates swung open.

Suddenly she recognized the voice. "Bear?"

"Yes."

"I'll be damned."

"No doubt, but come on in anyway."

CHAPTER FOURTEEN

"Friend of yours?" Mac asked.

There was no way to answer Mac's question without talking for several hours. Even then, he probably wouldn't understand. She drove through the gates and down a long, curving driveway, finally arriving at the main building of the retreat. Mel stood at the front door.

Shelby hadn't seen Mel in a of couple years, but she looked better than ever. Maybe it was the stress-free life of living at a retreat. Maybe it was the Native American ancestry coming to the surface. She stood several inches taller than Shelby and had a bearing that could only be called regal. Straight, black hair fell almost to her waist, which was still trim and toned at forty-eight. Shelby smiled. Damn. She should look so good in fifteen years.

She noticed that Mel's looks weren't lost on Mac, as they all piled out of the car. He was looking at her like he'd seen a goddess. Mel took everything in at a glance and opened her arms to Shelby.

"I assume you're in trouble?"

"Some things never change," Shelby said, returning her hug. "This is Mac, Zoe, Shannon, and Sam. We could all use a shower and a nap."

"And a meal, no doubt. Come. Bear will show you to your cottages, and I'll get something for you to eat while you clean up."

Bear was an extremely large African-American man. Shelby'd never known his age, and it could have been anywhere from thirty to fifty. His head was shaved, and his bulging muscles threatened to burst the seams of his black tee shirt. He still favored fatigue pants and commando boots, and his brown eyes were as warm and inviting as ever. Bear was a gentle giant who was ferociously protective of anyone he cared about. Shelby counted herself lucky to be in that small group.

"We're pretty full up, right now. I can put the child and his mother in a cottage, and you three will have to share one." Shelby, Mac and Zoe all nodded, too tired to consider an objection. They stopped at a small, one-room cottage, and Bear showed Shannon and Sam inside. They left them with the small amount of clothes and accessories Mac had gotten for Sam and continued on to another similar cottage.

"Clean up, then come back to the main house," Bear instructed with a nod that was almost a bow.

"Thanks, Bear." Shelby threw her arms around his

broad shoulders and gave him a fierce hug before he left.

"Nice place," Mac said looking around the room. Mel's cottages were each designed around a theme. Egyptian, Japanese, Medieval, French Country there were a dozen of thcm, cach one different. They had the Tropical cottage. One bedroom had a king-sized bed surrounded by a mosquito net suspended from a bamboo frame. Across from the bed, a teak cabinet hid a large television and stereo system. Next to that, a door opened to a walk-in closet with drawers and shelves. The second bedroom was smaller, with only a full-size bed and a small desk. The bedrooms were on either side of the main room of the cottage, containing a sitting area and small kitchen. A few feet from thc sofa and two mama san chairs, French doors opened onto a small private patio that bristled with tropical plants. A waterfall trickled down artfully arranged rocks into a shallow pool.

"Beats the safe house." Shelby dropped her small duffle bag on the bed and unzipped it. "Mind if I shower first?"

"Go ahead. I think I'll just relax out on the patio." Mac walked out through the doors and dropped into one of the chaise lounges.

"No problem," Zoe said. I don't have anything to change into anyway."

"I'll see what Mel can come up with for you to wear," Shelby said on her way to the bathroom. "But there are extra robes in the bathroom. You can use one until we find you something else."

After a quick shower, she brushed her teeth and ran a comb through her damp hair. Dressed in clean shorts and a tank top, Shelby joined Mac on the patio. Zoe almost ran to the bathroom for her turn in the shower.

"My turn." Mac rose from his chair.

"Not yet. Zoe's in there."

Mac dropped back into the chair. "What's her story?"

"I haven't had time to talk to her yet. I know she was at The Center against her will, and that's about all. She seems a little reluctant to go into any detail."

"I wasn't aware that she was there." Mac frowned. "But, I wasn't able to find Shannon either."

"She said she'd only been there since Wednesday. I take it the doctors didn't let you into the lab area?"

"No. I didn't even have the code for the lock." Mac shook his head. "I wish I knew what the hell they're up to."

"We'll find out. I sent all the files I downloaded to the FSA. They should have them unencrypted soon."

"Can't be too soon for me," Zoe said as she came out onto the patio, wrapped in one of Mel's fluffy, white robes, damp hair hanging down her back. "I'm still puking several times a day."

Shelby nodded at a chair. "Want to tell me how you came to be there?"

"I'm going to take my turn in the shower." Mac smiled and lifted his eyebrows at Shelby. Seconds after he'd left, there was a knock at the door.

"Come on in. It's open," Shelby called.

Mel opened the door grinning at Shelby and holding a thermal pot of coffee. "Thought you might want some coffee."

"You know me. There's no such thing as too much caffeine. You want some, Zoe?"

"No, thanks." Zoe shook her head and continued running a comb through her hair.

Mel swiped two mugs from the counter and brought the coffee out to the patio. "This smells like FSA, and I could have sworn you left the FSA to open your own PI shop."

"I did. Parker Security and Investigation," Shelby said.

Mel lifted her finely arched brows in question.

"Ethan hired me to do this op." Shelby savored the smell of the coffee and sipped. "And it's a black op. Well, almost. Ethan calls it gray."

"He would." Mel laughed. "So, tell me everything."

Shelby brought her up to speed on the op, including that Mac was a psychiatrist for the FBI, Shannon and Sam were obviously psychic, and that she didn't have a clue what the demented doctors at The Center were up to.

"And how did you come to be there?" Mel asked Zoe.

"I was doing a job. Someone conked me over the head, and I woke up several days later at The Center with Dr. Jonah Thomas pretending to be my caring doctor."

"Doing a job?" Shelby asked.

"Yeah." Zoe concentrated on a tangle in her hair.

"What kind of job?" Shelby asked with frayed patience.

"Doesn't matter. Just a job."

"It matters," Shelby said.

Zoe stared at her for a minute. Mel chuckled. "Don't worry, Zoe, Shelby isn't going to turn you in."

Zoe seemed to consider that and finally shrugged. "I was stealing something for someone. From Jonah Thomas' house. I was in the bedroom when he knocked me over the head with something, and the next thing I knew I was waking up strapped to a hospital bed."

"What were you stealing and who sent you there?" Shelby asked.

"Some photographs and negatives. The woman said her name was Janet Johnson." Zoe shrugged. "Probably made that up. Most of my clients don't give me their real names."

"You steal for a living?" Shelby asked.

"I'm going to school to be a CPA." Zoe's back straightened. "Stealing is the only thing I know how to do, but I'm getting out of it. I only have another six months in school."

"I'm not judging you, Zoe." Shelby smiled. God knows she'd done worse. "That was Tuesday night?"

"Yeah. I woke up on Saturday. I was really dizzy and groggy and puking. The jerk told me I'd been in a motorcycle accident and had internal injuries. The only injury I had was where he conked me." Zoe frowned.

172

"I'd like to know where my bike is."

"What else did he say?" Shelby asked.

"Told me I'd been restrained so I wouldn't injure myself, that I was locked in my room for my own safety. I pretended to go along with it, and waited. Then you came along and took us to that house."

"Which brings us to here. And me wondering just how the hell The Center knew where I'd taken them," Shelby said.

"You're sure no one followed you either time?" Mel asked.

Shelby shot her a look, and Mel laughed. "I know, I know. Just checking out all the possibilities." Mel sipped her coffee. "And Mac didn't call anyone at all?"

"No, I didn't." Mac walked out to the patio wearing shorts and sandals, pulling a tee shirt over his head, but not before Shelby got a look at his chest. It was definitely nice. Not the kind of chest you'd expect a psychiatrist to have. Unless he was seriously into sports or the gym.

"Not even your SAC?" Mel asked.

"Especially not my SAC. I've been avoiding unnecessary communication with her since I'm disobeying her direct orders."

"Wise man." Mel grinned at him, and Shelby remembered that Mel had always had an unhealthy attraction for men who break the rules. "And Shannon didn't have access to a phone? No cell phone?"

"Nope." Shelby shook her head. "She left The Center with nothing but jammies and slippers, just like Zoe."

"I suppose we can rule out Sam." Mel said.

"Well, I wouldn't rule out him being able to make a phone call, but I don't think he would have done it."

"Of course not, I'm just going through all the possibilities, no matter how extreme," Mel said.

"So, we weren't followed, no one made a phone call—except mine to Ethan." Shelby looked at Mel who'd raised her delicate eyebrows. "No. No way did Ethan tell The Center where we were."

"I didn't say that. However, you don't know who else Ethan might have told."

"You mean there could be a mole in the FSA." Shelby had thought of that before, but she didn't want to believe it. She'd told Ethan that she'd taken Zoe, Shannon, and Sam to the safe house. On the road, she'd left a voice mail saying that they were leaving the safe house because The Center had found them, without telling him where she was going.

"It's happened before." Mel sighed.

"I know. I just don't like to think it could happen again." Shelby set her cup down and got up. "I guess I need to talk to Ethan about this."

"Good idea." Mel rose and walked to the door. "I'll find some clothes for Zoe and Shannon." Mel let herself out as Shelby punched the speed dial number for Ethan into her cell phone.

"Ethan?"

"Shelby! Where the hell are you?"

"We had to leave the safe house."

"I got your voice mail about The Center finding you.

How the hell did that happen?"

"I've been trying to figure that out myself. No one followed us, no one made any phone calls. You were the only one who knew where we were."

"Damn! I only told Chambers."

"Could someone have overheard you?"

"Not unless his office is bugged." Ethan paused. "I'll have to tell him about this. Maybe he let it slip to someone."

"We're in a safe place. I'm just going to sit tight until we know something."

"I want to bring Zoe, Shannon, and Sam to head-quarters."

"Yeah, I know. But until we know how The Center found us, I don't want to move them. They're safe here."

"Where are you?" Ethan asked.

"I don't want to say until we know how they found us at the safe house."

"Shelby, I need to know where you are."

"No, actually, you don't."

"How can I provide you with any backup then?"

"I don't need backup Ethan. I told you, this is my case. I'm doing it my way."

"Are you saying you don't trust me?"

Shelby could hear the tension in Ethan's voice. "No, it's not that I don't trust you. It's that I don't know how The Center is finding us. Until I know that, no one is going to know where we are."

"I'll talk to Chambers and get back to you."

◆ ◆ ◆

"What happened, Allan?" Ruth's voice was clipped and unemotional. Allan squirmed under her scrutiny.

"Like I said, we got there, confirmed that the targets were in the house. Kevin and Steve went in through the kitchen window. I stayed outside." Allan reached down and rubbed his shin where his pants were ripped. Ruth could see a big knot of bruised, scraped skin.

"Everything was quiet. We thought it was a sure thing." Allan sipped from the glass of water. "Then I hear some scuffling. I figure the guys are taking her out or something. Next thing I know, it's all quiet again, and she's coming into the kitchen. She had a gun."

"So you ran." Ruth looked at him in disgust.

"It was the plan," Allan protested. "If something happened I was to get out and come back."

"No. You were to get out and call in."

"I forgot," he mumbled. "But I didn't forget to put the long range transmitter on the car. We can track them."

"That's good, Allan. Not perfect, but good. I'm glad you didn't forget to do that." Ruth turned away and nodded to the guard. Incompetent. Unable to follow the simplest orders. And now they'd lost them again. "Take care of him." She walked out, closing the door behind her. Ten steps from the room, she heard the muffled shot and kept walking.

Jonah held up a finger to silence her as she entered his office. Ruth would have ignored it but she knew he was talking to Chris.

"Well, find out!" Jonah closed the cell phone and sighed. "Chris doesn't know where they are. She's checking her source. Whoever that is."

"It doesn't matter. Allan managed to remember to put the long range transmitter on the car. We're tracking them now."

Jonah rose and straightened his tie. "Let's go find out where they've gone."

They walked to the control center in silence. Frank was at the console, typing commands into the computer.

"What've you got Frank?" Ruth asked, peering over his shoulder.

"They're on I-10 headed north. Not a big surprise. Nothing but I-10 out there, and they had to take it north or south. They traveled for several hours, going about sixty consistently. Stopped twice for about ten minutes each time." Frank looked up and grinned. "They stopped about an hour ago. Sedona."

"Get a team on the road."

"Already done, Dr. Carlson."

"Ouch!" Shannon dropped the plate on the counter and grabbed her thigh.

"What is it?" Shelby asked.

"The cabinet door hit my leg, and it hurts."

She was delicate looking but really, how hard could that door have hit her?

"It's just that it hit right on the incision," Shannon explained.

"You have an incision?" Mac looked up from the newspaper he was reading. "What from?"

"I have no idea. Sometimes at The Center, they'd knock me out and when I came to, I'd have no idea what they'd done. A week ago, I woke up with a bandage covering an incision." Shannon shrugged, obviously not ready to talk about everything that had happened at The Center.

"I'd like to have a look at it," Mac said.

"It's fine." Shannon shook her head.

"No, I insist, Shannon. Come on, we'll go to your cottage."

"No need," Mel said. "You can use my bedroom. Right through there." She waved at the hallway. "Third door on the left."

"Really, Mac, it's nothing. It's healing fine."

"Shannon. They made an incision for a reason. Don't you want to know why?"

"Not really." She sighed. "But I see your point." She turned and headed down the hallway.

Zoe shuddered. "I'm going to go lie down for a while."

"Nausea again?" Mel asked.

"Yeah. But it's getting a little better." She dropped her dishcloth on the counter and left.

"I need to get them all to headquarters so they can be checked out by a doctor. God knows what Thomas and Carlson did to them." Shelby rinsed a plate and handed it to Mel to stack in the dishwasher. "So, business looks like it's pretty good."

"It is. Of course, that's probably because I tend to get a lot of burned-out agents who need a rest. They don't mind paying for the amenities." Mel chuckled.

"Nothing like a safe place to come to."

"And it is safe, if that's what you're wondering." Mel chuckled. "I have better security than a lot of places."

"Better than where we were, anyway." Shelby dried her hands on a dishtowel. "It just really burns me that they found us at an FSA safe house."

"Well, you know that 'safe house' is a relative term."

"Still, they shouldn't have been able to find us."

"What did Ethan say?" Mel asked.

"He said he only told Chambers where we were. I'm sure he's pretty horrified at the idea of a mole in the FSA."

"That still doesn't mean there isn't a mole. Someone could have bugged Ethan's office or phone. Or the director's for that matter."

"I don't like to think there's a mole either."

Mel smiled. "It happens."

"I know. I just don't like it." Shelby put the dishtowel down and leaned against the counter. "You've got a nice set up here. You happy with this? You miss the ops any?"

"Oh, I absolutely do not miss the ops. I had enough of that." Mel laughed. "As for this. I figure it's the best place for me now. This is as safe and happy as I'm gonna be after what I did for the past twenty-odd years. God knows some of them were odder than others."

"Regrets?" Shelby asked, a little surprised.

"No. Not really. I did a lot of good for my country, and I had a lot of good times doing it."

"They weren't all good times, though."

"They never are," Mel admitted. "Still, it was my choice, and I don't regret it."

"There are some people who weren't satisfied that you just retired. People who want to retire you permanently."

"That's why I'm here, doing this. I figure I can help out a few agents and generally live a very safe and peaceful life."

"Helping out a few agents still puts your life in jeopardy, though."

"No, it doesn't. Because I'm the only one who decides who gets through these gates. A lot of agents—from all sides—know about this place. But not all of them are welcome here." Mel laughed again. "And I know all their tricks, so the ones who aren't welcome aren't ever gonna get in." Mel paused and looked at Shelby intently. "And how about you? How is it being out of the FSA?"

"It's good. I'm just barely breaking even, but the agency's only been open less than a year."

"Breaking even's not bad," Mel agreed.

"Making a profit is better. I hired another investigator so I can take on more jobs, but that means more expenses."

"Another investigator?"

Shelby nodded. "Paige Blackwell. She's young but she's already good. Worked for the Portland Police Department. We met on a case, and I hired her later."

"So, you've taken on a protégé."

"I don't know that I'd call her a protégé." Shelby frowned.

"It's good to have someone in the wings. Keeps your own game sharp."

"Well, this protégé wants to buy into the agency. I could use the money, but I'm not sure I want to sell part of the business."

"I'm sure Ethan is paying you well for this."

"Absolutely. That's the only reason I took the job. Actually, it feels weird, you know?"

"Working for Ethan or taking money from him?" Mel laughed.

"Both I guess. Kind of like moving out and then asking your parents for rent money."

Mel didn't get to answer because Mac came back into the kitchen, worry creasing his forehead.

"We have a problem."

"What kind of problem?" Shelby asked.

"I think Shannon might have a tracking device implanted in her."

"Crap." That would explain it. "Are you sure?"

"No. There's no way to be sure until we open that incision."

Shelby barely suppressed a shudder. "Is she okay with that?"

"If there's something in there, I want it out and I want it out now!" Shannon sat down at the table and dropped her head into her hands.

"Can you do it?" Shelby asked Mac.

"I don't have anything to do it with. No instruments, no anesthesia."

"We have that here," Mel said.

Mac's head snapped up.

"What? Doesn't everyone have a first aid kit?" Mel asked.

"Who needs a first aid kit?" Bear asked, walking into the kitchen with Sam sitting on his shoulder.

"Mommy! Look how high I am!" Sam squealed. Shannon's face relaxed as she smiled at her son. Her love for him was etched on every feature.

"If Bear took me outside, I bet I could touch the stars!" Sam declared. Mel looked at Bear and nodded her head at the door.

"The stars are very far away, little man. But there is no greater occupation than to reach for them." Bear pulled Sam off his shoulder, tucked him under one arm, and jogged out the door, Sam giggling all the while.

"It's nice to see Sam so happy. Bear is a very special man," Shannon said.

"That he is," Mel agreed. "Come with me, Mac." Mac obediently followed Mel into her bedroom.

Shelby sat down at the table with Shannon. "Are you okay with Mac doing this?"

"Absolutely. I trust him totally. And if he's right—if they implanted something in me . . ." Shannon shuddered.

"I can't imagine what it must have been like for you at The Center."

"It was pretty awful. The worst was not knowing how Sam was or what they had planned for him. Then there were the times they'd knock me out." Shannon made a noise that was half sob and half laughter. "I'd wake up feeling weird, you know? But no one would tell me what had happened."

"Once we get you to FSA headquarters, we'll get a complete physical done on you. And you'll have access to the best psychiatrists." Shelby tried to smile reassuringly. "I know it won't be easy, but you'll be able to put all this behind you."

"What about Chase?" Shannon asked. "He's still there."

"I'll make sure he gets out. Promise." Before she had to say anything more, Mac and Mel returned.

"We're all set. Mel has everything I'll need."

"Will Bear keep an eye on Sam?" Shannon asked Mel.

"Of course. He won't let him out of his sight. And Sam will never know what's happening here."

Shannon nodded and walked into Mel's bedroom with Mac. Mel and Shelby followed. While Mac was washing up, Mel pulled a small table over next to the bed and draped a clean cloth over it. Her first aid kit was a plastic drawer unit on wheels that must have contained just about everything you'd need for anything short of open-heart surgery. She laid out packages of bandages, sutures, surgical instruments, and hypodermic needles, as if she'd done it more than once or twice.

"This won't take long," Shelby assured Shannon, not knowing just how long it would take, but figuring that's what she needed to hear. Shannon took her hand and squeezed it.

"I don't think I ever thanked you for getting us out of there."

"No thanks necessary. All part of the job." Shelby heard Mel and Mac pulling on surgical gloves and got up from the bed. Mac placed a clean cloth underneath Shannon's hips and legs.

"Just lie still and try to relax. You really won't feel anything after I inject the lidocaine." Mac pushed up the leg of Shannon's baggy shorts and swabbed her upper thigh with betadine, while Mel stuck a hypodermic syringe into the bottle of lidocaine and withdrew a small amount. She tapped the hypo with her finger and handed it to Mac.

Shannon raised her eyes to Shelby and held out her hand. Shelby moved closer and took the hand. Not that it would help, but it seemed to be the thing to do. Mac inserted the needle, administered the lidocaine, and gave the hypo back to Mel. After a few minutes, he picked up a pair of tweezers and raked them over Shannon's thigh.

"Can you feel that?" he asked her. Shannon shook her head.

"Good. Let's get this done then."

Mel handed Mac a scalpel and moved next to him

holding several gauze bandages. Mac sliced along the original incision, and Mel swabbed it with the bandages. Using a couple of instruments, Mel and Mac pried Shannon's flesh open. Mac probed with a pair of tweezers, while Mel swabbed the blood away. Shelby kept her eyes averted.

"Here it is!" Mac held up a small, rectangular object. Mel held out a metal dish, and Mac dropped the device into it.

"Almost done, now," Mac said to Shannon. He quickly stitched the incision while Mel disappeared into the bathroom with the metal dish. Placing a clean bandage over the incision, he applied some surgical tape.

"Just what you thought," Mel said when she returned. "I'll have to check my sources, but this looks like a state-of-the-art, GPS tracking device."

"Any idea of the range?" Shelby asked.

"Hard to say. If they have direct access to a satellite, they can track it anywhere. If they're using portable receivers—probably at least twenty miles, could be as much as a hundred." Mel dropped the cleaned device into a bowl and nudged Mac, pointing to several plastic bottles of pills.

"Oh, yes." He looked at the bottles, chose one, and opened it. "The incision was pretty minimal, but you should take these." He handed two pills to Shannon. "It'll ease any discomfort after the lidocaine wears off."

"Thanks," Shannon said, and gulped the pills without water. "I'm really glad that thing is out of me. You don't think they put one in Sam, do you?"

"I gave him a bath last night, and I didn't see any signs of incisions or any scars, so I'm betting they hadn't had time to do it yet."

"Thank God!" Shannon said. "I think I'll take him and go to bed now. He's probably ready for a nap."

"Come on, I'll give you a hand." Mac reached out and pulled Shannon to her feet. "I'm sure you could use some rest."

Shelby put her hand on Mel's arm to keep her from following them. "This means The Center probably knows we're here."

"I'll be shocked if they don't have at least one car out front." Mel looked at her for a moment. "Come on, you're about to see something I don't show to many people."

CHAPTER FIFTEEN

Shelby followed Mel down the hall to a metal door where she punched in a code on the keypad and opened the door. They walked down another short hallway to a larger metal door, and Mel entered a code again. Shelby stepped into a small room filled with electronic equipment. One wall was covered with television monitors. There must have been two dozen. Each screen displayed a part of *Serenity Retreat* or the surrounding streets. Another wall held a large console with buttons, dials, and switches along with two computer keyboards.

"I can monitor just about everything from here. The only thing I can't see or hear is the interior of each of the cottages."

"Where do those doors go?" Shelby pointed to two doors on the far wall.

"Safe rooms," Mel said. "I can sustain about half a dozen people down here for two weeks. We have water, a generator, food, and satellite communication ability." Mel sat down at the console and typed in some commands. The display on four of the monitors changed, and Shelby turned her attention to them. The displays changed again and then a third time.

"There," Mel nodded at one screen. "That white SUV." She typed in more commands, and the screen zoomed in on the SUV. They could clearly see two men drinking out of paper cups. "My guess is they're from The Center."

"Which street is that?"

"Right outside the front gate. They probably think we can't see them because of the walls."

"What about the back?"

Mel entered more commands. "It appears that there's only one entrance to this place. Of course, that's not true." The screens showed empty streets surrounding the retreat.

"So, they've already found us. I guess the good news is that there's no reason to worry about a mole in the FSA."

"Probably, although I'd never discount that possibility completely."

"You know, Mel, sometimes you're kind of negative."

"Occupational hazard." Mel shrugged. Shelby knew what Mel meant. She had her own share of negativity.

"So, The Center knows we're here." Shelby sighed. "I need to get Zoe, Shannon, and Sam to FSA headquarters." There was no telling what The Center had done to them. They definitely needed to be checked out medically. And they needed to be out of danger.

"What's your plan?" Mel asked.

"I'll talk to Ethan. I'm thinking if I can distract the guys from The Center, then Ethan can send agents in for them."

"Ethan isn't fond of his agents deliberately putting themselves in danger."

"I don't see any other way to get them out of here safely. Besides, I'm not one of his agents any longer. If Ethan doesn't like it—he can bite me."

"I always did like your attitude, Shelby." Mel laughed. "So what kind of distraction are you thinking of?"

"If I can make them think I've left with Shannon and Sam, they'll follow me. I don't know how important Zoe is to them, but I know they want Shannon and Sam back. Once we're gone, Ethan can send in a team of agents to pick them up. By the time The Center figures it out, Shannon and Sam will be safely on their way to Denver."

"Easy. Simple. I like it." Mel nodded and considered Shelby for a moment. "What about Mac?"

"He can make his own choice. I'll call Ethan, and then I'll tell Mac what's up."

"Let me know what you want. I can pretty much supply anything you'll need."

✦ ✦ ✦

After Shelby talked over some possibilities with Mel, she headed back to the cottage to call Ethan. Zoe's door was closed and Mac wasn't there. Shelby assumed he was probably still with Shannon or watching Sam while she rested. Shelby pulled out her cell phone and punched in Ethan's speed dial number.

"Ethan, Shelby here."

"I was about to call you. I spoke with Chambers. He didn't mention the safe house location to anyone. I don't know how they found you."

"Yeah, well, we figured that out. Shannon had a tracking device implanted in her leg. Mac took it out, and she's all right. But The Center has already followed us here. Right now, there are two men sitting outside in an SUV. No doubt they're waiting for us to leave."

"Waiting? Why aren't they just storming the place?" Ethan asked.

"They're probably trying to figure out how to do that. We're at Mel's retreat in Sedona."

"Her place is like a fortress," Ethan agreed. "I can have an extraction team there tomorrow."

"I'll provide a distraction for them."

"I doubt that's necessary. You should return here with the others."

"We still need to get Chase out of The Center. From what I've seen, these people are up to something that's pretty horrible. I don't think they'll stop at anything to get Shannon and Sam back."

"We're still working on the files you copied. A lot

of them are encrypted. Hopefully we'll find out what they're up to soon."

"I'd really feel better if there was some distraction while you're extracting Zoe, Shannon, and Sam." Shelby paused. "In fact, I insist on it."

Ethan sighed. "All right. You set something up, and I'll let you know when we'll be there."

"Will do."

Shelby already had an idea of what she wanted to do. She walked back to the main house, asked Mel for some maps of the local area, and then returned to the cottage. She'd spent over an hour studying the maps when Mac returned.

"How's Shannon?"

"She's all right. I watched Sam while she slept, and then we talked some." Mac settled in the chair next to Shelby.

"What she went through must have been really hard on her. Especially worrying about Sam."

"It was. But Shannon's a lot stronger than she looks. And Sam probably could use some counseling, but otherwise he's dealt with it pretty well."

"What they did to her was so invasive."

"Yes, and we don't even know everything they did to her. It was just dumb luck that we found the tracking device." Mac paused for a moment. "Shannon got sick again this afternoon."

"Really? Was it the medication you gave her?"

"I doubt it. That isn't a common side effect of lidocaine or the painkillers."

"Does she have any ideas about it?"

"No. The only thing she could relate it to was when she first became pregnant with Sam."

"She mentioned that to me too." They looked at each other for a moment. "Mac, what about all the nausea Zoe's been having?"

"Could be a lot of things. They kept her drugged for three days, although that should all be out of her system by now." Mac frowned. "Could be any number of things."

"Sure," Shelby said. "Maybe she's pregnant."

Mac stood up. "Or in the process."

"What?"

"In the in vitro process, the first thing they do is give a woman hormones so she'll produce more ova than usual. Then they fertilize the ova and implant them into the woman's uterus."

"Right. Then they have a better chance of one of them surviving." Shelby suppressed a shudder thinking about stories she'd heard of women giving birth to litters of babies, because all the implanted eggs survived. "You don't think they impregnated Shannon, do you?" Shelby asked.

"I wouldn't put it past them." Mac shrugged and dropped into one of the chairs.

"And they could have been giving Zoe hormones, planning the same thing for her." Shelby shook her head. "Those people are sick and twisted."

"The few pages from Sam's chart that I looked at mentioned a program. It sounded like Sam wasn't the only child they were going to experiment on." Mac rubbed his eyes and leaned his head back. "Of course, that could mean they have other children picked out, or that they are trying to breed them."

"You can breed psychic ability?"

"I have no idea. Thomas and Carlson have been researching psychic abilities for years. Maybe they found something that indicates it's hereditary."

"Did you talk to Shannon about that?" Shelby asked.

"She wants to take a pregnancy test immediately. God, I hope it's negative."

"Well, she can probably have one tomorrow. Zoe too. Ethan is sending an extraction team for the three of them tomorrow."

"What about you?"

"I don't need a pregnancy test," Shelby answered with a straight face.

"Very funny."

"I'm going to try to distract The Center guys so Ethan's agents have time to get them out of here."

"I'm not sure I'm in any hurry to face my SAC." Mac chuckled. "Need any help with your distraction?"

"No, but you're welcome to come along for the ride." She considered him for a moment. "Mac, I have to tell you, this could be dangerous." She wanted him to understand just how dangerous she believed The Center to be.

"I think that if The Center wanted Shannon and Sam so badly that they'd implant a tracking device, they're pretty serious. If they've gone so far as to impregnate her . . ."

"I agree. I think they will stop at nothing to get them back." Mac stood up and stretched. "If it gives Shannon and Sam a better chance of escaping, I'm in."

Shelby gathered up the maps. "Let's go see Mel, and I'll tell you about the plan."

"I need more information." Chris braced herself for the protest.

"What? And how am I going to get it? I'm not privy to everything, Chris."

"Chambers tells you everything. You can get the information I need." Chris paused but heard no further protest. "I know that Parker took Shannon and Sam to Sedona. I need to know what they're planning now."

"Chris, I don't like doing this. It feels like I'm betraying the FSA."

"You're not. I'm not using the information for anything but to protect myself. You told me once that you'd do anything for me. I'm not asking for that much." There was a long silence, and Chris waited impatiently.

"I heard them talking in Don's office."

"Yes?"

"They're sending two agents in tomorrow to bring Shannon and Sam back here. And there's another woman with them. Shelby took her out of The Center when she rescued Shannon."

"What about Parker and McRae?" Chris didn't really care about the other woman.

"They said something about them creating a distraction so the agents can get the others out."

"What else?"

"That's all I know. Really."

"Keep your eyes and ears open. I'll call back later." Chris hung up the phone. McRae hadn't contacted her, and that was a surprise. Did he know something? Parker wasn't taking any chances. And Chris couldn't either. She punched in Jonah's number.

"Jonah Thomas."

"I've got some information for you."

"Good girl."

Chris cringed at his patronizing tone. God, how had she dropped so low? She swallowed hard and pushed the feeling aside. "Parker and McRae are providing a distraction tomorrow morning, so FSA agents can get Shannon and Sam out. They're taking them to Denver."

"By plane?"

"I have no idea, Jonah. I can only get so much information."

"Fine." Jonah sighed into the phone. "I'll just have to cover all the contingencies then."

"I'm getting a lot of heat on this, Jonah. Headquarters is assuming that something has happened to McRae. Word is that as soon as Shannon and Sam are safe, the FBI and the FSA are coming after you."

"Then, you'd better hope they don't get me. You've had such a stellar career, I'd hate to see it go up in flames."

Her anger flared. "Listen, asshole. As soon as

McRae talks to headquarters, they'll know that something is wrong here. They'll ask why I didn't tell them everything. I'll be suspended or up on charges. I won't have access to the information, which means I'll be useless to you."

"I'll make sure McRae never gets a chance to speak to headquarters."

Chris shoved a fist in her mouth to stifle the gasp she couldn't prevent. She'd just sold out McRae. She'd been able to ignore the fact that she was sacrificing Shannon Masterson and her son. But a fellow agent?

Chris turned off her phone and laid her head on the desk. How much longer could she do this? And what the hell had happened to that thief she'd hired to get the photos and negatives? The woman had never contacted her, and Jim Bottoms swore that he hadn't heard from her either.

Without the negatives, the only way to protect her life, her career, was to do what Jonah wanted. But eventually that would ruin her career too. To what lengths would she have to go just to save herself?

"You guys ready for dinner?" Mel asked when they'd finished going over the plans.

"Definitely. I'm starving." Mel led the way to the dining room. Bear was there with Sam, who had become his shadow in the short time they'd been there.

"Where's Shannon?" Shelby asked.

Bear nodded toward the bathroom down the hall. Mel caught Shelby's eye. "Shannon told me about being sick, so I gave her a test. Zoe too."

"You mean a preg—" Mac caught himself and glanced at Sam, who was happily scrambling over Bear's back in a game of leapfrog.

"Thank God!" Zoe came into the dining area and dropped into a chair. "Shannon's still in the bathroom?"

"She'll be out in a minute." Mel disappeared into the kitchen and returned just as Shannon appeared. Shelby took in Shannon's face. Pale. Frightened. A trace of disgust. She could guess the results of the test.

"Dear God, what have they done to me?"

CHAPTER SIXTEEN

"Two FSA agents will be here early tomorrow morning. They'll escort Zoe, Shannon, and Sam to the airport." Shelby gave Shannon an encouraging smile. "You'll be flown to FSA headquarters, just outside Denver."

Shannon nodded as she repeatedly wadded the napkin in her hands. "What happens then?"

"You'll be guests of the FSA until Carlson and Thomas are taken care of. After that, it's up to you."

"Will you be going back with us?" Shannon asked Mac.

"No. I'll be staying here for a bit, but I'll join you soon." Mac and Shelby had decided not to tell Shannon and Zoe about their plans to create a distraction while the agents took them to the airport. Mac thought that Shannon would worry, and Shelby was sure Zoe would want to be a part of it, since she wasn't really keen on going to FSA headquarters anyway.

Zoe seemed to be a very private person. She didn't talk about herself much and didn't involve herself in conversation with the others. Probably a habit she'd developed due to being a thief. From the little Zoe had told Shelby, she'd been a thief since she was a young girl. When she was a teenager, she'd hooked up with a series of older thieves who had mentored her. That had to be an interesting story, and someday Shelby would get it out of her.

With Zoe's desire to stay away from everyone, Shelby had decided to share the larger bedroom with Mac. All day, she'd been avoiding thinking about how she'd awakened with her legs entwined with Mac's. And how good it had felt. Which was bad. She was in the middle of an op. It was no time to start *feeling* something for someone—even if it was just purely sexual. She gave herself a mental slap. She wasn't a teenager, after all. She had reasonably good impulse control— when she was awake anyway.

Nevertheless, she was dead tired. They could sleep in the same bed without a problem. It's not like they would be naked or anything.

That brought up a visual that Shelby could have done without. Mac without any clothes on. Lying on the bed. She could almost see his tanned form through the gauziness of the mosquito netting. When she found herself squinting to see through the netting, she jerked herself back to reality. She had another three hours before they would go to bed. She'd stay busy. Be really tired and sleep like a baby. Shelby glanced around the room. Nothing to do in the cottage. Zoe's door was closed, as usual. Maybe Mel could use her help.

"I'll be back in a while," she said to Mac. He looked up from the book he'd borrowed from Mel.

"Where're you going?"

"Just thought I'd check on Mel's preparations for our distraction tomorrow."

He unfolded his tall frame from the mama-san chair. Heavens, his legs were long. And tan. And muscular. What kind of psychiatrist had muscles like that in his legs? Mac stretched, and her attention moved to the muscles in his arms and chest as they flexed. Why was he wearing a tank top? It hadn't been more than ninety-five degrees today. Couldn't he wear a regular shirt with sleeves?

"Good idea. I'll come with you. Nothing to do here."

Crap.

"She probably has it all under control."

"Then why are you checking on her?"

"No reason. I just want to make sure we have everything handled."

"Me too."

They walked across the common garden to the main house. Bear was just coming out of the control room Mel had shown Shelby earlier.

"Falcon, I was just coming to get you. Mel wanted to go over the plans again." Bear turned back down the hallway to open the doors to the special room for them.

"Thanks, Bear."

When he was out of earshot, Mac turned to Shelby. "Why does he call you Falcon?"

"It was my code name on some ops when we worked together."

"I see."

Really? Shelby doubted it. Mel and Bear were the only people she'd ever trusted enough to work with on an op.

Bear walked ahead of them across the room and opened one of the doors on the far wall. On the other side of the door, they walked down a long hallway and through another door into a large garage. Shelby was surprised to see her Mini parked there, doors open. There were two dummies in the back seat. One wore a wig that matched Shannon's hair pretty well. The other one was a child sitting in a car seat.

"What do you think?" Mel asked.

"They look pretty realistic."

"Check this out." Mel reached in and flipped a switch on the dashboard. The dummies started to move. Shannon's dummy moved its head and lifted an arm. Sam's dummy turned its head and lifted a toy. "I couldn't fit in a dummy for Zoe."

"I don't think that will matter." Shelby walked around the car. "They can't know for sure that we have her, and I think they're really only interested in Shannon and Sam at this point."

"Impressive," Mac said with a grin. "They'll most certainly believe we have them in the car."

"The female dummy is wearing the tracking device

around her neck." Mel moved to the trunk. "Since we don't know how soon you'll be able to lose them, I packed your trunk with some survival essentials."

"Thanks, Mel. Let's hope we don't need them." Shelby checked out the car for a moment.

"No time to put in bulletproof windows, so if they're shooting at you, you might want to get away from them."

"If they think we've got Shannon and Sam with us, they won't be shooting," Shelby said.

Mac nodded. "They certainly want Shannon and Sam alive and well."

"So, you just have to get away from them. Shouldn't be too difficult. I've seen you drive." Mel chuckled. "You better buckle up, Mac."

"She is a bit reckless behind the wheel, isn't she?" Mac was grinning, so Shelby assumed he was joking. Still.

"Hey!" She punched his arm. "I've never had an accident."

Mel arched an eyebrow at her.

"Not one that was unintentional, anyway."

"I probably don't even want to know," Mac said, shaking his head.

"Probably not," Mel agreed. "Well, we're done here. You two might as well get some rest. Tomorrow's gonna be a busy day."

"Busy. That's one word for it." Shelby turned to Mel. "You sure you don't miss this?"

"How can I miss it when it keeps coming to my doorstep?"

"Sorry."

"Don't be. You aren't the only one that's done it. Besides, it keeps my game sharp."

"Like it could ever be dull." Shelby opened the door and waited for Mel to turn off the light.

"Quarter after eight." Mac glanced at his watch. "A little early for bed."

"We were up early. Five, if I recall."

"So, you're ready for bed?"

"No."

"How about some cards then?"

"Sounds good." Shelby didn't want to think about going to bed with Mac. Because she'd had fantasies about that very thing. But they'd been brief—really brief. In fact, they were so brief, she figured they didn't count. Even if there'd been a couple hundred of them.

"Oh, wait!" Mel called as they were walking out of the main house. "I've got something for you." She ran across the room and thrust a bottle into Shelby's hand.

"Mel, I don't drink while I'm on an op."

"Yeah, like that's never happened before." She pressed two wine glasses into Shelby's other hand. "This is just one bottle. For two people." She grinned at Shelby and leaned forward. "Besides, I know that you could personally put away the entire bottle and not even need one of the magic pills to stay sober."

The magic pills. Shelby even had some of them

with her. All the FSA agents carried them on an op. Just in case. If you ended up in a situation where you had to drink in order not to blow your cover, you just popped a magic pill. The drug would jump start your adrenalin, which would burn off the alcohol, leaving you reasonably in control. Of course, some agents enjoyed the effects a little too much and ended up in rehab. The magic pills were very close to amphetamines.

"Hey, Mel, you have any playing cards?" Mac asked.

"There should be some in one of your nightstands," Mel said as she turned back down the hallway.

Back in the cottage, Shelby opened the wine while Mac searched the nightstands for cards. Shelby knocked softly on Zoe's door but didn't get an answer. By the time she had the wine poured, Mac was sitting at the small table shuffling the cards.

"So, what will it be? Gin? Poker? Blackjack? Go Fish?"

"Your choice." She handed him a glass of wine and took the chair across from him.

"Gin it is then." Mac dealt the cards and picked up his hand. "So, how did you come to be an FSA agent?"

"I met Mel when I was seventeen. She took a liking to me. Said I had a lot of potential. So, we kept in touch, and after college she recruited me."

"How did you two meet?"

"Ah, well, there's a story. I was spending the summer with my Dad in Tucson. He was a con artist and involved in some big scam."

"Your father was a con artist?"

"Oh, yes. So, this particular con was the one that was going to make him a millionaire." Shelby laughed at the memory. "Weren't they all? Unfortunately, he'd gotten hooked up with some pretty unscrupulous con men."

"Unscrupulous con men? Isn't that redundant?"

She shrugged. "Well, anyway, he thought this was his really big chance. He was using me as bait to draw in some marks."

"Using you as bait?" Mac looked appalled and outraged.

"Using might be too strong a word. I was well aware of what he was doing, and I participated willingly."

"Really?"

"I was seventeen. My rebellious period." Shelby laughed. "Just another way to rebel against my mother—although she certainly didn't know what I was doing. She would have had a heart attack. My parents divorced when I was five, and I only spent a few weeks in the summer and some holidays with my dad."

"So, Mel was one of your father's victims?"

"No, Mel was with the FBI. Seems the people my dad had gotten involved with had been running this particular scam for so long that the FBI was on to them. Mel was part of the sting operation."

"I'm surprised you didn't get arrested."

"If it hadn't been for Mel, I probably would have been." Shelby rearranged the cards in her hand.

"Anyway, my dad had me playing several roles in the scam."

"Several roles?"

"A nun, an ingénue, and a homeless pregnant girl. I was always good at that sort of thing."

"No doubt from years of practice?"

"Pretty much. But Mel saw through my disguises and took me under her wing."

"Did your father get arrested?"

"No. He agreed to help the FBI, and they cut him a deal."

"Lucky for him."

"So, Mel and I stayed in touch. By the time I'd graduated college, she'd moved from the FBI to the FSA, and she recruited me." She shrugged. "I was with them for ten years. Then I opened my agency."

"I see." Mac nodded. "So, you're atoning for your father's sins by being one of the good guys?"

"No, not at all." Shelby grinned at him. "Maybe atoning for my own sins—a bit."

Shelby slept restlessly, waking up for the third time at seven. Fortunately, Mac was sound asleep on his side of the queen-size bed. Unfortunately, she was curled up against him like a heat-seeking reptile. Their legs were entwined, her head on his shoulder, his arm wrapped securely around her. Crap.

She gently lifted his arm and breathed a sigh of relief

that he didn't wake up. But disengaging herself from the tangle of limbs and sheet with the weight of his leg on hers proved impossible. Finally, Shelby just jerked her legs free, and bounded out of bed before the movement brought him fully awake. Mac grumbled and raised up on one elbow.

"Oh, you're awake. I'm just going to grab a quick shower."

Shelby bolted to the counter to flip the switch on the coffee maker, and then into the bathroom, leaving him to wonder what the hell had awakened him, while she wondered what the hell was wrong with her. She was in the middle of an op, for God's sake. Normally she wouldn't have been the least bit affected by sleeping with a man. At least it wouldn't have shown.

She stripped off the tee shirt and shorts she'd slept in, turned the water on, and stepped under it. The blast of cold water slowly warmed up, and she quickly showered and shampooed. She then dried off with one of Mel's fluffy towels, forcing herself to think of nothing but the distraction she was going to provide for Zoe's, Shannon's and Sam's extraction. A part of her wished Mac had decided to go to headquarters with the others, and a part of her liked the fact that he was going with her. Shelby tugged on underwear, jeans, and a tee shirt, and opened the bathroom door to find Mac standing there in all his gorgeous glory.

Over six feet of tanned, hard-muscled man wearing nothing but boxers and beard stubble.

"My turn." Mac stepped into the bathroom as

Shelby stepped outside. She heard the shower start as she poured a cup of coffee. By the time she'd finished her first cup of java, she heard the hair dryer. Zoe emerged from her bedroom and joined her for another cup. Then Mac stepped out of the bathroom.

Shelby almost spewed her coffee across the room.

Zoe snickered. "You get that outfit from Land's End?"

He looked for all the world as if he were headed off to an archeological expedition, or perhaps modeling for one of those catalogs Shelby kept getting in the mail. Crisp white cotton shirt with the sleeves rolled up to the elbow over a pristine white undershirt, and khaki shorts with a multitude of pockets, flaps, buttons, and snaps. Heavy hiking boots with loose socks. All he needed was a backpack and a walking stick. Shelby handed him a cup of coffee.

"Thanks." Mac took a big swig of the coffee and smiled. Either he was impervious to the pain of heat or his coffee was considerably colder than hers. "When do we leave?"

"At 0830." Shelby finished her coffee, rinsed the cup, and put it in the sink. "Don't forget anything. We won't be coming back." She stuffed the tee shirt and shorts she'd worn into her duffle bag, along with the charger for her cell phone, and left the cottage, Mac and Zoe right on her heels. Her phone chirped, and she snapped it open.

"What?"

"Shelby, the agents should be there in half an hour.

You ready?"

"We're getting into the car now. The set-up's pretty good, so I think we'll be able to keep them away for a while. Mel will make sure they haven't left anyone behind to watch this place. If they have, she'll call you."

"Good. Although I still think you should come in with them. A distraction isn't necessary. Two agents can get the three of them out without a problem."

"I have to disagree with you. These people at The Center are really serious about what they're doing. And somehow Shannon and Sam are crucial to whatever that is."

"I should have an analysis of the files soon. I'll email it to you as soon as I get it."

"Good. That should tell us something. I'll keep in touch." Shelby closed her phone and waited, while Mac hugged Shannon and Sam and promised to see them shortly.

"You'll be met at headquarters by a man named Ethan. He'll make sure you're taken care of."

"Yeah, that's what I'm worried about," Zoe said.

"Don't worry, Zoe. Ethan won't really care about your past." Zoe probably didn't believe her, but there was nothing Shelby could do to convince her. She and Mac walked to the garage where Mel and Bear were making a last minute check.

"You're good to go," Mel said.

Shelby threw her small duffle in the trunk and gave Mel a hug. "Thanks for the hospitality." She hugged

Bear and then climbed into the car.

"You're always welcome here. You know that." Mel stood beside Bear as Shelby pulled out and drove around to the main gate.

"Take that tracking device and hold onto it," Shelby instructed Mac. He reached back and took the device off the Shannon dummy.

The opening of the gate had alerted the men in the SUV, and they pulled out immediately behind her.

"Not too subtle, are they?" Mac glanced back at them.

"I wonder if they're just clueless about following someone or if they really don't care that we know." Shelby checked out the SUV in her rearview mirror. The truck had been lifted and fitted with extra-large tires. They wouldn't be able to keep up with her if she took a few fast turns. But for the next half hour, she wanted them to follow her. Away from Mel's. Away from Zoe and Shannon and Sam.

When Shelby reached the middle of town she turned to Mac. "Drop the device out the window."

"Why?"

"Just drop it."

Mac dropped the device and then turned to her again. "Why?"

"Because wherever we end up, we probably don't want The Center people to know where that is."

"Good point."

Shelby led the SUV to the other side of town and headed west into the desert. Twenty minutes had passed, so she knew that the FSA agents probably had Zoe, Shannon, and Sam safely out of Mel's and on the way to the airport. In a few minutes she'd lead the SUV back into town and lose them there. Then she'd return to Mel's. At least that was the plan until the men in the SUV started shooting.

CHAPTER SEVENTEEN

Zoe shivered as a chill crawled up her spine and the small hairs on her neck lifted. Her eyes darted about nervously. Maybe it was just that these agents were taking her to the FSA headquarters in Denver. She'd spent most of her life avoiding cops and most other authority figures. Walking into the FSA of her own free will didn't sit well with her.

The car pulled up next to a hangar at the Sedona airport, and the agent who was driving turned to them.

"Stay here. I'll go make sure the plane is ready to take off." Both agents got out of the car. One stood a few yards away while the other one continued on into the hangar.

"What are you going to do when this is all over?" Shannon asked.

"Go back to my life, I guess. Finish school, so I can get a job as a CPA. What about you?"

"I haven't really thought about it."   Shannon

shrugged. "I doubt I could get my old job back. Besides, I think I'm ready to get out of Tucson."

"Where would you go?" Zoe asked. She wasn't really interested, but the conversation was taking her mind off the situation.

"Maybe California." Shannon snuggled Sam closer to her and smoothed his blond hair back.

"Is that where his father lives?"

"He's in the Marines. Stationed at Pendleton." Shannon shook her head. "But I don't know that he would want us close by. Besides, I'll have another child to take care of soon."

"Yeah. Still it would be nice for Sam to know his father."

"Yes, that would be nice. I suppose I should have made more of an effort to tell Chase about him. But at the time I didn't think he wanted to be saddled with a wife and child."

"But isn't that his decision to make?"

"You're right. It is his decision to make. I'll just have to tell him about Sam and see what happens."

Zoe's situation seemed easy in comparison to Shannon's. All she had to do was get through this and get back to what passed for a life. She wasn't eager to return to thieving, though. This had scared her. Black Joe had always told her that there would come a time when she should stop. He said that she'd know when the time came, and if she didn't stop then, she'd probably end up in jail or worse. She figured the time had definitely come, although she had no idea what she'd do to get through school for another six months.

"What's taking them so long?" Zoe wondered aloud.

"I wish they'd hurry too. I'll feel better when we get to the FSA."

"I'm going to go see what's holding them up." Zoe opened the car door.

"But they said to stay here."

Zoe laughed. "I've never been that good at following orders."

The agent who'd been standing close to the car was gone. Probably to check on the one who'd gone into the hangar. Halfway across the tarmac, she heard a shot. Damn! Zoe ran the rest of the way, stopping just inside the hangar, and ducking behind a stack of oil drums. She stayed crouched down, while her eyes adjusted from the bright sun outside to the darkness inside, and heard several more shots. After a few minutes, she cautiously peeked around the barrels. One of the agents lay on the floor, a bright red stain spreading over his starched, white shirt, his gun still in his hand. The door of the small plane was open, and she could see the pilot slumped forward in his seat.

Zoe scanned the hangar for the other agent, and found his lifeless body in the doorway to a small, glass-enclosed office. She ran over and saw another man sitting at the desk, his head lying in a pool of blood on the desktop. Then she heard footsteps. She slipped inside the office and crouched behind a filing cabinet. The footsteps continued past the office, and soon she heard the car peeling out. She edged out of the office and over to the hangar door. The car they had arrived in was gone, and her stomach soured as she realized they'd taken Shannon and Sam.

Zoe stood in the doorway wishing she'd gotten Shelby's cell phone number. The hangar was totally quiet, and she had the feeling that she was alone. Her mind sorted through the situation. She couldn't go back to Phoenix. The FSA, as well as the people from The Center, would be loooking for her. Since she'd cut back on her theft jobs, she'd lost a lot of the contacts she used to have. There was only one safe place to go. She left the hangar, walked across the tarmac and through the gate. Fifteen minutes on the narrow road that serviced the hangar brought her to the main airport building. She went inside, looked at the monitor displaying departing flights, and then went to the America West counter and bought a ticket for Phoenix. From there she could go anywhere.

Mac jerked around when the first shot glanced off the car. "So much for them not shooting at us."

Either they knew that Shannon and Sam weren't in the car, or they didn't care if they killed them. Neither made any sense, but Shelby didn't have time to think about it right now.

She gunned the car and shot away from the SUV. The shooter was using a handgun, and his shots were going wild. A couple shots ricocheted off the trunk of the car, and she was wishing they'd had time to install the bulletproof windows.

Shelby came out of a set of curves, and there was nothing but straight road ahead of them. She knew they'd try to gain speed and come up alongside her. She had only two choices. Turn around and force them to follow her back to town, where she could possibly lose them. But she'd be putting a lot of innocent people in harm's way. The other choice was to just deal with them in the desert. Shelby brought up a mental picture of the map she'd studied. There was a dirt road a few miles ahead. And about fifteen miles down that road was a ravine.

Her foot was pressed to the floor, and she glanced at the speedometer. At a hundred and ten, the spot she wanted would be coming up fast. Mac looked back at the SUV and then over to Shelby. His eyes were wide with apprehension, but at least he tried to smile. Although it might have been a grimace.

Shelby saw the turn-off she wanted up ahead. Waiting until the last possible moment, she slammed on the brakes, jerked the steering wheel to the right, and headed down a bumpy dirt road. Shelby watched in her rearview mirror as the SUV sped past the turn-off and then slammed on the brakes. In a couple of minutes the SUV appeared in her rearview again. All she'd gained were a few more yards of distance.

"I suppose you have a plan in mind?" Mac lifted his eyebrows at her.

"I always have a plan." That was a lie. A lot of

times, it was just by the seat of her pants. But Mac looked a little nervous, and she thought it might help if he thought she had a plan. And she did, somewhat.

After a few miles, Shelby let the SUV gain on her until it was practically kissing her bumper. She wanted their attention on her, not on what was ahead in the road. Which was a lot of nothing. She was kicking up a lot of dust, which helped. And the road was so bumpy they weren't even trying to get off a shot.

Mac watched the SUV for a few minutes and then turned back around. He stared out the front windshield, a look of stark terror spreading across his face.

Shelby sped toward the edge of a steep, wide ravine, ignoring the urge to slow down. At the last possible moment, she slammed on the brakes, pulled the steering wheel to the left, and prayed. The crunch of the car slamming into a boulder was echoed by the loud pop of the airbags inflating. She heard a hissing sound and pushed the deflating airbag down. Steam was pouring from the radiator.

"So, does this count as an unintentional accident?" Mac asked.

"No, not at all."

"Right." Mac looked around us. "I don't see the SUV anywhere."

Shelby hadn't expected to see the SUV. She got out of the car and walked over to the edge of the ravine. The SUV was a crumpled, smoldering heap at the bottom. It was unlikely that they had survived, and she certainly wasn't going down there to make sure.

Shelby turned and walked back to the car. The dummies were still lifting their arms and turning their heads repetitively. Mac looked at her, reached over, and flipped the switch that turned them off.

"What now?"

She took stock of their situation. They were probably about forty miles from Sedona. There didn't appear to be anything within sight other than rocks, desert, and the occasional cactus. From the bashed-in front end of the car, it was clear that they were without transportation. She pulled out her cell phone. No service available.

Crap.

"We've got about ten hours of daylight left." Shelby opened the trunk of the car to check out the supplies Mel had given them. "I figure we can make it back to the main road. Hopefully, we'll run into someone, or at least reach a place where my cell phone will work."

"Nice day for a walk." Mac grinned. She was relieved at his positive attitude.

"Let's see what we can take with us."

Shelby peered into the trunk of the car with Mac leaning over her shoulder. Evidently, Mel wanted them to be prepared for any eventuality. There were blankets, bottles of water, pouches of dehydrated food, flashlights, and a couple of backpacks. She handed Mac one of the backpacks, and they started loading as much as they thought they could carry without slowing them down.

Mac hoisted his full pack onto his back. "The shooting doesn't make any sense."

"I know," Shelby said, putting her arms through the straps of her own pack. "I still don't think The Center would take a chance on killing Shannon or Sam. Somehow they knew we only had dummies in the car."

"I don't think they got close enough to be able to tell they were dummies," Mac said.

"Let's just hope Ethan was able to get them out."

By early afternoon, they'd made about ten miles. Shelby thought they were doing pretty well until the rain started. The rain itself wasn't much of a problem. Given the heat of the desert, it was a welcome relief. It was the accompanying lightning that was worrisome. Other than some rocks, Mac and she were the tallest things in the immediate vicinity, and their backpacks had metal frames. Human lightning rods.

"That lightning's getting kind of close," Mac yelled over the steady thrumming of the rain. I think we should head back to the caves we passed."

"This will blow over soon," she yelled back at him.

Mac looked up at the sky and shook his head. "I don't think so."

Shelby looked up. The sky was dark as far as she could see. She counted the seconds between the lightning bolts and resulting thunder. Crap. It was close and moving toward them.

"Shelby, come on." Mac grabbed her hand and tugged.

She knew he was right. They needed to take cover quickly. But a cave was pretty much the last place she wanted to be.

She swallowed her fear and trotted after him. They reached the rock outcropping in less than half an hour. The lightning had moved closer, and the ensuing thunder seemed to almost shake the ground. Mac headed toward a small opening in the rocks but Shelby hung back, searching for a larger cave, or at least a larger opening. She finally spotted one and ran toward it, ducking just inside the opening. Mac crouched inside the smaller cave about thirty feet away from her.

He waved his arm in a motion that she took to mean he wanted her to run over and join him. That wasn't going to happen. He cupped his hands around his mouth and yelled something, but between the rain and the incessant thunder, she couldn't hear him. Finally, he gave up the communication efforts, grabbed his back-pack, and dashed through the rain to join her.

"The other cave is better." Mac rubbed rain out of his eyes.

"This one is bigger."

"The other one has a smaller opening, so less rain gets inside." Mac walked inside the cave and looked around. "Hey, someone's been here. There's a pile of firewood."

"Lucky us." Shelby watched the sky, but there was no sign of the storm moving on.

"Come back here and get out of the rain."

"I'm fine."

"Are you claustrophobic?"

"No, not at all."

"You *are* claustrophobic!" Mac chuckled, earning him a glare.

"I just said I wasn't."

"No, you said, 'No, not at all.' When *you* say that, it's a definite yes."

"What are you talking about?"

"You mean you aren't even aware you do that?" Mac was laughing, and if she hadn't been so terrified, she might have smacked him. But that would have meant going further into the cave.

"I don't know what you're talking about." She opened her backpack and took out a tarp and some twine. In a few minutes she'd attached the tarp to the rocks surrounding the cave opening, providing a little more shelter from the rain and a place they could build a fire.

"Bring some firewood over here."

"What about a match?" Mac dumped an armful of wood at her feet.

"You mean you can't start a fire without a match?" Shelby shook her head in mock disdain. "What's the world coming to? Didn't you belong to one of those organizations where they take young males out into the wilderness and teach them to survive?"

"Like your Boy Scouts?" Mac laughed. "Sure, we had something like that in Australia."

"Really?"

"Absolutely. When I was eight, my dad took me out in the bush and left me with the aborigines." Mac dropped more firewood on the pile and grinned at her.

"Maybe after we get the fire started, you can tell me all about it."

"Maybe," Mac said cheerfully, as he stacked logs into a perfect pyramid. "First, we need to light this."

Shelby dug out a box of matches and a small can of sterno Mel had included in their supplies. She tossed the matches to Mac and poured some of the sterno fuel over the logs he'd arranged.

Mac struck a match and tossed it onto the stack. The wood caught with a whoosh, and then settled into a respectable flame. "We make a pretty good team."

Shelby wasn't going to comment on that. "We're still wet. And it's going to get cold soon." There were still a few hours until sunset, but the clouds didn't show any signs of breaking up, and the air had cooled considerably. They were both totally drenched. "Did you bring any extra clothes?"

"A shirt."

She'd brought a shirt and a clean pair of panties. A throwback to her mom telling her to always wear clean underwear. At least the shirt would help.

"Did you happen to stuff a blanket in that pack?" She pulled a wool blanket out of her pack and shook it out.

"Of course." Mac pulled a blanket out of his pack. "We should probably get out of the wet clothes and hang them up to dry by the fire."

"At least by the time this blows through, we'll have dry clothes to put on." Shelby shimmied out of her shorts, toed off her shoes, and pulled her wet socks off.

"You really aren't going to come any further into the cave?"

Shelby looked up at Mac and realized she was still standing in the opening. The fire was warm, but she could still feel the cool air blowing in. "I'm staying close to the fire." She shrugged.

"Right. Even though the rain is still blowing in under your makeshift awning."

She turned her back to him, hastily removed her wet tee shirt and bra and pulled on a loose cotton shirt. Her cold fingers fumbled with the buttons, as she listened to the rustle of his clothing being removed. When she turned around, his shorts and boxers were lying on a rock near the fire. A cautious glance revealed that he'd wrapped the blanket around his waist. She was relieved and disappointed at the same time.

"You don't have to be embarrassed about having claustrophobia." Mac moved closer and sat down by the fire.

"I'm not. I don't."

"Really?"

"I've had to be in close places plenty of times. Crawling through air ducts, under houses, in car trunks."

"So, is it just caves?"

Shelby sighed and gave up the pretense. "Not really. I didn't like the other places either. But it was part of the job, so I just got through it."

"I'm impressed." Mac took her hand and tugged her down to sit beside him. She was a little further into the cave, but it seemed all right. "Most people can't just force themselves to endure a phobic situation."

"I don't let anything get in my way. In the way of the job, I mean."

Mac chuckled. "Oh, I think you had it right the first time. I don't think you let anything get in your way, ever."

"Does that bother you?"

"It fascinates me. Makes me wonder how you came to be so determined."

Shelby shrugged and pulled the blanket closer over her legs. "Aren't our parents to blame for everything?"

"That's a popular theory," Mac agreed. "What were your parents like?"

"Like night and day. They were total opposites." Mac quirked an eyebrow in question. "My mother is a society matron. She's never worked a day in her life outside of charity functions."

"And your father was a con artist. Interesting marriage partners. How did they meet?"

"I have no idea. I always figured Dad was running a scam or something."

"And ended up marrying her?"

"Who knows?" She shrugged. "What about your childhood?"

"Mine? It was so terribly normal, I was forced to seek excitement in psychiatry." Mac kept a perfectly straight face, but his eyes twinkled with amusement. "Only way to experience anything even slightly abnormal." He shook his head when she chuckled. "I swear it's true. Mum stayed home and baked cookies, while Dad went to work everyday and coached my soccer team on the weekends."

"Poor little boy." Shelby patted his arm. "Forever scarred by a normal, happy childhood."

"I take it yours wasn't normal since you were working scams with your father."

"That was only during vacations. I lived with Mom most of the time. It was all about dance lessons and being a lady and having the right friends and doing the right things. So, when I stayed with my Dad, it was kind of a relief.

"So, you liked it better being with him?"

"Oh, I thought it was a lark. I didn't have to be the perfect little lady. I got to play a lot of different parts for Dad. And he wasn't really big on rules like bedtimes and curfews and eating sensible meals."

"And your mother never knew?"

Shelby chuckled. "Hardly." She stood and moved under the awning she'd put up. "It isn't showing any sign of letting up. We might be stuck here all night."

"It's already after five. Even if it clears up soon, we wouldn't have time to make it to the main road before dark."

"Might as well do something about food then." She rummaged through her pack and came up with several pouches of dehydrated food and a large bottle of water. "Did you get a pot or anything?"

"Of course. Mel outfitted us very well." Mac moved over to his pack and pulled out a small metal pot, a couple of plastic bowls, and some plastic forks and spoons. "I have no idea what this is, but it was next to the pot so I grabbed it." He held up three metal rods.

"Perfect." She took the rods from him, opened them up into a tripod arrangement and placed them over the fire. A chain dangled from the top with a hook on the end to hold the pot. After Mac poured water into the pot, he attached it to the chain and then threw more wood onto the fire.

"Beef stew. Beef stroganoff. Beef tips in tomato sauce. What's your pleasure?"

"I doubt there's any difference in them."

"Good point." She emptied a packet into each of the bowls and sat down to watch the water boil.

"This will make it better." Mac reached into his pack and waved a bottle in the air.

"Brandy?"

"Mel thought of everything. No cups though." Mac shrugged and took a swig from the bottle. "Oh, sorry, I should have offered it to you first."

"No reason to stand on ceremony." She took the bottle and drank a healthy swallow. It burned all the way down, creating a warm glow in her stomach. She checked the water. It still hadn't boiled.

"Don't keep looking at the pot. It'll never boil."

Shelby laughed. "There's nothing else to do." Except look at his chest, which she was trying to avoid.

"Here." He passed her the brandy. "This will take your mind off it."

"It'll take my mind off everything." She lifted the

bottle to her lips again. Was one mindless evening so bad? It was beginning to sound like a pretty good idea. She handed the bottle back, and he took a swig.

"See, it worked."

"What?" She was distracted by the play of muscle across his tanned chest.

"The water's boiling." Mac used his shirt to hold the pot and pour water into the two bowls. He then stirred the contents.

"Looks appetizing." Shelby picked up a pouch and read the directions. "Says to let it sit for ten minutes. Maybe it'll look better then."

"I doubt it. I think, in theory, people eat this stuff because they're so hungry it doesn't matter what it looks like. Or tastes like."

They shared another round of the brandy while they waited. Shelby stirred the stuff in her bowl. "Did I get the beef stew?"

"What's it taste like?"

She tentatively tasted the gelatinous mixture0. "Hard to say, but definitely not beef stew." She spooned some up and offered it to him.

"Definitely the beef stew. See it's got bits of tomato in it. Mine's all cream colored. Must be the stroganoff." He offered her a taste.

"They taste alike."

"Like soggy cardboard," he agreed. They both ate a few spoonfuls then set the bowls aside. "I say we stick with the brandy."

"We'll feel like crap tomorrow." She took another

swig of brandy. "And we have a long hike."

"It'll give us something to bitch about." He leaned over to take the bottle and gently kissed her lips.

Shelby's lips parted but no words came out. His tongue snaked out to lick her lower lip, and she felt something inside her quiver.

"You taste good."

"You like soggy cardboard?"

"I was referring to the brandy. And your lips." He kissed her again, and she was expecting something harder, stronger. But his lips just grazed hers. Somehow that made her want more, and she leaned into him, her hand flattening against his chest. He nipped playfully at the corners of her mouth and then held the brandy bottle up for her. She took a sip, and some brandy dribbled down onto her chest and ran between her breasts. His head dipped, and he lapped up the brandy, pushing the shirt off her shoulder.

Her hand seemed to move to his neck of its own accord, and her brandy-fogged brain refused to remove it, so she pulled him closer. For some reason she couldn't take her eyes off his mouth. She leaned closer and planted her lips on his with a bit more force than he'd used. He didn't object and returned the kiss full force.

Part of her mind was telling her that this probably wasn't such a good idea. But her body promptly told her mind to shut up and enjoy the moment. Mac continued to kiss her, softly, then deeply. His lips trailed down her neck then back to her mouth until she could hardly breathe. He unbuttoned her shirt and slowly drew it off, tossing it over a rock. His eyes burned a trail from her breasts to her bikini panties, down her legs and back up to her eyes.

"God, you're beautiful. You should walk around naked all the time." He pushed her back until she was leaning on her elbows.

Her mind was asserting itself again. She knew exactly where this was going, and while her body was clamoring for it, her head was arguing against it. Mac dribbled some brandy into her belly button and licked it up. He then tugged her panties off her hips with his teeth.

Her mind finally shut up.

CHAPTER EIGHTEEN

Shelby was up and dressed before Mac even stirred. Watching him sleep, regret rolled over her and settled into a sour lump in the pit of her stomach. Last night had been a mistake. Her mistake. And now she'd have to talk to him about it. Crap. She started stuffing supplies back in her pack.

"Morning, gorgeous."

Shelby turned at the sound of his voice, and her knees almost buckled at the sight of him sitting on the blanket without a stitch of clothing on. The sooner she did this, the sooner it'd be over with.

"Morning." She tossed his shorts and boxers to him and perched on a rock just outside the cave entrance. "We need to talk about last night."

"It was great, wasn't it?" Mac laughed and pulled his undershirt over his head. When he looked at her, the laughter left his eyes. "Well, it was great for me anyway."

"It isn't that. It was great for me too." He had to

230

know that. All the moaning and whimpering. She
blushed at the memory. "I don't get involved with anyone when I'm on an op."

"You don't?" Mac grinned at her. "Then I'm the
first?"

That wasn't exactly true. "It's kind of an unwritten
rule with agents. When I'm on an op, I have to be all
about the job. Anything less can result in disaster." She
shrugged. "I just didn't want you to get the wrong
idea."

"And what idea would that be?"

"That it . . . I mean . . ." Damn him for making this
so difficult.

"Don't worry about it, Shelby." Mac stood and
pulled on his boxers and shorts. "If you feel that this
wasn't right, it's not a problem."

"It's not that I think it was wrong—necessarily."
She groped for the right words, but didn't find them.
"It's just that I don't do this on an op. It doesn't
happen."

"It's a control thing for you, isn't it?"

"What?"

"Do you always have to be in control of everything?"

"Well, if I'm not in control, that means that someone
else is." He was starting to piss her off.

"And that's a problem for you?"

"I don't know how you feel about your job, but mine
is important to me. And to do my job correctly, I have
to be in control of the situation."

"Fine. I'm just saying that what happened last night

doesn't have anything to do with the op. It has to do with you and me. And you don't have to see it as a control issue."

"I don't see it as a control *issue*."

"Then there's no problem, is there?" Mac walked over and kissed her. His lips weren't on hers for more than a moment, but they were soft, inviting. Pulling her toward something that her body wanted but her mind rebelled against. She sucked up some moral strength and pulled back.

"There's no problem because it won't happen again."

"If you say so." Mac picked up his pack and started walking. "Come on. You want to get to where your cell phone works, right?"

As they walked, Shelby kept her eyes peeled for any sign of a vehicle. As much as a ride out of the desert would be welcome, she was more worried about The Center sending someone to check up on the two men who'd followed them in the SUV. They saw no one, and after a few hours, she decided that The Center had no way to track the SUV that lay at the bottom of the ravine. If they found it or ran into her and Mac, it would just be pure luck.

They stopped to rest for a few minutes, and Shelby pulled her cell phone out. Finally, she was back in a service area. Shelby punched in Ethan's speed dial number.

"Shelby. Where the hell are you?"

"Mac and I are in the desert, about thirty miles west

of Sedona." The connection was lousy, and she could barely hear Ethan over the static.

"Hold on, I'm having them triangulate your position."

"Did you get Zoe and Shannon and Sam?

"What?" Ethan's voice crackled. "I can't hear you."

"Did you get them to headquarters?"

"I've got your location pinpointed. I'm sending a helo for you."

"Where's the extraction point?" Static crackled so loud that Shelby had to pull the phone away from her ear.

"Five point seven miles due west of your current loca—" Static garbled Ethan's voice again. "—three boulders set in a triangle."

"We can be there in two hours tops," Shelby said.

"What? I can't hear you over the static."

"Two hours," Shelby repeated. The phone crackled and went dead.

"Ethan's sending a helo for us. About six miles from here."

"Did the agents get them to headquarters?"

"I don't know. We had a bad connection. I could hardly hear him."

Mac grinned at her then moved closer. "Hey, cheer up. We're going to be rescued." He leaned down and planted a soft, seductive kiss on her lips.

"I told you we're not doing this."

"We aren't doing anything. It's just a friendly kiss." He kissed her again and then traced her lips with his finger. It was all she could do not to lean into him. She managed a severe frown.

"Let's get moving."

They kept up a pretty good pace and made the extraction point in an hour and a half. No helo yet, and she didn't know where it would be coming from or how long they would have to wait. They sat in the shade of one of the large boulders and drank the last of their water. She wished they had another bottle to tide them over until the helo showed up and was relieved when she heard the familiar thwapping sound of helo blades in less than half an hour.

Seconds later the helo appeared from behind them. A standard Bell Jet, black with no markings. Exactly what she expected. She moved away from the rock and waved her arms. The helo made a tight circle and landed about thirty yards from them.

They grabbed their packs, ran toward the helo, and climbed in. There were two men on board in addition to the pilot, all three of them dressed in cammies.

That was unusual. Unless there was a need for camouflage, FSA helo teams usually wore dark blue jumpsuits. And these guys were wearing jungle cammies. If cammies had been called for, they'd certainly be wearing desert cammies.

She glanced at the biggest man standing next to the door. His left ear lobe sported a small gold cross earring. FSA agents weren't allowed to wear earrings on assignment unless it was part of their undercover persona.

They'd just gotten on a helo with the enemy.

Crap.

CHAPTER NINETEEN

"Man, we're happy to see you guys!" Shelby turned toward the rear of the helo and deliberately stumbled into Mac. His arms automatically went around her, and she pressed her mouth to his ear so the men wouldn't hear her.

"These men are not FSA. Probably from The Center."

Mac cursed under his breath and tightened his grip. "You sure?" he whispered.

Shelby nodded and pulled him down to the seat next to her with their packs on their laps. She pulled her gun out of the waistband of her shorts and pressed it into Mac's hand under the cover of their packs.

Mac and she were in the rear seats of the helo. One man was in the center seat; another in the front with the pilot. Both men carried semi-automatic rifles. The only chance they had was to get the rifle away from the man

LIZ WOLFE

nearest them. At least then they'd both be armed against only one of them.

The man sitting next to the pilot exchanged a look with the man in front of them. He then turned back around and seemed to relax. He let his rifle rest across his legs. The man in the middle seat propped the butt of his rifle on the seat next to him and held it loosely.

Sloppy. Careless. Perfect opportunity for Shelby.

She desperately needed to tell Mac what she wanted him to do, but she couldn't think of how to do that until she remembered him telling her that he and Sam communicated in ASL. American Sign Language, used by the deaf and hearing impaired. She didn't know much of it, but she could fingerspell a short message to him. She nudged his thigh to bring his attention to her hand. As quickly as she could, she spelled out her message, hoping that she'd gotten the letters correct and that he understood.

Mac nodded and gripped the gun a little more tightly. At her nod, he pressed the gun into the man's neck as she grabbed the rifle from him.

He grunted in surprise, and his leg kicked out to hit the back of the seat in front of him. The man next to the pilot turned abruptly, his rifle poised. But Shelby already had the rifle she'd taken from his partner aimed at him.

"You don't really want a gun fight in a helo, do you?" She was relieved that his eyes showed resignation. She climbed into the middle seat and took his rifle.

Mac held her gun on the man in front of him and

rummaged in his pack, coming up with a roll of duct tape that Mel had included in their supplies. He tied up the man's hands, pushed him into the back seat and taped up his ankles.

Shelby moved over and motioned the one sitting next to the pilot to climb into the rear seat so that Mac could tape his wrists and ankles.

"Turn it around." She pressed the rifle barrel into the pilot's shoulder to provide encouragement. The helo swung around and headed north.

Shelby punched Ethan's speed dial number into her cell phone. He answered on the first ring.

"Where are you? The helo just called to say you weren't at the extraction point."

"A helo showed up. We got on. Turned out to be people from The Center. How the hell are these guys finding out where I am?"

"I assume you have control of the helo now?" Ethan asked.

"Call the Flagstaff Police and tell them to meet us at the airport." She had to yell into the phone for Ethan to hear her over the noise of the helo. The rest of the conversation could wait until they landed. She closed the phone and turned to the pilot. "You know where the Flagstaff airport is?"

An hour later, the three men were in custody, and Mac and Shelby were sitting in a small office in the Flagstaff Police Department sipping bitter coffee from chipped mugs. She punched Ethan's speed dial number into her cell phone.

"Ethan, how the hell did The Center know where we were and that we were expecting a helo?"

Ethan sighed heavily. "The same way they knew we were picking up Zoe, Shannon, and Sam at Mel's."

"Oh, no." She felt sick. Her stomach rolled over, and she swallowed hard. "Please don't tell me they took them."

"When the agents got them to the airport, they were ambushed. One agent is dead; the other is in serious condition."

"Someone in the FSA is keeping The Center informed."

"I'll find out who it is."

"You do that," she snapped.

"When will you be arriving in Denver?"

"I won't. My job is to extract Shannon and Sam. And Zoe."

"We've been watching The Center. They didn't take them back there."

"That's not really a surprise, is it?" Thomas and Carlson wouldn't be stupid enough to go back to The Center. She'd have to figure out where they were.

"I think you should come back to headquarters, Shelby. We can find out where they took them and go after them again."

"I think I'd rather handle this my own way."

"Shelby, this is not sanctioned—"

"Sanction this, Ethan." Shelby snapped her cell phone shut and turned to Mac. His face was pale, his brow furrowed. "I'm sorry, Mac."

"How do we find them?" he asked.

"I don't know, but we will."

They begged a ride from the police, and half an hour later, they were escorted to a large suite on the third floor of the Flagstaff Inn Suites Hotel. Mac graciously offered to let her have the shower first, and she decided to let him be a gentleman about it.

The hot water relaxed her muscles, and she let her mind drift, not focusing on anything in particular. After fifteen minutes of steamy relaxation, she wrapped herself in the thick, terry robe the hotel provided, stuffed her clothes in a plastic bag, and joined Mac in the sitting room.

"Change into this, and I'll send our clothes down to be laundered." She tossed a second robe at him. Mac caught the robe and sat on the sofa while he pulled off his boots and socks. She didn't want to view the rest of his undressing, so she pulled her laptop out of her pack and plugged it into the high-speed Internet connection at the desk. When she heard Mac close the bathroom door, she gathered up his clothes and added them to hers. She then called room service to pick them up.

By the time Mac emerged from his shower looking better than she'd ever thought possible, the clothes were on their way to the hotel laundry and she was reading the preliminary analysis of The Center's files that Ethan had emailed to her.

Mac walked up behind her, and she felt his hands on her shoulders as he leaned over. "What's it say?"

"This is just a preliminary report. They haven't

unencrypted all the files yet. But, evidently, The Center is trying to create meta-humans with phenomenal psychic abilities. It says something about recessive and dominant genes."

Mac leaned over her shoulder to read the report. "It seems that if both parents have a certain pair of recessive genes, then they'll have a child with some psychic ability. But there are also some dominant genes involved."

"I don't understand all the biology of it, but it says something about two parents who have psychic ability and also carry the recessive genes."

"According to their research, chances are excellent that in that situation, the child would have outstanding psychic abilities and also carry the recessive gene." Mac kneaded her shoulders, and it felt just too good to ask him to stop.

"Sam?"

"I think so. Chase and Shannon must have both the recessive and dominant genes necessary to produce a child with outstanding psychic ability."

"Do you think they knew Chase was Sam's father?"

"Shannon didn't tell them, and Chase didn't know that he had a son. They could have done a DNA test. I think Chase was just there trying to find Shannon. The Center was interested in him because he had psychic ability."

"Look at this." Shelby pointed to the screen. "They have some notes about certain drugs being able to enhance psychic ability."

"All this is very frightening. And useless. What we need to do is get Shannon and Sam away from them."

"Zoe and Chase too. I promised Shannon I'd get Chase out." Shelby's email program kept dinging and blinking, telling her she had new email. She could imagine who it was from. She suppressed a sigh and opened the email from Ethan.

"Ethan wants to talk to me."

"Are you going to call him?"

"I don't know. I don't really believe Ethan is giving information to The Center. He has no reason to."

"That you know of."

"True. Still, Shannon is his wife's best friend." She shook her head. "I'm certain there's a mole in the FSA, but I'm also certain that it isn't Ethan."

"Then talk to him."

"Why don't you order us some dinner. I'm starved."

"And we aren't exactly dressed to go out." Mac picked up the phone. "What's your pleasure?"

"Red meat and lots of it. Something green for my health, and something sinfully rich and sweet for my psyche." She moved away from Mac and punched in Ethan's home phone number. It was after seven, and she was hoping he'd be home.

"Shelby!"

"Hey, Ethan."

"I'm glad you called."

"I didn't want to talk to you at the office."

"I understand. Don is having the offices swept for bugs tonight."

"You think that's it?"

"Honestly, I don't know. I guess I'd rather believe that than think that someone inside the FSA is a traitor. Besides, most of the information that's been leaked has only been discussed between us on the phone, or between Don and myself. I can't quite believe that Don is the mole."

"So, what is the FSA doing about locating Zoe, Shannon, and Sam?"

"Everything we can, which isn't nearly enough." Ethan paused, cleared his throat. "The doctors have definitely left the area. The Center appears to be closed up."

"Have you sent anyone in?"

"We're sending in a team in a few days. But, we don't expect to find anything."

"Why aren't you sending someone in sooner?" Shelby asked.

"I don't have any qualified agents available."

"You need to step up your recruitment program, Ethan."

"I need *you*. You're worth any three agents currently at my disposal."

"You've got me. But I'm doing this my way."

"No argument. So where are you, and what's your next move?"

Shelby hesitated and hated herself for that. If she couldn't trust her handler, then she was already dead. "We're at the Flagstaff Inn Suites. Just for tonight. Tomorrow, I'm going back to The Center. Maybe I'll find something."

"I hope so." Ethan sounded weary and frustrated.

"I'll let you know."

"Watch your back, Shelby."

"Yeah, you watch it too." She turned off her cell phone and called the concierge desk to order a rental car for the following morning. There was a knock at the door, and Mac let room service in with their dinner. Shelby ordered the car and sat down at the table. Mac had followed her instructions to the letter. Filet Mignon, steamed asparagus, new potatoes swimming in butter and parsley. She was pretty sure the covered dish contained the dessert she'd requested. Even better, there was an ice bucket with a bottle of very good champagne. Mac was going to try to seduce her.

It worked, but really, she didn't know if it was the champagne or the Death by Chocolate dessert.

CHAPTER TWENTY

Shelby and Mac were on the road before six the following morning. She knew there was no one at The Center, but she was still anxious to get there. Mac didn't grumble about the early hour. Better yet, he didn't mention the fact that she'd broken her rule about not getting involved with anyone during an op. Although, really, it wasn't an op—it was a job, a case. She wasn't an FSA agent now, but a private investigator. She needed different rules.

Not far outside of Flagstaff, she noticed a car following them. Of course, anyone leaving Flagstaff heading south would be on Highway Seventeen. And there really was no reason to suspect that anyone would be following them. The Center had pulled up and moved. She didn't know where they were, so why would they have someone following them? Then again, why not?

"You keep checking the rearview mirror," Mac said.

"There's been a car behind us for some time. Probably nothing to worry about."

"Then why do you keep looking at it?"

"Force of habit." The car edged over to the middle line of the road. "Looks like he's going to pass us." They were on a straight stretch of road, so she slowed a little to give the car a chance to pass before they hit a curvy stretch.

"Good. One less thing to worry about." Mac glanced at the car behind them. "Isn't he coming up pretty fast?"

"The Highway splits into two lanes up ahead." She nodded toward the sign at the side of the road and slowed the car a little more. The car following them kept gaining speed but didn't move into the passing lane. "Mac, make sure your seatbelt is fastened."

"Oh, boy."

Shelby moved into the right lane, designated for slower traffic, and kept an eye on the car. It stayed in the left lane but made no move to pass them. The car crept up to a position just behind Shelby. She looked over the rail, and her stomach clenched. If she'd wanted to run a car over the edge of a steep embankment, it was exactly what she'd do. Stay behind and to the left, then bump the rear fender of the car just as it went into a curve.

"What the hell is he doing?" Mac glanced back at the car again.

"I think he's going to try to run us off the road."

"Oh. I'd rather not have that experience."

Shelby speeded up, thinking to move into the left lane, but the car moved with her, leaving no room to move over. She slowed down, and the car slowed with her.

"He's definitely messing with us." She spared a glance at Mac. "Brace yourself."

The car dropped back, then sped up and plowed into the rear left bumper. Shelby and Mac slammed against their seatbelts, and she worked to pull the car out of the fishtail he'd thrown them into.

"Mac, look in my backpack. There's a knife in one of the outside pockets." Mac reached over the seat and grabbed her pack. He checked all the outside pockets until he came up with the knife. "Now what?"

"Eventually he might hit us hard enough to set off the airbags. If that happens, you need to cut mine, so it deflates immediately."

Mac looked at her as if she'd lost her mind. Probably a fairly normal reaction. "What if I stab you instead?"

"Don't aim for me. Just hold the knife in your left hand. When you hear a really loud noise, stab in the direction of the steering wheel."

"Do you think it's someone from The Center?"

"Who else would try to run us off the road?" She kept moving her eyes from the road to the rearview mirror. With the angle of the rising sun, she couldn't be sure, but it looked like there were two people in the car.

Suddenly, the rear window of the car exploded, and Shelby felt a sharp, stinging pain in her left arm. Mac reacted according to her instructions and stabbed at the steering wheel, narrowly missing her right hand.

"Mother of crap!" Shelby glanced at her arm. The white shirt was ripped and beginning to turn red with blood. These guys were really pissing her off.

"Hang on!"

Mac nodded and lowered the knife in his hand.

She slowed, and the car behind her slowed. There was a sharp curve coming up, and the car slowed even more, getting into position behind her. No doubt it would slam into them again just as they got to the curve. Shelby waited until they were just going into the curve and punched the gas, shooting ahead of the car. They sped up again, and she kept most of her attention on the rearview mirror. She hit the brakes hard with her left foot and a split second later punched the gas with her right.

The driver of the other car reacted as she'd expected and hit his brakes hard when he saw her brake lights. Tires squealed, and the smoke and smell of burning rubber filled the air as the car maneuvered into the left lane to avoid hitting them.

Suddenly the car spun in a full circle, and crashed into the mountainside.

Shelby slowed and pulled off onto the shoulder. Slamming the car into park, she grabbed her gun and pulled her cell phone off her belt, tossing it to Mac.

"Call Nine-One-One and report an accident. I'm going to check on them."

She trotted back to the car and heard Mac following her.

"We're on Highway Seventeen just about thirty miles outside Flagstaff. Someone had an accident behind us. They crashed into the side of the mountain. We've stopped, and we're walking back to check on them." Mac reached the car just seconds after Shelby. "They're dispatching an ambulance and calling the highway patrol."

The man in the driver's seat sat with his head slumped over the steering wheel, not moving. His buddy in the passenger seat seemed to be in the same condition. She checked both of them for a pulse, and they were alive. Satisfied that neither man was in any condition to pose a threat, she tucked her gun in her waistband and pulled her shirt over it.

"Are you looking for identification?" Mac asked, as she started going through the men's pockets.

"Identification won't tell us anything. Besides, I doubt they have any on them." She pulled a cell phone out of the passenger's shirt pocket. "This is what I'm looking for." She pressed buttons on the cell phone until she had a list of outgoing calls. There was only one number listed. She memorized the number and times that calls had been placed, and then punched more buttons to get the incoming calls. All the incoming calls were from the same number. She grabbed her phone from Mac and entered Ethan's speed dial number.

"Ethan, Mac and I were almost run off the road by a couple of men."

"Where?"

"Less than an hour outside of Flagstaff."

"Son of a bitch!"

"Yeah, I'd say the leak hasn't been plugged yet. But the good news is that they're both still alive. One had a cell phone, and the memory shows calls to and from one number in the three-six-zero area code." She could hear Ethan tapping on his keyboard.

"That's in Washington State."

"I know, but it's a big area."

Ethan paused, and she knew he was checking a database on his computer. "Southwest quadrant of the state. From Vancouver up to Tacoma, west of the Mt. Rainier National Forest."

"Damn. That's a lot of ground to cover."

"If it's a cell phone number, they could be calling from anywhere. Give me the number."

She gave him the full number and waited.

"Bad news. It is a cell phone number. They might be located in Southwestern Washington, but all we know for sure is that the phone number was issued from there."

"Crap. Well, it's better than nothing." Her left arm was beginning to sting now that the excitement was over. "Ethan, we called Nine-One-One. They should be here in a few minutes."

"I'll take care of it, Shelby. Are you still going to The Center?"

"You bet your ass I'm going there. If the doctors have already left, there must be some reason they didn't want us to go there."

"More likely, they just wanted to get rid of you. But

it still can't hurt to check the place out."

"I'll check in later." She paused for a moment. "Ethan, please find whoever is leaking this information to them."

"I'm working on it."

Shelby snapped her cell phone shut just as the Highway Patrol cruiser pulled up, lights flashing, and an ambulance right behind it. She fished her FSA ID out of her back pocket and walked over to the two officers getting out of the car. The older officer was obviously in charge. The younger one had his hand on his gun as if there was going to be a problem.

"You called this in?" the older officer asked.

She nodded to both men and handed the older one her ID. "This is part of an on-going FSA investigation. The men are alive and need to be held until the FSA sends someone for them."

"Will do. Any idea when they'll arrive?"

"Probably today, although I can't be certain. Your Captain should be receiving a call right about now."

"They'll probably be in the hospital for a while." The older officer peered into the window of the car and waved the ambulance attendants over. He glanced at his partner and made a subtle motion for him to take his hand off his weapon.

"Just be sure to keep a guard on them at all times."

"I don't think they're in any condition to run."

"Probably not. But I'm more worried about someone getting to them." She was relieved to be dealing with an officer who knew the drill.

"I get your point." He gestured at her arm. "You want a ride to the hospital? Looks like you need a little mending yourself."

Shelby looked down at her arm. Three inches below her shoulder, the shirt was ripped, exposing a nasty wound from the bullet. The sleeve was slowly turning red from the blood.

"I'll be fine. I'm traveling with a doctor." No way was she going to take the time to go to the local hospital.

"Dear God, Shelby!" Mac had just noticed her arm.

"It's just a flesh wound." That hurt like hell. Still, she knew all she needed was a little clean up and some antibiotics. Mac grabbed her other arm and shoved her over to lean against the trunk of the car, where he ripped her sleeve open to inspect the wound.

The two paramedics had one man out of the car and on a gurney. They stopped by Shelby on the way to the ambulance. "That looks pretty bad. We'll check it out when we've got these two loaded up."

"No need," Mac said. "I'm her doctor. Do you have some supplies I could use?"

The paramedic nodded and motioned Mac to follow him to the ambulance. The older officer walked over to Shelby.

"I don't suppose you're at liberty to tell me what this is about?"

She shrugged and shook her head. "You know how it is."

"Yeah, I know. If you tell me, you'll have to kill me."

Shelby laughed at his joke, old as it was.

Mac trotted back over with an armful of stuff he'd gotten from the paramedics. He washed the wound out with a saline solution, which stung like hell, and then with something else that set her arm on fire. The bullet had taken a gouge out of her flesh, but not enough to require stitches. Mac slathered some ointment on it, slapped a pile of gauze on top of that, and then taped it up. Good as new, except for the burning pain.

"You want something for the pain?"

She was beginning to think he could read her mind. Shelby shook her head. "I need to stay clear for a while."

"I figured." Mac sighed. "When we get to a town, I need to get some antibiotics for you." She let Mac lead her back to their car and got into the passenger seat.

"I'm driving?" he asked.

"You know how, right?" She leaned her head back against the headrest and slitted her eyes to see Mac's reaction. He grinned at her. The paramedics had both men loaded up and were taking off back in the direction of Flagstaff. The older officer leaned down and tapped on Shelby's window.

"All set?" he asked as she lowered the window. "We'll keep an eye on them until the FSA shows up. Take care of that arm." He straightened and slapped the roof of the car to let Mac know they were good to go. Mac jumped a little.

Shelby grinned and waved at the officer.

✦ ✦ ✦

Ethan hurried down the hall, nodding to coworkers. He opened the door to Monique's office and waited while she ended a phone call.

"He's expecting you. Go on in."

"You look tired, Monique. Is Don working you too hard?"

"Doesn't he always?" Monique smiled and rose to place four cups and a carafe on a tray.

"Who's in there?"

"John Fields and Chris Jackson," Monique said.

"He's working me too hard too." Ethan winked at her and opened the door to the director's office.

"Ethan, come in. This is FBI Director John Fields and SAC of the Phoenix office, Chris Jackson." Don moved from behind his desk to the table by the window where Chris and John were seated.

Agent Jackson stood to shake Ethan's hand, but Fields merely nodded to him and scowled at Don. "I'm still more than a little perturbed by your actions, Don. You knew this was already in the FBI's hands."

"We've discussed this, John. I did what I thought was best, and I'll take whatever heat may come of it. But before you start blowing your top about it, you might want to consider your rather strained relationship with Ambassador Watkins."

The room fell silent. Ethan took a seat and accepted a cup of coffee from Monique.

"My concern at the moment is that Shannon and

Sam Masterson are being held against their wills. And there are others. We don't know what these people are up to or where they've taken them."

"I agree that the situation is unacceptable," Fields said.

"And, I understand that you had an operative undercover with them and basically got no information at all from him," Don continued.

"Sir," Agent Jackson held up a hand. "Dr. McRae was only there to gather whatever information he could without compromising either his own safety or the future of our operation. He's not an agent; he's a psychiatrist."

"And when he informed you that Sam Masterson was in danger, you still delayed sending someone in to extract him." Don accepted a cup of coffee from Monique.

"There were extenuating circumstances, sir. We didn't want to put Shannon's life in danger, and there was no reason to believe the child was in imminent danger. We had plenty of time to decide the best way to handle it." Agent Jackson folded her hands over a leather portfolio on the table.

"There's something just not right about this," Don said. "Your agent is now with my agent. I'd like to know why the hell he wasn't coming in with the Mastersons."

"Actually, I believe we may have a problem with Dr. McRae," Agent Jackson said.

"You certainly have a problem somewhere, Agent Jackson," Don retorted.

"Dr. McRae had a personal relationship with Shannon and Sam Masterson prior to this incident. He's done extensive research on psychic ability in the past, especially pertaining to children."

"Wasn't that why you sent him to The Center in the first place?" Don asked Fields.

"Actually, Dr. McRae volunteered. In fact, he insisted on being allowed to infiltrate The Center," Fields said.

"There are indications that McRae might be working with Thomas and Carlson." Chris turned in her chair to look directly at Don.

"What?" Don asked.

"At the very least, it appears that McRae has his own agenda and that it might not necessarily mesh with the goals of the FBI or the FSA."

Ethan felt a cold knot of dread form in his chest.

Agent Jackson cleared her throat. "We believe McRae has gone rogue."

They were less than an hour from Tucson when Shelby's cell phone chirped. She pulled it out and looked at the number on the display.

"Ethan. What's up?" She shifted in her seat and transferred the phone to her right hand.

"Is McRae with you?"

Shelby sat up straighter, wincing at the pain in her arm. "Yes."

"Chambers has been in touch with the FBI. McRae's SAC thinks he's gone rogue." Ethan paused a moment, but she didn't have anything to say. "Shelby, there's a mole in the FBI. It might be McRae."

Crap.

CHAPTER TWENTY-ONE

"McRae's SAC is full of it. She refused to go in for Sam for several days. Mac had no choice but to extract him without her approval."

"Calm down, Shelby."

"Calm down, my ass!" She glanced at Mac. He seemed calm enough. "And what's this crap about Chambers talking to the FBI? I thought the reason I was brought in was that he didn't want the FBI to know the FSA was investigating The Center."

"He really didn't have a choice once they took Shannon and Sam from us."

"I guess." She sighed. "Anything else I should know about? Any word on Chase Harmon's whereabouts?"

"None. I'm assuming they took him wherever they have Zoe, Shannon, and Sam."

"Great. I'll let you know what I find at The Center."

Shelby flipped the phone closed and leaned her head back against the headrest.

"What was that all about?"

"Your SAC is saying that you might have gone rogue, since she hasn't heard from you."

"Looks like I'll need that reference for my résumé after all."

"I wouldn't rush to any conclusions. But I have to wonder why she'd say that."

"I have no idea. Chris was very supportive of my involvement in the investigation." Mac's brow creased in thought. "This seems out of character for her."

They were silent until they approached The Center. Shelby was sure Mac was thinking about what his SAC was doing. She was thinking about Ethan's warning that Mac might be the FBI mole. God, she didn't want to believe that. And she was reminded of why she always had the rule of never getting involved with anyone on an op. It ripped your objectivity to hell.

"Sure looks abandoned," Shelby said as Mac pulled into the small parking lot. There had been no one at the guard gate. No cars in the parking lot. They'd only been gone for less than two days, and the place looked totally deserted.

Mac parked next to the front door, got out, and hurried around to open her door. Really. She didn't know whether to be impressed or aggravated. She'd taken some over-the-counter painkillers, and her arm had relaxed into a dull throb. She got out of the car, being careful not to jostle the arm any more than necessary.

Mac stopped just short of offering an arm to lean on.

Shelby pulled her gun, and they checked the front door. Locked. Not surprised, Shelby took the lead and walked along the front of the building, down the windowless, doorless side and to the back. The back door hung open; the lock blown off by a gun. Well, wasn't this interesting?

She motioned Mac to stay behind her, and he frowned but didn't argue. She stepped inside, quickly assessing the hallway, which was empty except for the faint, dusty trace of heavy boot prints in the carpet. She paused and examined the prints. Not enough detail to tell what kind of boot, but the prints were large. Had to be a big man wearing lug-soled boots designed for working or combat. This was definitely not a random B&E of an abandoned building.

Shelby cautiously made her way down the hallway, trying doorways as she went. Nothing. When they reached the lab doors, she saw that the lock had been shot off and the door hung open. Shelby motioned Mac to stay behind her, as she cautiously entered the lab.

It looked like everyone had just walked out. Medical equipment was still in place; charts were still in folders.

"Look through those charts," she told Mac, nodding toward a wheeled cart. She headed down the hallway where Shannon's room had been. All the rooms were empty.

She stopped and checked the computer at the nurses' station. Nothing. It wouldn't even boot up. She pulled the tower around and immediately saw the problem. The hard drive had been removed. They wanted the data, but the equipment was expendable. And this was state-of-the-art equipment.

She walked back to Mac and glanced at the charts he'd looked at.

"Nothing important. Nothing that would imply there was anything going on here. Mostly these are older charts. Patients that aren't here any longer."

They moved to the other rooms that were unlocked and found a similar situation. They'd taken all the data but left expensive equipment behind. Hard drives had been removed from every computer and server in the building.

"Let's check out the rest of the place." Shelby led the way to the doctors' offices. Both doors hung open, the locks shot off. Shelby entered Dr. Carlson's office and then motioned Mac to follow her. The laptop was gone, and a few drawers hung open in the desk and the credenza behind it.

"Check those drawers," she instructed Mac. He went through the credenza while she checked out the desk drawers and then the small closet. Nothing.

There had been no sign of whoever had shot off all the locks and left boot prints on the floor. Mac and Shelby moved to Dr. Thomas' office and found the same situation as in Carlson's office. Laptop missing, drawers hanging open. No data, no clues.

Crap.

Shelby slumped down in the plush leather chair

behind his desk and turned to gaze out the window. Mac shuffled through the open credenza drawers in front of her. That's when she heard the noise.

"Don't move!"

The deep, commanding voice matched the reflection in the window. He must have been about six feet two, heavily muscled. He wore desert fatigues, and his hair was cut in the traditional jarhead style of a Marine.

Shelby slipped her gun in between her knees and lifted her arms above her head slowly. "No problem. I'm an agent with the FSA. This is Mac. He's with the FBI."

"Doc?"

"Chase." Mac nodded.

"You're with the FBI?"

"I was investigating Shannon's disappearance."

Shelby slowly turned to face Chase. Seeing him again, she was struck by his resemblance to Sam. His hair was a dark golden blond rather than the lighter shade of Sam's. But his eyes were the same shade of blue, and his mouth turned up at the corners in the same way as Sam's did.

His eyes narrowed as he turned to Shelby. "Who are you?"

"Shelby Parker. I'm working with the FSA to extract Shannon." She almost added Sam's name, but figured she'd probably better leave that revelation for later.

"Let me see some identification." He still held the gun on them.

Shelby slowly pulled her FSA ID from her pocket with two fingers and handed it to him. He stared at it a moment and then lowered his gun, sagging a little. That's when she noticed the bloody tear in his pants' leg.

"What happened?" Shelby asked, nodding to his leg.

"Bastards shot me while I was getting away." Chase moved to half sit on the corner of the desk.

"Me too." She turned to Mac. "You want to take a look at that?"

Mac moved to kneel next to Chase. He pulled apart the torn fabric and inspected the gash. "The bullet cut a pretty deep gouge. Must hurt."

"I've had worse." Chase shrugged. "So, what are you two doing here?"

"Same as you, I suspect. Looking for a clue as to where they took Shannon."

"I've been through everything here. Nothing."

"Then we have to look another way."

"How do we do that?" Mac asked.

"We find out who owns this building. If they leased it, we might be able to find them by whatever information they gave the leasing company, or by the checks they used to pay the rent."

"What if they own it?" Chase asked.

"Then we trace them through that paper work." She looked from Mac to Chase, knowing they weren't going to like what she had to say. "Unfortunately, that can take some time."

"We don't have time." Mac shook his head. "They don't have time."

"I know. The FSA and FBI have probably already done a lot of the work on this. Hopefully, that'll speed everything up."

"They?" Chase asked. "They took people besides Shannon?"

"Shannon's son, Sam, and another woman." Chase nodded but said nothing. Shelby decided she'd let Shannon explain.

"How did you escape?" she asked him.

"Wasn't that hard. They came in a couple of days ago in a heated rush. I could hear a lot of activity, and I figured that might be my chance to get out. After a while, they sent some rookie security guard to get me." Chase shook his head and grinned. "He wasn't much of a challenge."

"You're Marine Force Recon, aren't you?" she asked.

"Yes, ma'am."

"That explains how you got into The Center initially and how you got out."

"Chase, why did you come here? How did you even know that Shannon was here?" Mac leaned against the credenza and crossed his arms over his chest. "Had you been in touch with her?"

Chase glanced down and shrugged. He then looked back at Mac. "No, I hadn't heard from her since I went into the Marines."

Mac lifted his eyebrows, and Shelby watched the interplay with interest. Chase looked like he really didn't want to say something, but had to.

"I had a feeling," he mumbled.

"A feeling?" she asked.

"Actually, it was more than a feeling, wasn't it?" Mac spoke softly, as if he didn't want to upset Chase.

"Yeah, it was more than a feeling," Chase admitted with a sigh. "Shannon and I always had this connection."

"Can you communicate with her?"

"Some." Chase shifted again.

"How much?" Mac demanded.

"I don't know. I mean, we used to do it a lot. Not words or anything, but feelings, emotions." Chase stood and grimaced a bit from the pain in his leg. "But that pretty much ended when I left. Until about a month ago." He shook his head. "I don't know how to explain it. I just had this feeling that she was in trouble, that she needed me."

"So you came here?"

Chase nodded. "I talked to some of her friends. They didn't know much except that she'd been coming to The Center for a while. So I decided to check them out. They said they didn't know what had happened to her, but I knew they were lying."

"You knew? How?" she asked.

"It's just something I can do." Chase shrugged and looked embarrassed. "I can read emotions in people."

"So, you hung around?"

"I hung around. They were looking for volunteers for psychic research, so I signed up. I knew I had enough ability to keep them interested for a while. And

I figured that would give me a chance to find her."

They all stood silent for a moment. Shelby guessed Mac was considering what Chase had told them. She was just amazed. Psychic stuff wasn't something she'd ever dealt with or even thought much about. Go figure.

"If we're done here, I'd like to get someplace where I can clean up his leg." Mac shot her a look. "I'm fairly certain taking him to a hospital is out of the question."

Actually, she'd have been pleased to dump Chase in a nice safe hospital. The last thing she needed was someone getting in her way. She already had enough obstacles.

"No hospital." Chase stood again, and Shelby could see him gritting his teeth against the pain.

"Why doesn't that surprise me?" Mac asked.

Shelby punched the redial button on her cell phone and waited for Ethan to answer.

"Shelby. Did you find anything?"

"Yeah, I found Chase. Unfortunately I didn't find a single clue as to where they've taken Zoe, Shannon, and Sam."

"Nothing?"

"Not a damn thing. They took all the hard drives out of the computers, no papers around. But they left a lot of very expensive equipment. Maybe they're planning on coming back for it."

"And they left Chase."

"Well, they didn't really leave him. He escaped

while they were getting ready to leave. Then he just hid out and kept looking in The Center for a clue as to where they'd gone."

Ethan cursed vividly. "So, we've lost them again."

"Only for now. I need you to find out what the FSA and the FBI know about them. Did they own this building? Did they lease it? We might be able to track them through a paper trail."

"I'll see what I can find out. I'm sure they buried everything in dummy corporations, so it'll take a while to find anything."

"Crack the whip, Ethan. We're dead in the water until we know where they are."

"Yes, Ms. Garrett, we can do that for you." Paige Blackwell stifled a sigh and rolled her eyes since there was no one in the small offices of Parker Security and Investigation to see her. Another woman who was sure her husband was having an affair. "Absolutely, I'll get on it as soon as you come down and sign the contract." Paige held the phone away from her ear for a few seconds to get some relief from the woman's sobbing hysteria. "Fine, I'll see you then." She replaced the phone as the door opened to admit a petite woman dressed in jeans and a tee shirt.

The woman's eyes darted around the office, and she tossed a long red braid over her shoulder. "I'd like to see Shelby Parker."

"Ms. Parker is out of the office. May I help you with something?" Paige stood and pulled herself up to her full five feet nine inches. The woman had to look up at her as she walked to the desk, but didn't seem the least bit intimidated.

"Are you her secretary?"

"No. I'm her partner." Well, not really a partner—yet. "What did you want to see her about?"

"It's personal."

"I see." It was always personal. "She's out of town on a case right now. I don't know when to expect her back."

"Oh, I thought it was over, and she'd be back. Do you know how to reach her?"

"I might," Paige said. "If you tell me who you are and what this is all about."

"Just tell her Zoe Drummond needs to talk to her. I'll be back tomorrow."

"Wait!" Paige almost yelled. "Zoe? The one she got out of The Center?"

"You know about that?"

"Well, I am her partner." She really needed to stop lying about that. "Anyway, Shelby emails in her case reports whenever she has the chance, and I read them. The last one indicated that you and the others had been taken by The Center again."

"I got away, but they got Shannon and Sam."

"Hold on. She's going to want to talk to you." Paige lifted the phone receiver and punched in the speed dial number for Shelby's cell phone. After a few rings, she got Shelby's voice mail. "Shelby, Paige here. Call me. Soon."

"Where are you staying?"

"I don't know yet. I just got off the plane this morning. I guess I'll get a hotel room."

"No need." Paige waved her hand. "You can stay with me. I have an extra bed."

"No, that's all right."

"It's necessary. Shelby might call me at anytime." Paige pressed the phone button to send all calls to voice mail and picked up her purse. "I was just about to close up. We'll go to my place and order a pizza. Shelby will probably call soon." She wasn't about to let Zoe out of her sight.

"All right. No anchovies though."

"Deal." Paige closed up the office and led Zoe the four blocks to her loft apartment over The Zen Tea Garden and Bookstore.

"Nice place," Zoe said as Paige dropped her purse and mail on the small table next to the door.

"I like it." Paige looked around her large, single room apartment. "I refurbished it myself. Used to be some kind of sweatshop, I think." Paige picked up the phone and punched in the number for pizza delivery. "Make yourself at home. You want a beer?"

"Sure." Zoe accepted a beer from Paige and walked over to the large windows that ran along the street side of the apartment.

Paige placed the order for the pizza, and then sat on the sofa and pulled out a roll of blueprints, spreading them across the coffee table. Zoe didn't seem to be the talkative type, and Paige decided to let her settle in while they waited for the pizza and for Shelby to call.

"What are those?"

Paige jumped, startled at Zoe's voice. She hadn't heard her move across the apartment to stand next to the coffee table. Must be her size, Paige decided. Zoe was decidedly tiny.

"A client wants us to recommend an electronic security system. From the layout he's got, I'm thinking he probably needs a Zenador Maximum system." Paige hunkered over the floor plans to hide her smirk.

"That would work on the doors, but the Zenador is a little weak when it comes to window access. He's got a lot of floor-to-ceiling glass, even on the first floor. You'd do better with a Tricor system. It works on pressure sensitivity and has the best motion detection."

Paige gaped at her. "How do you know that?"

Shannon stood at the small, barred window of the sterile, chilly room and stared out at the pine trees just beyond the high walls. She didn't even know exactly where they were. Somewhere in Washington State. She could see Mt. Rainier to the northeast and Mt. St. Helens to the south. She'd memorized the way they'd traveled after they left the plane. But it wasn't going to do her any good if she couldn't get out.

Part of her mind just didn't want to accept that

they'd taken her and Sam. Again. If the FSA and FBI couldn't keep them safe, then what was going to happen to her and her son?

The worst was not knowing where they'd put Sam. As soon as they'd entered the big, gray building, they'd taken Sam away from her. She tentatively reached out to him with her mind. A smile spread across her lips when she touched the bright, energetic essence of the four-year-old.

"Mommy. Where are you?"

"I'm here, Sam. Are you okay?"

"I miss you. I don't like these people."

"I know, honey. I'll find a way to get us out of here."

"Mac's going to come for us. And Bear too."

"I hope you're right."

"I saw it, Mommy. They'll come."

"I love you, Sam."

Shannon broke the connection with her son, worried that if she held it too long, someone would know that she could communicate with him.

Tears filled her eyes and slipped down her cheeks. She just wanted her little boy back. And to escape from this place and these mad people. She thought of Sam again and envisioned his white-blond hair and big, blue eyes. He looked so much like his father. *Oh, God, Chase. I wish you were here now.*

CHAPTER TWENTY-TWO

"I know where Shannon is."

Mac and Shelby both turned to stare at Chase. "How could you know where she is?" she asked, thinking that maybe the stress had gotten to him. Mac seemed to take it at face value.

"Where?" Mac asked.

"I don't know exactly, but Mt. Rainier is to the east and Mt. St. Helens is to the south." Chase looked down, seemed to realize that he was only wearing boxer briefs and an undershirt, and blushed. "I'll be right back."

After he'd closed the door to the bedroom, Shelby turned to Mac. "Is this possible?"

"Oh, absolutely. Chase said he and Shannon had a deep connection. He knew that she was in trouble of some kind. Now that Shannon knows Chase is in the picture, she's probably sending out very specific messages to him."

"Unbelievable." Shelby shook her head. Chase hurried out of the bedroom again, this time fully dressed in his dirty fatigues.

"What exactly do you know, and how?" Mac asked.

"I was almost asleep. Just lying there, drifting, you know? Then I started to get these pictures." Chase paced across the room and back again. "At first, I just thought I was starting to dream, but it felt different." Chase shrugged and grinned. "This must sound kind of crazy."

"Not at all, Chase." Mac quirked an eyebrow, poured a cup of coffee, and handed it to Shelby. She wasn't sure if he was the kind of guy who bothered to notice that she drank it endlessly, or if he just figured it would be a way to keep her mouth occupied for a few minutes. She knew what the eyebrow quirk was about, though.

"After a few minutes, I realized that it felt like Shannon. And she was sending the images in a loop. First there was a large, gray building with a wall around it, then a snow-capped mountain, and then Mt. St. Helens. I recognized it from pictures of when it erupted."

"And you're convinced she's there?" Shelby asked, in spite of Mac's warning glance.

"Absolutely."

"The snow-capped mountain could have been Mt. Rainier." Shelby opened up her laptop and turned it on. "Is she sending you pictures of what she's seeing?" She opened her browser, did a search on Mt. Rainier, and clicked on a photo.

"That's it, but from a different angle. Chase pointed to a spot on the map. "It was more like it might look from here. How soon can we get there?"

"Hold on, cowboy. What do you mean 'we'?" Shelby held up a hand. "There's no way you're going there with me."

"There's no way I'm not." Chase straightened and clasped his hands behind his back in a military stance. Respectful but determined.

"We could use him, Shelby," Mac said.

"We?" She lifted an eyebrow at him. "You aren't going either."

"Why not?"

"This is my op. I don't work with partners. Besides, neither one of you is trained for this."

Mac frowned. "You think I'm not capable? I *did* complete the basic field agent training at Quantico."

"I'm Force Recon. I'm trained for anything," Chase said, taking some of the wind out of Mac's sails.

"Training at Quantico is not the same as being on a dangerous op." Shelby looked at Chase. "And I know that you are well-trained and experienced, but not for this."

"Actually, I don't see how you can do this without us," Mac said mildly as he poured a cup of coffee for himself.

"How's that?" She leaned back in the chair and folded her arms across her chest.

"You need Chase to help you pinpoint where they are holding Zoe, Shannon, and Sam," Mac pointed out.

"And what do I need you for?"

Mac turned so Chase couldn't see his face and waggled his eyebrows at her. Shelby frowned to prevent a fit of giggles.

"Actually, I have the most firsthand knowledge of Carlson and Thomas, and I might be able to increase the communication between Shannon and Chase."

Shelby could have argued, but what was the point? Mac was right. She could use both of them and would probably need them at some stage. Especially since she was about to cut Ethan out of the loop.

"Mac, you take Chase out and do some shopping. Get whatever clothes you'll need for a week. It'll still be chilly at times up there, so shop accordingly. I have to make some calls, and then we'll leave." After Mac and Chase left, she punched in Ethan's number.

"Got anything yet?"

Ethan sighed, and she could visualize him rubbing the furrows on his forehead. "I told you it would take some time."

"I know." Shelby hesitated. This wasn't going to be easy. "Ethan, I've decided that I need to go alone on this for now."

"Go alone?" Ethan chuckled, but there was no humor in it. "That's ridiculous. And unnecessary."

"I think it's the only way. I'm not saying you're leaking information deliberately, but everything I've told you has gotten back to The Center."

She waited a few seconds, but Ethan was silent. "It's the only way until you find the leak."

Ethan sighed heavily. "I understand, but I don't think it's a good idea, Shelby."

"I don't like it myself, but I don't see any other way."

"Do you have a lead on them? Did you find something?"

Shelby said nothing, and it was one of the hardest things she'd ever done.

"Where will you be going?"

"I'm not telling you. I can't risk it this time. You just find the leak."

"I don't like you being out there with no backup."

"There's no other way. Listen, I'll call in. See how things are on your end."

"I'll find the leak, Shelby."

Ethan disconnected, and she felt like she was adrift at sea. Suddenly everything was different. She'd worked ops alone for years at the FSA. But Ethan had always been there with resources, intel— whatever she needed to get the job done. Now, she not only didn't have that, she had Chase and Mac along for the ride.

Then she had an awful realization. Ethan had given in pretty easily. And for a good reason. He had resources. He figured he could track her and find out where she was going. He also could track her credit card use and know exactly where she was. Even using cash wouldn't stop him completely. He had the access to find out if she bought airline tickets or rented cars. And she'd told him about the phone number on the cell phone after the highway chase, so he'd be suspecting that they were heading to Washington.

Crap.

✦ ✦ ✦

Shelby's cell phone chirped, and she looked at the number before answering. Crap. She'd forgotten to return Paige's phone call last night.

"Paige, what's up?" She'd hired Paige about four months earlier. Shelby had been investigating a case for a lawyer, and Paige had been on the police team assigned to the same case. They'd ended up in tight quarters with some bad guys and found that they worked pretty well together.

"There's someone here who wants to talk to you," Paige said.

"Paige, I really don't have time right now. Whatever it is can wait."

"No, this can't wait. Just a sec."

"Shelby?"

"Zoe? What the hell are you doing there? I thought The Center had taken you and Shannon and Sam."

"They got Shannon and Sam. I'd gotten out of the car to find the agents. I guess they didn't realize that I was even there." Zoe paused. "Shelby, they killed the pilot and both of the FSA agents and the guy who was in the office."

"I know, Zoe."

"I didn't know what to do, so I got a flight to Phoenix and then to here. I figured if I could get to your office, I could find you."

"You did the right thing." Shelby was impressed with her ability to think in a crisis, to take action. "Just stay there with Paige. Do you have a place to stay?"

"Paige is letting me bunk with her."

"All right. Just stay there. After we get Shannon and Sam, I'll come pick you up and we'll finish this."

"You found them?"

"We think so."

"Don't let those bastards get away with this, Shelby. Can you use my help?"

"No! I've got more help than I need right now. Just stay put with Paige and put her back on the phone." Shelby waited until Paige answered. "Paige, I'm going to be in Washington soon. I might have to call you to help with this."

"No problem. Hey, I thought I'd use Zoe for the next bouncer gig. Is that all right with you?"

"If you think she can handle it."

"Shelby, she's a biker. And I don't mean a biker chick. She can handle herself, and I could use the help."

"Good. Just be ready for my phone call."

"I thought we'd be flying to Washington."

"We will, tomorrow." Shelby glanced over at Mac and then in the rearview mirror at Chase. He was sacked out in the back seat. How did everyone in the military acquire the ability to sleep at will?

"Tomorrow? Why the delay?"

"I need to see Mel for something."

"Really?" Mac smiled. "It'll be nice to visit with her again."

Four hours later they were rolling through the gates of *Serenity Haven*. Bear's warm, deep voice through the intercom welcomed her back like a big, comfortable hug. Mel pulled Shelby into her office, gave her a cup of coffee, and listened silently while Shelby briefed her on the situation.

"I'll need IDs for Mac and Chase, radar detector, radar jammer, something to conceal the weapons from airport security." Shelby paused. "And weapons. All I've got is my Desert Eagle. Chase has a Glock 9MM. That's about it until I can get back to my agency."

"Don't worry about weapons. I've got anything you need. No way I want you walking in there not fully armed."

"You're an angel."

"Not according to my enemies," Mel said with a chuckle. "Let's get the boys in here for a photo session."

Shelby stepped out of Mel's office to the large common room and motioned to Mac and Chase. "Come on. This is your photo op."

Mel led them into another room, took their pictures, and waved them away. Shelby watched as she sat down at the computer and punched in commands. A few seconds later, another machine whirred to life.

Minutes later, Mel handed her two perfect Washington State Driver's Licenses.

"That should do it."

"You sure you don't need anything?" Mel asked. "I can set you up with some sweet ID. License, library card, credit cards, the works."

"Thanks, but I've got mine with me."

"FSA stuff?"

"No. It's an ID I've been growing for a few years. It'll stand up to anything. It's as real as my regular ID."

"Good girl! I knew you'd learn something from hanging around me." Mel put an arm around her. "Must be hard cutting Ethan off like that."

"It feels strange." She shrugged. "But I've worked cases without him since I opened my agency."

"This isn't a case, Shelby, it's an op—there's a difference." Mel sat back and crossed her arms. "How did he take it?"

"About how you'd expect. He wasn't thrilled. And knowing Ethan, he'll try to track me. That's why I wanted the fake IDs. Crap!" Shelby slammed her fist down on the desk as another thought exploded in her head. "I'll bet he's going to go a step further than that."

"Have the airports watched?" Mel asked.

"He wouldn't have the manpower to do it normally, but the FBI is working this op too. They have offices in every major city."

"It'd be easy enough to have them stake out the airports for a couple of days," Mel agreed. "Better get you and the boys some disguises and some ID to go with

279

them. No point in taking any chances."

A couple of hours later, Mac, Chase, and Shelby all had disguises and IDs that matched. They weren't deep but they didn't have to be. Just good enough to get them on a plane without Ethan's men recognizing them.

"Now, is there anything more I can do?" Mel asked.

"There really isn't, Mel."

"I'm still amazed that Zoe had the presence of mind to get away from The Center, and even more amazed that she went to your agency."

"Me too. She's a smart cookie."

"You could use someone like her." Mel nodded.

"Yeah, if I had any work for her to do. Besides, she might be smart, but she's not a PI. I'd have a lot of training to do."

"That's what I thought when I recruited you." Mel cleared her throat. "Besides, I made a few phone calls. You'll probably be getting some work soon."

"Mel, what did you do?" Shelby asked.

"Nothing really. I just called a few friends and told them about a very good PI agency."

"And of course, you'd have friends who would need a PI agency."

"Of course."

"Thanks, Mel. I really appreciate it. And I won't let you down."

"I know that." Mel logged off the computer and turned to Shelby. "I'm fond of Sam and Shannon. Anything you need—me, Bear, equipment, anything at all—we'll be there."

"I'll keep that in mind." Shelby glanced at her watch. "Time to roll." They had reservations on a flight from Phoenix to Seattle, leaving in five hours. Mel had shipped the guns to a private mail center to be held until Shelby arrived.

Shelby left the car at Mel's to be returned to the rental company in Flagstaff in a few days. Mel loaned her a car for the trip. They left the car in long-term parking where Mel would have someone pick it up later.

Shelby entered the airport first, leaving Mac and Chase instructions to follow her at ten-minute intervals. After picking up her ticket at the counter, she slung her briefcase strap over her shoulder and wheeled her carry-on suitcase to the gate. She spotted one agent in the open eating area of a fast-food restaurant and another reading a paper in the sitting area of a gate. Neither of them took a second look at her as she clipped along smartly in her two-inch heels, business suit, red wig, and glasses. She stopped at a newsstand and perused the magazines while waiting for Mac and Chase to appear.

Chase walked by first. Since there was no disguising his military bearing, they'd dressed him in an army uniform and buzzed his head to get rid of the distinctive jarhead haircut. She doubted they would be looking very hard for him, and the disguise seemed to do the trick. He walked to the gate, got a boarding pass, and took a seat facing the windows at the next gate.

Shelby figured they'd be looking harder for Mac and her, so she'd spent more time on his disguise. He had a good tan, so she'd chosen cut off jeans, an old tee shirt with a surfing emblem, sandals, and a long, wavy, blond wig. The hardest thing to cover up was his Australian accent, so they'd decided to put his knowledge of sign language to use and have him pose as a deaf person.

She watched as Mac took a seat at the gate next to the one for their flight. Mac leafed through a surfing magazine, and Chase pulled a sheaf of papers with government and army emblems from his battered briefcase. The agent watching the gate didn't give them a second glance.

Part of making a disguise work was in the details. Give anyone watching every reason to believe you're the person you're pretending to be. Anyone catching a glimpse of the army documents Chase was reading would automatically assume that he was an army officer—why else would he have army documents with him?

Shelby paid for a *Wall Street Journal* and rolled her suitcase to a chair several seats away from Chase. The flight began to board, and she glanced at both men to make sure they weren't moving yet. She knew that if Ethan had been able to convince them to watch the airports, it would probably be on a limited basis. Only the major airports and for no longer than twenty-four hours. They were just past the twenty-four-hour mark now. Her guess was that as soon as this flight was boarded, the agents would all leave.

The last person trundled down the corridor for the flight, and the agent took a last look around. He checked his watch, and then walked away from the gate.

The attendant announced the last boarding call for the flight, and Shelby, Mac, and Chase walked over and disappeared into the corridor.

The flight was uneventful, and they landed at Sea-Tac three hours later. Shelby exited the plane first, checking the gate for agents, and was relieved that there were none. She walked to the restroom and took the large, handicapped stall. The wig, suit, and heels were packed into the suitcase, and she pulled on jeans, tee shirt, sneakers, and a baseball cap. Less than half an hour later, she cruised by short-term parking in the four-wheel-drive truck she'd rented and picked up Chase and Mac.

Shelby parked in front of the private mail center and told Chase to stay put while she and Mac picked up the crate Mel had shipped to them.

"I'm picking up a crate for Shelly Parton," she said when the pimply-faced clerk finally gave them his attention. "It was shipped to Nirvana Corporation." She had to wonder just how many corporations Mel had in different cities.

"Sure. That'd be the big one that came in this morning. Must be something special. Had a lot of insurance on it." He looked inquiringly at her.

"Collectible artifacts for a trade show," she said.

"Figured something like that. You want to pull your truck 'round back? I'll bring it out on a dolly."

"Sure." Mac and Shelby walked back to the truck.

"Lies just roll off your tongue, don't they?" Mac grinned and shook his head.

Shelby shrugged. "I practice. That's why it comes so easy to me." They got in the truck, and she pulled it around to the alley.

"I should be worried, but for some reason, I'm only amused."

She grinned at him and got out to help the clerk load the crate into the back of the truck.

It was only mid-afternoon. They had several hours to look for the place before the sun set. Shelby turned off I-5 and headed east toward the point Chase had identified on the map.

Shelby still had a hard time wrapping her mind around the existence of psychic ability. Especially at that level. But she really hoped it was true and the building Chase had seen was where they were holding Shannon and Sam. She drove past miles and miles of farmland, areas of forest, and a few small towns.

"We're getting closer." Chase sat in the back seat, leaning forward so that his head was almost between Mac's and Shelby's. "I can feel it."

Shelby could only wonder what that felt like, having not a smidgen of psychic ability herself.

"Chase, are you linked with Shannon now?" Mac asked.

"I think so." Chase closed his eyes and concentrated. "Feels weird. But it definitely feels like Shannon."

"Just stay with it," Mac encouraged him. Shelby sighed and had to admit that they'd been right. She did need both of them.

"Wait!"

Shelby slowed the truck and pulled off the road onto the shoulder.

"It's back there. About half a mile. There's a dirt road off to the right." Chase grinned. "This is getting easier. It's like she's showing me exactly how to get there."

She turned the truck around and headed off on the dirt road. The road started to climb a bit and after a few miles took a sharp turn to the east. Then they saw it.

A dark gray building stood in the middle of a clearing that looked to be about ten acres. The building was surrounded by a solid wall about twelve feet high with razor wire strung across the top. There were tall guard towers at each corner.

How the hell was she going to get into that place?

CHAPTER TWENTY-THREE

"You folks want some coffee?" The plump, middle-aged waitress hovered the glass pot over the cups on the table.

"I would, thanks." Shelby pulled her hand back quickly to avoid being splashed with the hot brew, as the waitress poured from a height of over a foot. Mac agreed to coffee, and Chase ordered a glass of milk.

"Special's meatloaf and mashed potatoes with green beans or peas and carrots." She pointed to their menus with her pen. "I'll get your milk and come back for your orders."

Shelby, Mac, and Chase had gotten motel rooms in a small town a few miles from the road that led to the big, dark building and were having dinner in a small café. Shelby was starving, and meatloaf sounded as good as anything else on the menu. She laid the tattered menu down and sipped her coffee, which she figured was just a couple degrees shy of boiling.

"So, where do we go from here?" Chase asked.

"We need to confirm that Shannon and Sam are there. Which means we need to find a way inside."

"I guess driving up to the gate is a bad idea." Chase returned to studying his menu.

"It's a dangerous idea," she said. The waitress was headed back to their table, and Mac and Chase put down their menus.

"Here's your milk. Now, what can I get for you?"

Mac and Shelby ordered the special; Chase chose a burger and fries, an order of chicken strips, and told the waitress to come back later for his dessert order. Shelby shook her head. If she carried that much muscle she could eat that way too.

"You folks just passing through?" the waitress asked.

"We'll be staying for a couple of days," Shelby said. "Thought we'd do some hiking."

"You want to be careful in that forest, honey. Somebody gets lost in there most every year." She tapped the pen on her order pad. "And stay away from the Fortress. Hear tell they don't appreciate anybody getting too close."

"The Fortress?" Shelby asked as casually as she could.

"Well, we been calling it that since it was first built, about ten years back. It was a prison then." She shook her head. "Thank the Lord that didn't last too long. I can tell you, nobody around here was too thrilled about having a prison so close."

"Did they close it then?"

"Sure did. Not more than five years after they built the dang thing. I heard it was too much trouble getting people to work out there and too expensive getting supplies in. Guess they shoulda thought of that before they spent our tax dollars building it."

"What is it now?"

"I couldn't really say. I heard it was bought up by some research company. Folks around here hoped that that might open up some jobs for the locals, but they didn't seem to need any help with whatever they're doing there."

"That's too bad."

"Well, who knows, you know?" The waitress cocked her head toward the kitchen and then turned around. "Howard, how many times I gotta tell you not to holler at me when I'm with the customers?" she yelled.

"Dang fool got no class at all." She shook her head and frowned. "Anyways, I suppose they're doing something up there. Folks tell me they see some kind of trucks turn onto that dirt road that leads up there every couple of weeks."

"Why do you say they don't want visitors?"

"Well, cause they don't. A couple of guys around here drove up there thinking to ask about some work, and they said it was guarded just like when it was a prison. They didn't even get inside to fill out an application. Guard just said they weren't hiring and sent those men on their way."

"Not very friendly of them."

"Not a bit. But whoever they are, they don't come into town." She shrugged. "Guess they just want to be left alone. I'll get your orders in now. Just holler if you need anything."

"Interesting," Mac said as she left the table.

"It's got to be them. We need to get in there." Chase leaned forward like he was about to bolt from his seat.

Shelby held her hand up to quiet Chase. "First, we need to confirm that it's really Thomas and Carlson in there."

"We need to recon the place. Find out what their security is and how we can get around it." Chase frowned. "We can check out the exterior security easily enough, but the interior will be tricky."

"The only way to check out the interior is to get someone in there," Shelby agreed. She really wished she could have contacted Ethan. He had sources that could get answers faster than she could. But it wasn't worth the chance. Besides, it wasn't like she didn't have any resources at all.

"Parker Security and Investigation."

That brought a smile to Shelby's face. "Paige, Shelby here."

"Hey, Shelby. What do you need?"

"Some research. I'm hoping to confirm Shannon and Sam's location."

"Sure. What can I do?" Paige's voice had taken on a note of excitement, and that was one of the reasons Shelby had hired her. She was always eager for something new.

"Basically, I need you to find out who bought an old prison located a few miles outside of Elk's Point."

"Where is that?"

"Washington. Just west of the Mt. Rainier National Park. It would have been sold a few years ago. Don't have an exact date."

"Sure. No problem. What all do you need on it?"

"Who bought it, whether it was a person or a corporation. Who's paying the property taxes. And any other businesses that person or corporation might have." Shelby paused for a moment, thinking of what else she could use. "After you get that, I'll have some other research for you."

"And I suppose you need all this tomorrow?"

"Nope. Needed it yesterday."

"I'll see how much of it I can get online tonight and then make some phone calls tomorrow. Anything else?"

"How's everything at the office?"

"Excellent, as usual. Why? Didn't you think I could handle it?" Paige's voice had taken on a tone of defensiveness. Shelby thought she'd have to do something about that someday. Then, again, maybe experience and time would take care of it better than she could.

"If I didn't, I wouldn't have left you in charge." Shelby moved the phone to her other ear and reached for a paper cup of coffee. "Any new business in the works?"

"Nothing to scream about. Had a woman in yesterday who wants us to find out if her husband is having an affair."

"Great. Can't have too many of those cases."

"I told her we'd check him out. It pays the bills, and it's no worse than the bouncer jobs."

"How's Zoe?"

"Hard to say. She doesn't talk much. But she went to the bouncer gig with me the other night. Did a bang up job."

"That's good to hear. I need one more thing from you. Call Ethan Calder and ask him if he has any information for me." She gave Paige Ethan's cell phone number. "And, Paige, you are not to even give him a tiny hint as to where I am. And just to be safe, don't mention Zoe either."

"Problem with your former handler?"

"No, but information is leaking that's getting in the way of me getting the job done. Ethan doesn't need to know where I am or what I'm doing. But if he has any info for me I could sure use it."

"More coffee?" Mac asked holding the thermal pot over her cup. Shelby nodded and held her cup out.

"Shelby, did I just hear a man's voice?" Paige's voice had a smirk in it, and Shelby thought she would have to do something about that too.

"It's business. He's with the FBI."

"Uh huh."

"Just call me on my cell as soon as you find anything." Shelby flipped the phone closed and sipped her coffee. She'd been refusing to consider the situation with Mac. Of course, she'd been busy, what with being shot at, finding Chase, getting to Washington. It wasn't like she was actively avoiding the issue. Besides, she didn't really know that there was an issue.

They made love. Which was good. Really, really good. And they liked being around each other. Most of the time. Probably, there was nothing to consider, really. Just let it go whichever way it was going. Until there was a problem. She was jerked out of her thoughts when Chase knocked and came in.

He had on an olive drab tee shirt tucked neatly into fatigue pants which were tucked neatly into combat boots. A matching camouflage duffle bag sat next to his combat boots. Where the hell had they gone shopping?

"I'm ready," he announced as if she should know what that meant.

"Ready for what?" Invading a third world country?

"We need to recon the Fortress. Find out what the exterior defenses are so we're prepared to take them down."

"Tonight?" Her thoughts had been centered on Mac and what might be happening in that king-sized bed later. Midnight reconnaissance maneuvers at the

Fortress didn't exactly figure into her plans.

"No point in waiting. We go in, check it out tonight. Then when we get the intel on the interior security and come up with a plan, we're good to go."

He had a point. Still she didn't like the fact that it wasn't her idea.

Shelby, Mac, and Chase were about fifty yards from the southeast guard tower, lying on their stomachs on the forest floor. Just beyond their position, the land surrounding the Fortress had been cleared. It looked like someone had used Agent Orange on the ground. No grass, no bushes, not even a dead tree stump. A few hardy weeds struggled out of the ground. Figured. The same weeds populated her yard.

They watched and made note of how many men occupied the tower. Then they moved to the next tower. And the next, and the next. Finally, they were back at the southeast tower. It appeared that each tower was manned by a single guard, while two guards walked the perimeter inside the wall. The walking guards and the tower guards changed places every two hours. Shelby didn't know where the other two guards came from, but assumed they were on some kind of guard duty inside the building.

Chase used hand motions to direct her vision to the tall poles about twenty feet outside the walls. Some kind of electronic equipment was mounted at the tops of the poles. Chase had brought a pair of night vision binoculars, and she motioned for him to pass them over. The boxes appeared innocuous enough, but they had to be there for a reason. Shelby looked at their positions in relation to each other and figured they had to provide some perimeter detection.

She motioned Chase and Mac back into the forest another twenty yards, told them to expect some commotion, and returned to the edge of the trees. Her hands fumbled around on the forest floor until she came across a pinecone. She crouched and threw the cone toward the wall. Nothing. Probably wasn't big enough. But anything bigger might garner the attention of the guard in the tower closest to her. She picked up a section of a fallen branch and waited. The ground guard passed by the front gate and out of sight. Then the tower guard stood up and stretched, and turned away from her. She heaved the branch with all her strength and was rewarded by a flash of lights that burst from the southeast and southwest towers on either side of the front gate.

Shelby hurried back to where Chase and Mac waited, motioning them to silence. The front gates opened and three armed guards walked out. They checked the ground, walking toward the forest. Shelby held her breath as they ventured several yards into the trees with powerful flashlights.

"Nothing here. Must have been another freakin' animal," one of the guards said.

"You think so?" another one asked.

"Yeah. Happens a couple times a week. Some creature crawls into the laser beam field and sets off the lights and alarms."

Laser beam field. Crap.

CHAPTER TWENTY-FOUR

Shelby motioned to Chase to hand over the night vision binoculars again, which he did, although he looked like a kid parting with one of his favorite toys. She slung them around her neck and climbed up a tree until she was high enough to be able to look down into the Fortress. Not that there was much to see in the wee hours of the morning. But, she got a good look at the guards in the towers and could see that inside the gates there was a short driveway leading to a small parking area. The wall stood about thirty yards from the building all around. The building was massive, and she felt her confidence fade a bit as she considered how they were going to get in, and then how they were going to find Shannon and Sam.

The limb Shelby was sitting on jiggled, and she looked down to see Chase coming up after her. He paused at her limb, motioned for the binoculars, and climbed higher. He'd been observing the Fortress for several minutes when Shelby felt the tree move and saw that Mac was joining them. Noisily. She put her finger to her lips in the universal sign for *be quiet* and frowned at him. He slowed down a bit but finally made it up to her limb, then tugged on Chase's pant leg, and motioned for the binoculars.

Great. It was a little party. She was going to have to explain about this being her op again. After Mac had a minute or two with the binoculars, she took them back and motioned him down the tree. Chase and Shelby followed, and they all crawled away from the Fortress for a ways, and then jogged back to the truck.

"Impressive," Chase said as they headed back to the motel.

"Makes me wonder what all they've got going on in there. They didn't have anything near this for security in Tucson." The thought of them doing something even worse than they were doing in Tucson made her blood run cold.

"Looked like military guards to me," Chase said.

"Not possible," Shelby argued. "It would have to be a government operation to have military guards. Maybe they're mercenaries."

"That might be, but they were definitely military at some point. You can tell by the way they walked, the way they stood." Chase frowned. "You're sure this isn't a government operation?"

"God, I hope not." Shelby shook her head. "If it is, it's gone real wrong somewhere."

"It just feels weird," Chase said. "Mercenaries usually aren't so disciplined. Even the ones that are ex-military. And they're too straight, too clean, too neat to be mercenaries."

"True," she agreed. "Most ex-military go into the mercenary arena because they can't hack it in the military."

"Former military, then," Mac said. "But I'd bet they think they're guarding a government center."

"That could be." Chase nodded. "My dad is retired military, and he gets called occasionally to do a job just because of his military career."

"That would explain why all the guards were older. I don't think any of them looked under late thirties, early forties." Shelby pondered the situation for a moment. Was this to their advantage or not?

"One thing for sure," Chase said. "If they're ex-military who think they're guarding a government center, we sure as hell don't want to get caught by them."

"I would imagine that the doctors have instructed them to shoot first and ask questions later," Mac said.

Well, that was a happy thought. Getting shot at by her own government while trying to do a job for them.

"Shelby?"

"What?" She recognized Paige's voice but it took her a moment to remember why she'd be calling. Untangling her legs from Mac, the sheets, the blankets, and a pillow that had somehow ended up at her feet, she sat on the edge of the bed. Mac grunted so she stuffed the pillow into his arms. He smiled and seemed to drift off again.

"Did I wake you?"

Shelby checked the clock. Nine in the morning. "No, not at all. What've you got?"

"I did wake you."

"I just said you didn't. Now spill."

"No, you said 'no, not at all.' That always means yes when you say it."

She really had to stop saying that. "What do you have?"

"Okay. First of all a message from Ethan. He said to tell you that some of the files you downloaded from The Center's computers started to self-destruct as soon as they opened them."

"Self-destruct?"

"Evidently there was a virus attached that just ate the files as soon as they were opened without a password."

"None of the files were password protected?"

"Exactly. Somebody named Josh said they didn't appear to be password protected just so if anyone tried to open them, the virus would be activated." Paige paused, obviously reading from her notes. "He said that if they'd known about the password, then they would have broken that first and the files would still be intact."

"Did Ethan say what files they were?" She'd

already gotten the analysis of some of The Center's files about their experiments. What files could be more important than those?

"He said it was files that he believes would have led them to The Center's financial source and to the people who were willing to buy the meta-humans."

That must have pissed Ethan off. Pissed her off a bit too. "What else have you got?"

"I found out who bought the prison lands and building. A corporation called New Millennium. Haven't found a person's name associated with it yet, but I'm still working on it."

"That's all?"

"Nope. I also found a research center owned by the same corporation. Called Fortress Bio-Psychological Research. Again no names yet, but I did find a list of suppliers."

"You got supplier names?"

"Yep. Everyone has a credit history. Even corporations. No real surprises. Medical suppliers, linen suppliers, and a food service supplier. I'm working on getting more information on that."

"I'd rather know that Ruth Carlson or Jonah Thomas are linked to the Fortress."

"I'll see what I can do. At least I have an opening in one of the suppliers."

"What's that?"

"I have a friend who works for one of them in the billing office. She can get me details on what they've bought, how often, stuff like that."

"Good work. Call me when you have more." Shelby flipped the cell phone shut and looked at Mac.

He was sleeping peacefully, hair tousled, long, muscular body stretched out in a tangle of linens. He looked comfortable. Too comfortable. If she was awake, he should be too. And she knew just how to wake him up. But first, maybe she'd brush her teeth and take a few tangles out of her hair.

Shelby slipped into the bathroom, brushed her teeth, ran a brush through her hair, and then used her fingers to fluff it up a bit. Then the bathroom door opened.

"Morning, love." Mac smiled sleepily at her.

"You're awake."

"You sound disappointed."

"No, not at all." She pulled the brush through her hair again. "I'm going to take a shower."

"Good idea."

Yeah. Not as good as the idea she'd had about five minutes earlier, though. She turned the water on, waited for it to warm up a smidgen, and stepped into the stall. She lathered her hair, rinsed it, and slathered on some conditioner.

"Mind if I join you? It'll save time." Mac stepped into the shower stall, which was a bit small for two people, so they ended up pressed up against each other.

"Save time? Are we in a hurry to get somewhere?"

"Well, I don't know about you, but I'm starving." Mac bent his head and started to nibble on her neck.

"Really? Then we should hurry up so we can have breakfast."

"That isn't what I'm starving for."

Yeah, neither was she.

By the time she'd showered a second time, and she and Mac had dressed, Chase was knocking at the door. Over breakfast, Shelby filled them in on the information Paige had given her.

"Look, we know that Thomas and Carlson are in there along with Shannon and probably other innocent victims." Chase shook his head and shoveled in more eggs, hashed-brown potatoes, and bacon. "I say we just go in and get the job done."

"I need to make sure before we move." She sighed at the look of disgust on Chase's face. "Otherwise we're opening up a huge can of worms."

"Trust me, Shelby. This is the place. I can feel it."

Crap. That psychic stuff again.

"Tell you what. If I can't get confirmation by tomorrow one way or the other, we'll go in. Happy?"

"No, but I can deal with that." Chase ate more food and then looked up again. "I'm getting that Shannon and her kid haven't been touched yet. But it's only a matter of time."

"Can you get actual thoughts from her?" Mac seemed to be fascinated by all this psychic stuff. Shelby was fascinated too, but in a way that made her a little queasy.

"Not really thoughts. Not words, anyway. Mostly I just get emotions. Right now she's tense but unharmed."

"I gotta go make a couple of calls." Shelby wiped her mouth on a napkin and pulled a twenty out of her pocket. "See you guys back at the motel."

Mac picked up the twenty and stuffed it in her breast pocket, copping a subtle feel. "I'll get breakfast."

"Bring me back a large coffee." She resisted the impulse to kiss him and hustled her butt out of the restaurant. Shelby punched in Mel's number as she walked the half block to the motel.

"Serenity Haven."

"Hey, Mel. Shelby here."

"Is everything all right? Do you have Shannon and Sam?"

"Not yet. I need a favor."

"What?"

"I want Bear."

"I know, dear. Most women feel that way about him eventually."

"Not sexually."

"Oh." Mel snickered. "I guess you have that all wrapped up, huh?"

"Mel!"

"Lighten up, Shelby. I'll have him there—hold on."

Shelby heard the tapping of the keyboard.

"He'll be there at four-fifteen. Alaska Airlines. What else do you need?"

Shelby rattled off a list of items that she absolutely

needed; then a list of stuff that she'd like to have, but could do without.

"No problem. He'll have luggage, so have someone pick him up at the baggage claim at four-forty."

"Mac will be driving a black Ford 250." Shelby paused. "I can't thank you enough for this."

"You will. Someday I'll call in this chip."

"Anything, Mel. I mean that."

"I know, and I'll hold you to it"

Chris looked at the caller id on her phone before she picked it up. Three-six-zero area code. She started the trace and then picked up the call at the start of the third ring.

"Jackson."

"Chris. How is everything? I haven't heard from you in so long."

"Because I haven't had anything to tell you."

"That's too bad, Chris."

"Listen, Jonah, I can't beat information out of anyone. I have to be subtle." Only another twenty-five seconds.

"Oh, I understand. I just wanted to remind you of the photos."

"Believe me, I haven't forgotten about them."

"You wouldn't be holding out on me, would you?"

"No way, Jonah. My career's too important to me." She paused a moment. "But you know that."

"Indeed, I do. That's why I'm keeping them close to me. You might say they're in a virtual fortress." He chuckled in a way that made her shiver.

"I'll try to get something for you, but I have to tell you that right now the FBI and the FSA are at a stand-still. Wherever you've gone, they've lost you." Fifteen more seconds. Please, God, let him stay on the line that long.

"That's what I wanted to hear. Still, I think I'll keep the photos for insurance. I'm sure you understand."

"Damn you, Jonah!" Chris snarled and glanced at the trace. Only a few more seconds and she'd have his location.

"I'll be in touch."

Chris looked at the trace. Damn! The trace hadn't completed. But at least she'd narrowed it down to a location in southwestern Washington. She punched up a map and scanned it. It was good enough. She'd gotten within a few miles of the actual location from which he was calling. That wouldn't have been good enough in a city, but this area was in the middle of nowhere. No large towns nearby.

She punched in the URL for the travel page and checked flights. She could be there by four this after-noon. Chris leaned back in her chair and considered the implications of what she was about to do.

It didn't matter. Her career was at stake. She had to get those damn photos and negatives away from Jonah. Otherwise, she'd be at his mercy forever. She couldn't live with that.

"Shelby? I still don't have any names. And that can mean only one thing. Anyone going to this much trouble to keep the name a secret has a reason," Paige said. "But I have some excellent info for you."

"Shoot."

"I got a copy of the original building plans from the state archives, and my friend who works at the supplier for the Fortress? Her boyfriend is the truck driver who delivers to them."

"Building plans will help a lot. Have you interviewed the driver?"

"No need. This is the really good news. My friend said that the sales representatives ride along with the drivers on the remote deliveries sometimes and make their sales calls while the drivers are making the deliveries."

"Has the sales rep gone with this guy before?"

"Nope. There was no reason to because they weren't ordering much. But suddenly, last week, the order just about quadrupled. Perfect time for the sales rep to make a call, wouldn't you think?"

"That fits. They would have upped their order because they knew they were moving here from Tucson. What does this company deliver to them?"

"Food, mostly, and some linens. Some bulk food, frozen meals, fresh fruit and veggies, baked goods. According to my friend, it's just about everything you'd need for a lot of people."

"How many people?"

"Before the order was upped, she thinks it was enough to feed four to eight people. Deliveries were once a week. With the increased order, she figures it's enough for twenty or so people, and they get deliveries twice a week."

"That fits too. Before it would have only been the guards. Now they're feeding themselves, additional staff, and probably a few prisoners."

"So, he's making a delivery this afternoon, and I'm going along with him as the sales rep."

"Whoa! Paige, I'm not sure about sending you in there."

"It's cool, Shelby. I've already made business cards, I've got a really cool suit, and I'll be up there in a few hours. Come on, Shelby. You need this information, and you can't go in because they know what you look like."

"I could change my appearance," Shelby argued, but she knew Paige was right. It would be better for her to go in. The only disguise Shelby had with her was the business suit and red wig. The doctors would see through that in a heartbeat, and it would be impossible to get a really good disguise together in a few hours.

Paige was waiting somewhat patiently while Shelby talked herself into letting Paige do it. For someone who always worked alone, she was certainly ccumulating a lot of people. Still, it seemed to be the thing to do. Just felt weird.

"Okay. Get up here now. I want to have time to brief you before you go in." Shelby was sure she heard a little squeal of delight, but Paige managed to contain it before she could change her mind. "But first, look in the closet in my office. There's a large black case on the floor. Bring it with you."

"No problem."

"And Paige? Bring Zoe with you."

CHAPTER TWENTY-FIVE

"Hold still." Shelby was trying to get the tiny camera attached to Paige's lapel pin.

"So, what's this guy like?"

Shelby looked up at her and shrugged. "He's nice."

"You don't go for nice guys."

"Mac is different. Besides, it's not like it's a relationship or anything. We enjoy each other, that's all." She got the camera nestled in among the silver roses on the pin and stood back. It was good. The pin completely camouflaged the tiny lens. She slipped the wire down the inside of Paige's jacket to the battery pack taped under her arm.

"There. Now move around the room." Paige walked around while Shelby watched the screen of her laptop. "Good. Now give me an audio test."

"Okay, why don't we talk a little more about your new boyfriend?" Paige giggled.

"He's not a boyfriend. I'm too old to have boyfriends."

"Whatever." Paige waved a hand, acknowledging that they weren't going to have any girl talk about Shelby's love life.

"You're sure you're ready for this?" She was worried about sending Paige into the Fortress. She was talented and eager, but she was also young and inexperienced.

"I'll be fine. It's just a sales call. Barbara gave me a little crash course on what to say. I have my business cards, and I'll only be there for half an hour." She held up her hand to prevent Shelby's imminent interruption. "I won't say or do anything to make them suspicious. My only job is to check out what kind of security they have on the inside."

"Good girl. Let's get this equipment in the truck." Shelby carried the laptop and the receiver to the door. Paige grabbed her briefcase and opened the door for her.

Zoe was talking to Chase and Kevin, the delivery truck driver. Kevin opened the back door of the truck, and Chase helped Shelby set up the equipment and cover it with boxes.

Kevin checked his watch. "Time to go. I'm due there in half an hour." Paige climbed into the truck beside him and waved at the others as they took off.

Shelby was still watching the road they'd driven down when Mac drove up in the rental truck, Bear in the passenger seat beside him.

Bear gave her a big hug and smiled at Zoe. He then went to the back to pull out his luggage. Chase grabbed one of the crates.

"Chase Harmon," he introduced himself. "You can bunk with me. I've got two beds."

"Uneventful trip?" Shelby asked.

"Almost," Bear said and looked at Mac. "Tell her."

"It's possible I saw Chris at the airport."

"Who's Chris?" Chase asked.

"Mac's SAC." Shelby turned back to Mac. "You're not certain?"

"Well, it certainly looked like her. But we were at a distance, so I can't be sure. Besides, what would she be doing here?"

"It's possible the FBI and FSA were able to locate the Fortress. They have a lot of resources."

"But then it would be a team. Why just Chris alone?"

"Are you sure she was alone?"

"I didn't see anyone around her. It's possible that she flew in separately from the team, but that doesn't really make any sense."

"Actually, it doesn't really make sense that she'd be here even if they found out about the Fortress." Shelby said. Chase and Bear reappeared, and the five of them walked back to the motel room. "Chris is the SAC of the Phoenix office, but she's not in charge of this op. I can't see why she'd come out here."

"It was probably just an over-active imagination," Mac said. "She was a distance away, and it's entirely possible that she just resembled Chris. It could have been just a coincidence."

Shelby exchanged a look with Bear. She knew from working with him that he didn't believe in coincidence any more than she did.

In the room, they gathered around the small round table and laid out what they'd observed the previous night to Bear. They then spread out the building plans Paige had brought, taking some time studying them and looking at each section carefully.

"First thing is to disable the laser beams," Bear said. "To do that I'll have to climb up one of the poles. We'll figure out which one when we get there. Usually one pole will hold the master unit that powers all the others. Once that's taken out—"

"I have to get past the gate," Shelby added. "Or go over the wall. There's a lot of light around the place, even when the laser beams don't set off the search lights."

"Shouldn't be a problem to take out a couple of lights. All we need is one dark area."

"I'm really hoping they haven't changed the floor plan too much." She looked at the blueprints again, committing them to memory a little more each time.

"They wouldn't have taken out any of the support walls. That's about all we can be sure of," Bear said.

"What do you want me to do, Shelby?" Zoe asked.

"Nothing. You'll be staying here."

"No. I want to go in. I want to be a part of the team that takes them down."

"Zoe, there's nothing for you to do."

"But I'm really good at getting into places undetected."

"I know you are. But, this is my op. We do it my way."

Zoe scowled at Shelby. "Fine."

Shelby stood up and stretched. "You guys go get some rest. I'll let you know when Paige gets back." The men left and Shelby put on a pot of coffee.

"What are you going to do when this is over?" Shelby asked Zoe.

"That's funny. Shannon asked me the same thing right before—" Zoe cleared her throat. "The weird thing is that I don't really know. I can't be a thief any more."

"Really? Why is that?"

"A friend once told me that one day something would happen, and I'd know that it was time to quit." Zoe shrugged. "And something happened."

"I see."

"Besides, I was trying to get away from it anyway. I was just doing enough to live on and get through school, until I could take the CPA exam."

Shelby laughed. "Somehow, I can't see you as a CPA."

"Why? I'm pretty good with numbers."

"I don't know. I guess I just see you as kind of active. Can't really imagine you sitting behind a desk crunching numbers."

"I hadn't thought of it that way. But it doesn't matter. I'm going to be a CPA."

"Is it just another way to steal? Maybe a safer way?"

"No! I'm tired of the stealing. It's just that I'm really good at it."

"How did it start? The stealing, I mean? I don't suppose there's a school you go to?" Shelby chuckled.

"Well, there is a school, kind of. I started when I was a kid. Stealing stuff from stores. I got caught a few times before I got good at it."

"What happened then?"

"The foster parents I was living with would send me back to the orphanage. Then I'd go to another foster family. Finally, I just ran away."

"How old were you then?"

"Fourteen. I supported myself stealing. It was better than what most runaways did."

Shelby knew she meant prostitution, and she had to agree. "And you just kept doing it? How did you graduate to the big time?"

"The big time? You mean stealing jewelry and stuff?" Zoe shrugged. "I hooked up with some other thieves. They were older, better, knew more. And they taught me what they knew."

"I see. So that was your school?"

"Pretty much. When I got older, I got my GED and tried to stop stealing for a while. I got a job with a security company." Zoe shook her head. "That just made me a better thief. Before that, safes had been my specialty. Once I knew security systems too, I was in demand."

"So you went back to being a thief?"

"I got laid off, and it was the only thing I knew how

to do. After a few years, I remembered what Black Joe had said to me about knowing when it was time to quit. So, I started school and made my plans." Zoe laughed. "I don't know why I'm telling you all this. I don't normally tell people about my life."

"I understand. I used to be the same way. Probably still am." Shelby poured two cups of coffee and handed one to Zoe. "When I was growing up, my dad was a con artist. I used to help him."

"You did?"

"Sure did. Right up until I was seventeen and met Mel. I still don't know what would have happened to me if I hadn't met her. She turned my life around."

Zoe smiled. "By the way, working with Paige was great. We had a lot of fun. She doesn't think I can't do anything just because I'm small."

"She told me you had some natural ability at handling the bikers in that bar."

"That was easy." Zoe shrugged. "I hang out in biker bars, so I know what they're like."

"You know, Zoe, you have developed a lot of interesting skills."

"I have?"

"Sure. Not everyone can sneak into a house and steal something without getting caught. You know about safes and security systems and bikers." Shelby laughed. She liked Zoe. She reminded her of herself a while back.

"Yeah, I guess. But it'd just be nice to use my talents legally, you know?"

Shelby looked at Zoe and made up her mind. Mel had reached out to her when she was young, and she figured it was time to pay that back. Whenever she'd tried to thank Mel for what she'd done, Mel had told her no thanks were necessary. Just pass it on when the time came.

"You could."

Zoe just stared at her.

"I might be needing another investigator at my agency." Shelby sipped her coffee. "You'd have to be trained, of course. At first, you'd just be answering the phones, maybe doing some bouncer gigs. And God knows I could use some help with my accounting."

"Are you serious?"

Shelby nodded. "I think I am."

"Where do you want this stuff?" Kevin carried the laptop and receiving unit. Shelby motioned him to put them both on the table and then hurried to plug everything in.

"I think I got some good stuff, Shelby. Zoe, can you help me get this thing off?" Paige motioned for Zoe to follow her to the bathroom. By the time they came back, Shelby was ready to play the footage.

"Well, that was fun, but I gotta run. Still have another delivery to do." Kevin shook Paige's hand and then everyone else's.

"Thanks, Kevin. You've been a big help.

Remember, not a word of this to anyone," Shelby said.

"And lose my secret agent status? No way!" He laughed and waved as he left.

"Okay, let's see what we've got." Shelby tapped in the commands to replay what Paige's camera and microphone had recorded.

There were good shots of the entry. The gate appeared to be electronically locked and operated by the guard who stood in the guard tower next to it. There was a camera where visitors were stopped and asked for an ID and the reason for their visit. After Kevin and Paige had been cleared by the guard, the gates swung open. Kevin had dropped Paige at the front and then driven off toward the delivery area.

She was met at the front door by another guard and escorted to a small office. Paige had fiddled with her lapel pin in order to show the cameras tucked into corners all over the place. Soon the door to the office opened, and Ruth Carlson stepped inside. There was a collective intake of breath. Absolute proof that they had the right place.

"I tried to get her to show me the kitchens. Told her I could help her with the ordering, but she didn't go for it. This was pretty much all I got on tape." Paige pointed to the monitor. "But right here Carlson left for a few minutes. She was having a conversation with someone just outside the door."

The view from Paige's pin camera shifted and moved as she walked to the door. "Damn. I was hoping the microphone picked it up."

"Give me a minute," Bear said as he settled at the keyboard and began typing in commands.

"Don't worry. You got what we needed the most. Proof that we have the right place," Shelby said.

"I've got it." Bear turned the volume on the laptop up and sat back.

"I told you, Jonah, I'll be ready to start the course of meds on three of the children tomorrow."

"I'm just anxious."

"Have you given any thought to controlling Shannon?"

"I'm actually leaning toward the lobotomy. It won't affect the fetus, and it's not like we need her psychic abilities. Only her breeding ability."

"When will you do it?"

"I suppose tomorrow. I'm growing weary of her tantrums and demands. It'll be a welcome relief to have her docile for a change."

"Dear God," Mac whispered. Bear shook his head and turned off the monitor.

"That was definitely Carlson and Thomas," Shelby said.

"So, when do we go in?" Paige asked.

"Uh uh. You don't go in at all." Shelby shook her head. "You, Zoe, Chase, and Mac will stay here and wait."

"Not likely!" Mac shook his head. "I've been in this from the beginning; I'm going to be there at the end."

"Not going to happen, Shelby." Chase crossed beefy

arms over his chest and shook his head.

"Me too." Paige planted her hands on her hips and frowned.

"I could help, Shelby. As I told you before, I'm good at getting into places undetected," Zoe said.

"No. I go in alone."

That brought on arguments from all of them. Shelby looked at Bear and jerked her head toward the door. They stepped outside, and she heard Mac tell the others to give them a few minutes as the door closed.

"What do you think, Bear?"

"I think it's your op, and you do it your way."

"No, that's what *I* think. Or what I've always thought." Shelby shook her head and leaned against the wall. "What do you really think?"

"I think you're going to have a hard time getting Shannon and Sam out of there all by yourself."

Not the words she wanted to hear, but Bear had always been honest with her. "I can get in easier by myself."

"That's true, but what about getting out with two people? And it seems like there are more people in there than just Shannon and Sam."

"It's really hard to bring others in when I'm so used to working alone."

"You called me in." Bear gave her his blindingly brilliant smile.

"Yeah, but I've worked with you before. I know I can count on you."

"Trust has never been your strong point, Falcon.

But you can't go through life never trusting."

"I trust you and I trust Mel. I even trust Ethan, pretty much." Shelby sighed as Bear continued to smile at her. "I guess I can trust Chase and Mac too."

Bear wrapped his arm around her shoulders and squeezed. "I knew you'd come to the right decision."

Bear opened the door, and they stepped inside. Shelby held her hands up to quiet their questions.

"I can't stop Mac or Chase, but I can stop you two." She pointed at Paige and Zoe. "Direct order, Paige. You don't go anywhere near the Fortress. Besides, I need you back here with the building plans. I'll be wired in case I need information from you. And you'll be here in case something goes wrong."

That wasn't exactly true. Shelby had a feeling that if things went wrong, there wouldn't be anyone left to rescue. But it placated Paige, or Paige figured there was no point in arguing.

"Why not me?" Zoe asked.

"I agree that you have some exceptional talents, Zoe. But, not this time." Zoe's face fell and Shelby grinned. "Believe me, you'll have plenty of other opportunities to get in trouble with me and Paige."

Zoe grinned.

"She will?" Paige asked. "When? What happened?"

"Shelby offered me a job," Zoe said.

"Great." Paige smiled, but it looked a little forced. Shelby decided she'd deal with that later, if it became necessary.

"I'd suggest that we all get a little sleep while we can. We'll meet back here at 1700 hours." Shelby held the door while everyone left for their own rooms.

Chris crouched in a dense clump of bushes and thought about how she was going to get inside the gates. She'd had no idea it would be so well guarded. But it was still early, and maybe they'd reduce the number of guards in a couple of hours. She'd hiked several miles to get here, and she could use the time to rest and plan.

So far, her only plan was to get the photos and negatives from Jonah. If that involved killing him, she really didn't have a problem with it. He was not going to rule her life any longer.

She sat back and considered the possibilities of getting in. She had the equipment to scale the wall, but they probably had that alarmed. The only other option seemed to be just walking up to the front gate and announcing herself. Jonah would let her in, thinking that she had information for him. At the very least, he'd want to know how she found him. Still, she preferred getting in unannounced. She would wait and see if some of the guards went off duty in a while.

She was almost dozing off when she heard the noise. She crouched down further into the bushes and watched as people walked past, not more than fifteen feet from where she sat. She almost gasped when Mac walked by. What the hell was he doing here? The woman must be that Parker bitch. The woman paused for a moment and looked around. Chris felt like she was looking right at her. But then they all moved off again.

She had to think quickly. The last thing she'd heard from Monique was that Parker had cut off all communication with the FSA. Chambers and Calder didn't know where Parker was or what she was doing. Evidently, she'd been looking for Jonah, and she'd found him. Chris hadn't expected this, but it could work to her advantage. After Parker and her group got inside, Chris could just stroll in behind them.

Shelby stopped about twenty yards from the edge of the clearing that surrounded the Fortress and motioned Bear to go check to see which pole held the power source for the laser beam units. He was back in less than five minutes. He pointed to the pole he'd need to climb, and she checked her watch. The guards would be changing positions in about ten minutes. Shelby nodded and signaled everyone to take their places.

Bear crouched at the edge of the forest, just a few feet from the pole. Mac and Shelby positioned themselves between two other poles. Chase was between them. If it looked like Bear was going to be discovered, he'd signal them, and they'd throw a stick to activate the lights on their side, drawing the guards' attention away from Bear's location.

Shelby and Mac crouched low in the bushes, tensely

watching Chase for a signal. It never came, and a few minutes later they all moved back into the cover of the forest again.

"We got a bonus," Bear said with a big grin. "The pole also has a light on it. I rigged the light so I can make it go out from here. He pulled a small black box with an antenna on it from his pocket. "Watch." He pressed a button, and the light flared and died.

The guard in the nearest tower looked over at the light when it flared and then checked the ground around the wall. He picked up a notebook, wrote something in it, and sat down again.

"It's not as dark as I'd like, but it'll do," Shelby said.

The two guards that walked the inside perimeter moved in opposite directions. Their paths crossed at the front gate and at the back. Shelby had timed their walk at twenty minutes from the front to the back. When they walked the length of the front and rear of the building, the darkened area was out of their sight for ten minutes, and then in their sight for ten minutes. The tower guard would have to stand up and turn around to see the area, and his attention was on the area in front of his tower. It was tight, but Shelby figured they could make it if they were quiet and didn't make any mistakes.

The building plans had shown a door leading to the kitchen area just across from the wall in that spot. Shelby was counting on the doctors not having bothered to relocate the kitchen and hoping that the blown light would leave the door in a shadow. She signaled everyone to move into position.

Counting from the time she'd seen the guards pass each other at the front gate, she waited until they would pass each other at the rear. When that time came, she tossed the grappling hook over the wall and hoped that they hadn't changed their pacing.

The grappling hook had been covered in black rubber to minimize the clanking and scraping of metal on brick. She scrambled up the wall and quickly snipped the razor wire. She hooked another grappling hook over the wall, dropped the black rope to the ground, and lowered herself as silently as possible. Scanning the area, she ran full out for the building and tucked herself into a dark corner.

In a few minutes, the guard walked past. Shelby held her breath hoping he wouldn't notice the rope in the shadows, or her pressed into a corner.

After he passed and turned the corner, she let her breath out. The door she wanted was about fifteen feet away, and she bolted for it, pulling her digital decoder out as she ran. Shelby pressed it against the coded lock and pushed the button, glancing over her shoulder to see Chase coming over the wall. The decoder had two of the five numbers when Mac came over, and by the time Bear heaved over the wall, she had all five numbers. Shelby committed them to memory, signed the numbers to the men, and punched them into the key lock. The door swung open into a dark hallway. Checking each of the doors, she found that the entire side of the building housed the kitchen, laundry, and utility rooms.

They passed through the kitchen and adjoining room that must have been the original dining room for the prison. Now it held crates of equipment, still shrink-wrapped. On the other side of the dining room was the center of the building, with open stairways going up to the second floor. Shelby surmised that that would be where the cells had been before the doctors remodeled the place. Now the walls were lined with solid doors on both floors.

Shelby moved to the rear of the Fortress and opened the double doors, using the same key code. Laboratory area. Tons of equipment, lots of individual rooms. No one present. Which meant they were keeping Shannon and Sam somewhere else. She motioned the men to check out the rest of the lower floor. Then they met up again in the deserted dining room.

"What'd you find?" Shelby whispered.

"Lab stuff, a few offices," Chase whispered back.

"Storage for medical supplies," Mac whispered.

Bear nodded. "Same here."

"Upstairs." Shelby took the lead.

They silently made their way up the stairs and paused. She turned toward the front of the building. If she were in charge, that's where she'd put her living quarters. She found two doors marked *Private Quarters*.

Shelby pulled two cylinders out of her pack and handed one to Bear. They both knelt down and quickly threaded plastic tubes under the doors. The doors were hung about a half-inch off the floor to accommodate the plush carpeting inside the living quarters. They turned the canisters on and heard a soft hissing as the sleeping gas spewed into the rooms.

Shelby signaled everyone, and they moved along the walkway to the rear of the building. Both sides and the rear of the second floor held rows of doors that had retinal scanners and coded locks. She was betting that only the doctors' eyeballs would allow entry to any of these rooms.

"Hands in the air and freeze!"

Shelby turned slowly, hands above her head. A big guard in a khaki uniform held an AK-47 on them.

Crap.

CHAPTER TWENTY-SIX

This had definitely not been in her plans. She hadn't even heard him approaching. That no one else had heard him was little consolation. Her hopes that the guards were washed-out ex-military fled.

Shelby forcefully stopped the self-chastisement and string of excuses that were running through her head. She had to think of a way out of this. There were four of them; only one of him. Since she didn't hear the pounding of boots running up the stairs, she assumed he hadn't called for backup—yet.

"Lieutenant Greenley?" Chase asked, peering through the dim lighting in the hallway.

"What?" The guard advanced a few steps, not taking his weapon off them. "Harm? What the hell are you doing here? You go over the wall or something?"

Of course, he had, literally. But Shelby knew that Greenley was referring to the metaphorical wall that meant Chase was now working for the bad guys.

"Actually, I think you went over. Unknowingly, of course, sir."

Shelby glanced over and realized that Chase was standing at attention. Interesting.

"You want to explain that, son?"

"You probably think you're guarding a government research center, sir." Greenley nodded, and Chase continued. "The fact is that Parker and Bear here are with the FSA." Shelby raised a hand in a mock salute to Greenley. "McRae is with the FBI. We're here to rescue the people Thomas and Carlson are calling patients, but are actually prisoners."

Greenley seemed to consider that for a moment. "Downstairs. Now. All of you." He held the weapon on them as they trooped down the stairs and then pointed to one of the offices with a coded lock.

Shelby started to punch in the code she'd memorized and thought better of it. Never taking his weapon or his eyes off them, Greenley punched in the code and pushed the door open. Inside, he slapped restraints on everyone and told them to be seated.

"Now. Out with it. The whole story." He pointed the AK-47 at Shelby. "You seem to be in charge. Talk."

So she did. Shelby explained the entire situation as quickly as she could. Greenley looked at Chase and shook his head. "You go along with this?"

Chase nodded and explained his connection to Shannon and his experience at The Center in Tucson.

"Well, I'll be damned." Greenley lowered the

weapon and removed the restraints from their wrists. "Let me go tell the guards what's going on, and then we'll decide what to do."

"I take it he's a friend of yours?" Shelby asked Chase after Greenley left.

"He was the leader of the first Force Recon unit I served in."

"Okay, that explains why I didn't hear him in the hallway. You think he'll convince the other guards that we're the good guys?"

"Not a doubt. If I know Greenley, his team is totally loyal to him. They'll do whatever he says."

"That would be good." Excellent, actually. Instead of having to avoid or take out guards, she'd have a commando unit at her fingertips.

"They're gonna catch hell for letting us get inside, though." Chase chuckled and seemed pleased by the idea.

Half an hour later, after a heated debate in Greenley's now-crowded office, they had a plan. Actually, Shelby had a plan, and she'd finally convinced Greenley that they were doing things her way. She could tell he wanted to be in command, but even more he wanted the op to work, and he had to admit she had the knowledge and the skills to lead the maneuver.

"First, we need one of the doctors' eyes." Most everyone blanched at that statement. Shelby was sure they thought she was going to cut out someone's eyeball. She motioned to two of the guards. "You're with me."

They trotted upstairs to the private quarters doors. "Which one is Thomas'?" One of the guards motioned to the door on the left. Shelby slapped the decoder on the lock and pushed the button to activate it. The numbers came up in a few seconds.

She'd really have preferred using Carlson for this, but she'd pegged Jonah as the weaker one, and she had to make her decision based on the success of the entire op. Carlson would get hers later.

Shelby pushed the door open to a luxurious suite of rooms, but she didn't have time to admire the furnishings. The sleeping gas wouldn't start to affect her for at least five minutes, but she wasn't taking any chances. She moved directly to the second room where Jonah lay sleeping peacefully in his king-sized bed. Taking a handful of his pajama top in her fist, Shelby jerked him off the bed. He barely opened his eyes as she muscled him out the door, closing it behind her.

Shelby thrust him toward the guards. "Bring him along." His bare feet dragged the ground as the guards pulled him down the hallway. She jogged ahead and used the decoder on the lock. At the first door, she pulled him over to the retinal scanner. His head was lolling on his chest, so she took a handful of that silver hair, jerked his head up, and pried an eyelid open. He looked pretty stupid, hanging on the guard's arm, drool running from the corner of his mouth, and that pleased Shelby.

The scanner glowed red, and then green. She punched in the code and pushed the door open.

Shannon was sitting up on the edge of her bed, fully clothed. Chase pushed past the guards, and Shannon launched herself into his arms.

Damn, this felt good. She left them together and took the rest of the guards with her, as she used Jonah's eye to open each of the doors. All told, there were eleven prisoners. After they'd gotten dressed in whatever clothes they had, the guards led them downstairs, under Greenley's eagle eye. The guards were pretty gentle with them, letting them know that they were taking them to safety. Their nightmare was over.

Bear walked ahead of Shelby holding Sam in his arms.

"Mommy! I told you Bear would come!"

Bear handed Sam over to his mother, and Shelby watched the look on Chase's face as he looked at them.

"Sam, this is Chase," Shannon said. Sam lifted his head from his mother's shoulder and gave Chase a smile. Shannon took Chase's hand. "I have something to tell you."

"Chase, take Shannon and Sam, and go join the others. Greenley is loading everyone into the trucks, and getting them out of here."

"Where are we taking them?" Chase asked.

"To the nearest hospital. They'll all need to be checked over. Be sure the doctors know that they might have received unknown drugs. As soon as we're done here, we'll join you."

"Am I with you or them?" Bear asked.

Shelby looked around. The only thing left to do

here was to get into the doctors' offices, take their laptops, AND get all the hard drives from the other computers. Jonah and Ruth were both drugged from the sleeping gas, so she wouldn't have any problem with them. "Go with them. Mac and I'll finish up here."

Jonah was mumbling and showing signs of coming out of the drugged gas. Shelby flagged Greenley down. "Mind if I borrow a couple of those restraints?" He didn't and handed them to her as the last of the prisoners trundled down the stairs with the guards.

"You probably want to slap a set of those on Dr. Ruthless before she wakes up," he advised.

"Dr. Ruthless." Shelby chuckled. "I like that. Fits her."

Greenley grinned, lifted a hand in a mock salute, and followed everyone down the stairs. Moments later, she heard the first of the trucks pull out of the gate.

"Let's get the doctors' laptops. Then I'll call Ethan and tell him to pick up our evil scientists."

Mac pulled a semi-conscious Jonah down the hallway, and Shelby repeated the retinal scanner procedure with his eye and opened the door to his office. She quickly unplugged his laptop and stuffed it in her pack.

"Now, we need to leave him somewhere and get Dr. Ruthless to open her office for us."

"Can't we just leave the computers to the FSA and FBI?" Mac asked, dragging Jonah after her.

"After everything we've been through, I don't know who to trust anymore. I want all this taken care of, and *then* I'll call in the feds. They can figure it out from there."

"Good point."

They were almost at Greenley's office when she heard a noise from Jonah's office. Mac must have heard it too, because he stopped and turned back.

"Did we leave the lights on in there?" he asked. Shelby shook her head. Motioning him to stay behind her, she approached the office. Definite noises. Drawers opening and closing, papers being shuffled around. She took the safety off her gun, paused at the doorway, and then charged in.

"Freeze!"

A tall, slender, blond woman turned to face Shelby. Her eyes were frantic, and she held a sheaf of papers in her hand. Mac shuffled up behind her, still holding onto Jonah.

"Chris! What are you doing here?"

"This is your SAC?" Shelby asked, giving Chris a once over. She wore a set of night cammies with a knit hat pulled over her short hair. The look in her eyes was that of a half-demented person.

"Where are they, Jonah? Tell me!" Chris lunged at Jonah, and Mac pulled him out of her path. Chris caught herself and stepped back a few feet.

"Chris, calm down. Tell me what you're doing here. What is it that you want from Jonah?"

"How the hell do you even know him?" Shelby asked. Especially on a first name basis.

The slightly crazed look slipped from her eyes, and she looked from Mac to Shelby. Mac moved Jonah into the office and sat him on a sofa like a rag doll. He was coming to a little more, but he had restraints on, so Shelby wasn't worried about him.

Chris dropped into the chair behind his desk, which apparently she'd ransacked in the few minutes they'd been gone.

"He's been blackmailing me with some photos." Chris sighed. "I didn't want to give him the information about the investigation, but he said he'd send the photos to the FBI, my family, magazines. I'd have been ruined." Chris frowned and choked back a noise in her throat. "I even dragged Monique into it. I threatened to tell her lover about us if she didn't give me the information from the FSA."

Shelby became wary. This was not good. In any way. Chris was confessing to giving classified information to Jonah Thomas. Because he was going to ruin her career. Like this wouldn't ruin it? Of course, if Mac and Shelby weren't alive to tell about it, she supposed it wouldn't have any effect on Chris' career.

"Chris, stay calm. We'll figure this out. We'll work everything out. Jonah is in custody now. He can't hurt you any longer." Shelby saw the gleam in Chris' eye and the subtle movement of her arm. Before she could react, Chris had pulled a gun out and shot Jonah in the head.

"You stupid bitch!" Another shot fired from behind Shelby, and she turned to see Ruth standing in the doorway. Shelby glanced back to see that Chris had a hole in her forehead similar to the one in Jonah's. She whirled to aim her gun at Ruth, but Ruth had already moved to Mac.

Ruth held him with an arm around his throat, her gun pointed at his temple.

"Where did you come from?" Shelby cringed inwardly at the stupidity of the question, but it had just popped out of her mouth.

"You thought you'd drugged me with that tricky little canister, didn't you?" She was right. Shelby had thought that.

"Unfortunately for you, I have asthma."

"You have asthma." Shelby remembered her using an inhaler at The Center, but what the hell did that have to do with this?

"I use a breathing machine at night. It forces oxygen into my breathing passages." Ruth smiled, and she looked truly evil to Shelby. "It helps with the asthma. Tonight, it had the added advantage of bypassing most of the noxious fumes you pumped into my quarters."

Crap. That sucked.

Mac grimaced, and a strangled groan escaped his arm-clasped throat. Shelby looked into those deep green eyes and, in a hot second, realized what Mac meant to her. Her only thought was his safety and survival.

Shelby was taking this bitch down.

"Now that I have a hostage, I suppose we can negotiate."

"There's a flaw in your plan, Dr. Ruthless."

"Really? I fail to see it."

"Well," Shelby explained in a patient tone, "a hostage is only good if he's alive." She took careful aim and shot Mac.

Ruth gasped as Mac slid from her grasp, blood running from his upper arm.

Shelby didn't hesitate to fire a second time. That one went into Ruth's shoulder. From the placement, she figured she'd probably shot through Ruth's clavicle, but she was really hoping she hadn't hit anything vital. Shelby wanted Ruth alive to suffer for everything she'd done.

Shelby had already reached Ruth when the gun slid from her hand. She whipped Ruth around, pulled the restraints over her wrists and tightened them.

"Ouch!"

Good. She wasn't going to die.

"Shut up!" Shelby pushed her over to sit on the sofa with her dead colleague and knelt down to Mac.

"Mac?" Shelby whispered. Please God, don't let him be unconscious. Or dead. Surely she was a better shot than that.

"Shelby," he whispered. She jerked her gaze from his bleeding arm to his dark green eyes.

"What Mac?"

"We're really going to have to talk about these spontaneous displays of affection."

CHAPTER TWENTY-SEVEN

"I want to know whose bastard sperm they used to impregnate Shannon!"

Shelby could hear Chase's voice from down the hall as she approached Ethan's office. She thought she should probably give them a moment, but then she wanted to know who the bastard was too, so she slipped inside his office.

"I know, Lieutenant Harmon. I have all the data here." Ethan held a manila folder out to Chase.

Chase ripped the folder from Ethan's hand and opened it, scanning the contents. "Where is it?" he demanded.

Shelby took pity on the poor guy and took the folder from him. She skimmed the pages, found the data he wanted, and handed it back to him. "Right there."

He snatched the folder from her hand and looked at it. "Oh, my God!"

Shelby grinned at him.

"I'm the bastard."

"I don't know if I'd put it that way, but it's true. The Center impregnated Shannon with your sperm. Evidently they were trying to create another child with Sam's unusual abilities."

"Does Shannon know?" Chase asked.

Ethan smiled and nodded. "She does."

Chase looked like he was going to be sick. "What did she say?"

Ethan shook his head. "I wouldn't want to interpret her reaction. She's downstairs. Maybe you should go talk to her."

"Yes," Chase agreed. He turned to Shelby and grinned. "I'm going to have a baby. Again." He bolted from the room without waiting for a reply, not that she had one for him.

"I can't believe the mole was Monique." Ethan dropped into his chair and leaned back. "Of course, I didn't know that Monique had been Chris Jackson's lover either."

"Nor should you have." Shelby sneaked another look at the check he'd handed her. Between this and the retainer she'd gotten in the beginning, Parker Security and Investigation could stay open for another six months, even without the bouncer gigs she and Paige had been doing. She slipped the check into her pocket to prevent looking at it again.

"What about the people behind Thomas and Carlson? Any luck on finding them?"

"Some. We've managed to get into some of the files that were on their laptops, and we're tracing some financial transactions. All we really know so far is that they call themselves The Dominion Order. We're working on finding out exactly who they are and what else they might be up to. We've alerted Interpol and the intelligence organizations of our allies."

"The Dominion Order? Sounds presumptuous."

Ethan leaned forward and twined his fingers together. "So, you ready to come back?"

"No way."

"Come on, Shelby. We both know you love the job."

"I love the work. And I have my own agency to provide the work now. I don't need the FSA."

"That's probably true," Ethan admitted. "But the FSA needs you."

"No. I'm done with the FSA. You have all those trainees. Use them."

"Not a damn one of them shows half the promise you did." Ethan slammed his palm on the desk.

"Like I said, you need to improve your recruiting methods." Her cell phone chirped, and she pulled it off her belt.

"What?"

"Hey Shelby. Paige here. You busy?"

"Not really. What's up?"

"I just wanted to ask you again about buying into the agency. You said I did a good job with the Fortress and—"

"Sure," Shelby said, grinning when Paige gasped.

"You mean it? Really?"

"Absolutely. I've discovered I actually like working with a partner."

"Oh, Shelby, you won't be disappointed. I promise."

"I know. But just so we're clear, you're only getting thirty percent."

"That's good. That's fine. Oh, one more thing. I got a call about a case."

"And?"

"Well, do you want to hear about it?"

"No. You're a partner. You make the call. Just make sure Zoe is able to handle the office if you have to be out for any length of time. Tell her not to accept or decline any cases. Just keep her busy with the accounting books."

"You got it! See you when you get back."

Ethan leaned back in his chair. "You're working with a partner now?" He shook his head. "I'd never have believed it." He looked up as someone knocked on his door and gestured.

"Excuse me. Ms. Parker, you have a visitor." The fresh faced young man looked apologetic.

Shelby swiveled her chair around and saw Mac through the glass walls of Ethan's office. They hadn't had a chance to talk since they'd been picked up along with Dr. Ruthless and the dead bodies. His arm was in a sling, but otherwise, he looked good. Really, really good.

"Excuse me, Ethan, I need to speak to Mac."

"Sure, but first, Shelby, how about another op? Just one more."

"I don't think so." She rose and walked to the door.

"It's something you'd really like. It's in the Caribbean. A real piece of cake."

"Why me?" She forced herself to turn back to Ethan.

"It requires a chameleon."

She looked back at Mac. He was smiling. There was a certain heat in his eyes. "Find another one. Maybe Mel's available." She heard Ethan snort as she opened the door.

"How's your arm?" she asked Mac.

"It'll be fine in a few weeks. Flesh wound."

"That's good."

"I'm sure that's what you planned."

Shelby blushed, wondering just how to explain to a man that you shot him for his own good.

"Shelby, just consider it." Ethan's voice had turned into a pleading whine. She ignored him.

"I've been thinking about us."

"You have?" Was this good or bad? She really wished she had better social skills. Maybe she'd have some answers to questions like that.

"It's never easy to start a relationship. And it's even harder when it's started under . . . well, let's say dire circumstances."

Shelby couldn't argue with that so she didn't. But she didn't think Mac was sounding real positive right now.

"I thought we should take some time to think about what we want, where this might eventually lead." Mac spoke softly, and Shelby felt a hard lump form in her throat. She swallowed hard.

"Sure. I understand." Crap.

"See, this is perfect timing, Shelby," Ethan broke in. "You do the op in the Caribbean, then you two can have time to consider everything. You always said you think best when you're on the job."

Mac pulled a brochure out of his breast pocket and handed it to her. "I thought this might be a good place to start."

Shelby took the brochure he handed her and stared dumbly at the pictures of couples frolicking in the ocean, riding horses, and dancing under the stars.

A luxury island resort? She opened the brochure and found two airline tickets tucked inside. The significance sank in, and she looked back at Mac and smiled.

"Sounds like a great place to me."

L.G. Burbank Presents

The Soulless

Book One in the Lords of Darkness Series

An unlikely hero...

Mordred Soulis is the chosen one, the man ancient legends claim will save the world from great evil. There's only one problem. Before Mordred can become the hero of mankind, he must first learn to embrace the vampyre within.

A forgotten race...

With the help of a mysterious order, a king of immortals and a shape-shifting companion, Mordred is set on a dangerous course that will either save the human race or destroy it.

A timeless struggle...

Journeying across the sands of the Byzantine Empire; in the time of the Second Crusade, to the great Pyramids of Egypt and then on to the Highlands of Scotland, Mordred will face the Dark One. This evil entity is both Mordred's creator and the Soul Stealer he has become. As champion of mortals, Mordred must accept his vampyre-self...something he has vowed never to do.

ISBN# 0-9743639-9-5

Gold Imprint continued...

The Soulless by Leslie Burbank
ISBN 0974363995 *Paranormal Vampire Fiction*

Wintertide by Linnea Siclair
ISBN 1932815074 *Fantasy*

Silver Imprint

All Keyed Up by Mary Stella
ISBN 1932815082 *Contemporary Romance*

To Tame a Viking by Leslie Burbank
ISBN 0974363928 *Historical/Paranormal Romance*

Illustrated Fairy Tales
for Adults

Ellie and the Elven King
by Helen A. Rosburg
ISBN 0974363901

Once in a Time of Dragons
by Shannon Drake
ISBN 0932815023

www.medallionpress.com